THE DARKEST LULLABY

ELLE BEAUMONT

KATYA DE BECERRA

JESSICA CRANBERRY

MARLENA FRANK

C. VONZALE LEWIS

D.M. SICILIANO

Midnight Tide
PUBLISHING

CONTENTS

To all those caretakers who tended to little monsters, this one is for you.

FOREWORD
BY MEG DAILEY

"Out of the mouths of babes," goes the saying, a phrase which by modern interpretation means that children are often smarter than we give them credit for. Smarter and—even if they don't know it—much more honest.

Whether that's a good thing or a bad thing is a matter of perspective.

Many of the nursery rhymes we grew up with and teach our kids today also have ever-evolving interpretations, not all of which are particularly cheerful.

Take, for instance, the quintessential "Oh my god, why do we let kids sing this?" rhyme: "Ring Around the Rosie."

Ring around the rosie
Pockets full of posies
Ashes, ashes
We all fall down!

Aside from the fact that some iterations of the game have children throwing themselves dramatically to the ground upon singing the last line, this version of the nursery rhyme carries some potentially awful implications, believed by some to be referencing the bubonic plague: a ring of roses equates to a rash, posies reference the scents and flowers carried as a deterrent for the illness, and the falling down at the end is a representation of death.

Or is it?

Professional folklorists will point out that this version of the song cropped up long after the plague had passed and probably wasn't in reference to it at all. But as readers and writers we have to ask: does that matter? What weight does history hold to a child singing a song? If it's ingrained in a whole culture of kids that this is a song about death, then at the end of the day, isn't that what it becomes?

Out of the mouths of babes, indeed!

Here's one that makes no secret of its scary implications:

Ladybug, ladybug, fly away home.

Your house is on fire, and your children are gone.

All except one, and her name is Ann,

And she hid under the baking pan.

Once again, the jury is out on what exactly this rhyme is about. It could be a reference to the religious persecution of Catholics in the 16th century, as ladybugs are sometimes used as a reference to Mary, mother of Jesus. It could also be a much more innocuous rhyme spoken by farmers to their pest-eating friends, the ladybugs, just before the dregs of a crop are burnt to encourage new growth in the next season. Or it could be a spell cast to send someone home, away from unknown danger, back to family.

In any case, the imagery isn't quite what you'd imagine a group of kids singing cheerfully about on a summer day, is it?

Think back to your own childhood: What other rhymes come to mind that could have terrifying connotations?

"This Little Piggy"? Consider what "went to market" might mean for a pig.

"Baa, Baa, Black Sheep"? Your younger self might never have guessed that the wool going to the master and dame were tax payments.

"London Bridge is Falling Down"? Seems self-explanatory, and this one even comes with a game that implies its own deaths, as the "bridge" of hands "falls" on whomever is under them when the rhyme ends.

Here's another from my childhood that's stuck with me out of pure catchiness:

Cinderella, dressed in yella

Went upstairs to kiss her fella.

By mistake, she kissed a snake!

How many doctors did it take?

One, two, three, four…

The last bit requires jumping over the rope as many times as you can while everyone around you watches and counts. Meaning if you're a really good rope-jumper, it could take tens of doctors to keep poor Cindy around!

This one doesn't have a long historical background to follow into the dark—even the classic Cinderella tale didn't have much to do with snakes, just people cutting off bits of their own feet and dancing until they died. You know, stories for kids. But that makes this jumping rhyme almost worse, doesn't it? Sure, the words were probably chosen because they rhymed and fit a rhythm, but why did they have to be about a beloved fairytale character being bitten by snakes?

What are we meant to take away from that?

There are many who believe that fictional stories, rhymes, and songs are good ways for children to experience and learn from danger and heartbreak in a safe environment, one they know they can come back from when they need to feel safe and whole again. Even the scariest stories can impart lessons to be carried forth into adulthood.

In this strange case, perhaps a game of jump rope might just make some young players a little more wary of snakes—literal or metaphorical—hiding in place of their own prince charming.

Finally, consider this little riddle:

Little Nanny Etticoat

In a white petticoat

And a red nose.

The longer she stands

The shorter she grows!

Can you guess who this attentive nanny is? Maybe it will help to imagine her with fiery red hair, her white dress pooling beneath her as she slumps, tired from a day of work.

Little Nanny Etticoat is a candle.

The original nightlight and the last vigil of young children, back before screens acted as our go-to babysitters. Losing height and losing light as the night wears on. A protection against the dark—with her own tinge of danger, the threat of fire uncontrolled.

A nanny, as a stand-in for a parent, should be someone a child can trust. And in turn, the nanny should be able to trust that their charge is willing to be guided, protected, and taught.

But we all know children aren't always the most willing students.

This collection carries the weight of these spooky songs, these riddles and rhymes with their mysterious meanings and hidden histories, then sets that weight squarely upon the shoulders of the unsuspecting nannies. Will they be able to bear the burden of childhood secrets and pranks beyond explanation? Or will they topple like candles left lit too long?

From the mouths of babes comes wisdom, truth . . . and often more than a little horror.

Sleep well.

Meg Dailey

The Silver Whistle

by Marlena Frank

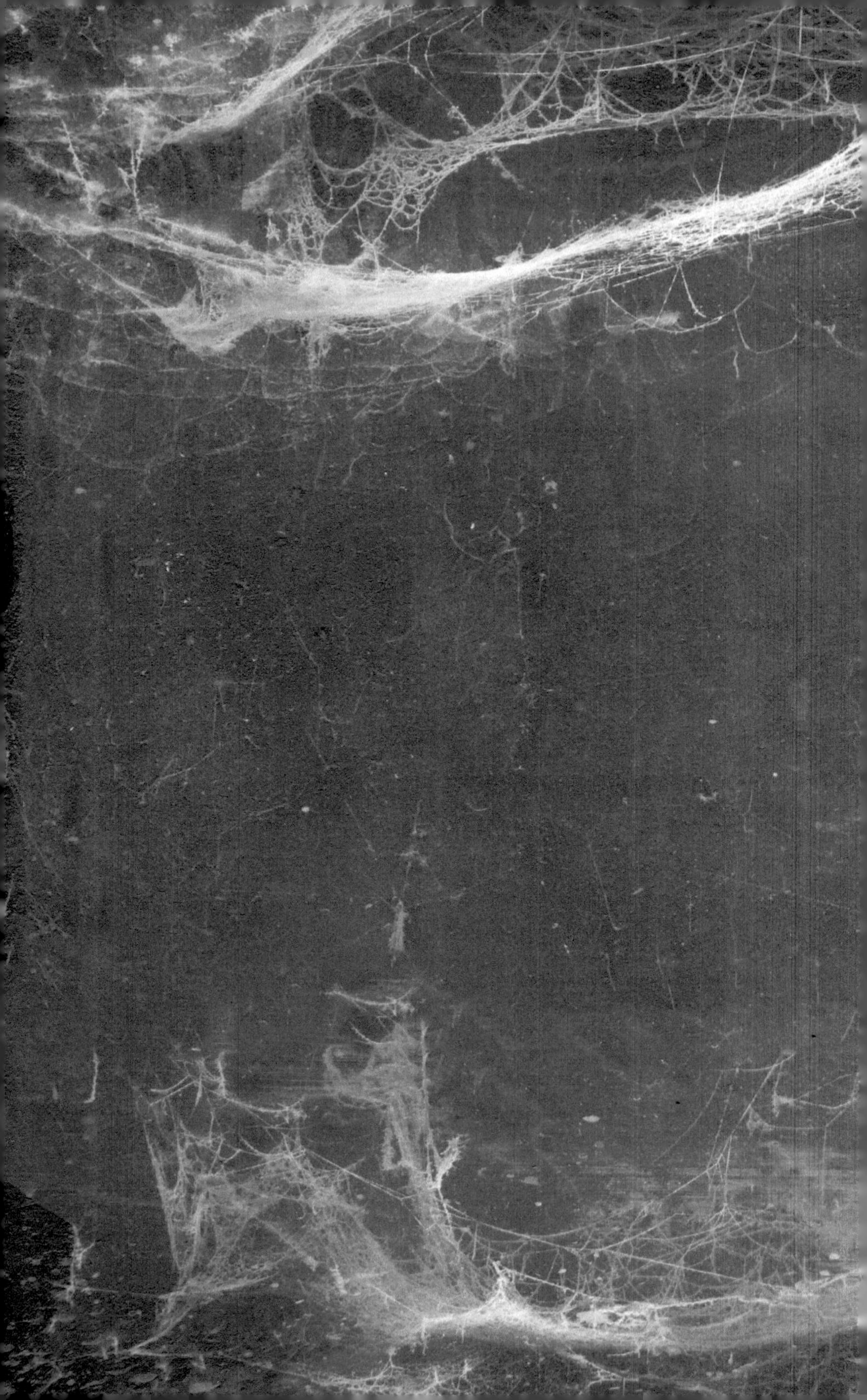

1

LITTLE DEVILS

Marion's eyes shot open. She shook from head to toe. The cotton sheets of her bed clung to her sweaty skin as she tried to make sense of where she was.

This was her bedroom, the second-floor guest room located in Rose Manor. The one she had been given when she first started working for Dominic Rose and his son, Peter. She had lived here for two years, and yet it felt like nightmares tormented her every night. Sometimes she wondered if she was awake or asleep. It was difficult when the lines blurred so often.

The horrible nightmare that had yanked her back to wakefulness faded. She put a trembling hand to the side of her head, trying to recall the details. Trying to recall any of it. She felt like remembering them would help her unlock the terror, shed light on what truly plagued her. As if knowledge could release her from the endless prison of her mind.

She reached down beside the bed to drag her fingertips against the space between the box spring and the mattress, where she kept her personal journal. It was a private diary she had kept ever since she left home and came here to work as a nanny. Her fingers fumbled against the harsh springs and the soft cotton of the mattress. She pushed down the familiar depression and reached inside. But there was nothing. She leaned over the edge of the bed farther, sticking her whole hand inside. It was gone.

Marion pushed up to a sitting position, tangling her hands in her hair. All the homesickness she had written about was lost. All her hopes and fears gone. She took a deep breath, trying to calm the panic inside that threatened to overflow. Most importantly, her dream logs were gone. She had logged them for weeks, noticing that they were getting worse and the nightmares more frequent. Sometimes when she read through them it felt like the dreams belonged to someone else.

The dream from last night, she needed to remember it. Marion closed her eyes. Maybe she could commit it to memory even if she couldn't write it down. Something bad had happened to her in the dream. It felt so real. Or at least, her terror was real.

But try as she might, the nightmare slipped through her fingers like the delicate strands of a spider web dissipating in the breeze. She wrapped her arms around her knees and hugged herself tight, trying to ease the pounding of her heart in her chest.

"Just a nightmare," she whispered. "That's all."

If that were true, why did she feel like she needed to convince herself?

Marion got to her feet and slid on her slippers. It was dark still. Dawn hadn't quite broken the surface of Rose Manor and the lush gardens that surrounded it. She pulled on her thick bathrobe, the one her mother had made herself and given her years ago. She padded over to the small balcony and pulled open the doors.

Icy wind swept over her face, drawing tears from her eyes. It was the beginning of spring, but the bite of winter still lingered. She breathed in the air, felt the cold fill her lungs. The pond in the distance was just visible as the sky shifted from purple to orange. Despite the freezing temperature, the pond had no ice floating on top. She had learned over the years that the pond worked as the actual indicator of the seasons; dates be damned.

It was wild to think that she, a small, frail girl from an impoverished village, would be given the chance to live amid such beauty, to dwell in a lavish room with its own private balcony and look out at a lovely pond every morning. Mom had cried when she left to be a nanny. She said Marion was meant to do amazing things someday. Marion wouldn't be stuck in the small village for the rest of her life. Dad, on the other end, had said he didn't like Dominic Rose. He said the man had a suspicious air about him but wouldn't elaborate. Honestly, Marion wished she had taken her father's advice and turned the offer down. Though trying to justify it to her mother or the rest of the village would have been impossible.

Marion settled in the wicker chair and watched the sun rise over the Rose property. Fog rolled over the pond and dispersed as the first rays of sunlight streaked over the water. The sun brought the dense forests around the edge of the property alive like fire. Then lit up the chapel and the carriage house. Finally, once it had risen fully over the horizon and a flock of ducks alighted upon the surface of the pond for their morning breakfast, Marion knew she needed to get to work. Peter would be awake soon and she had a full day ahead of her. Watching the boy was hardly simple work.

At least she could face him without the terror of that nightmare hanging over her. She shivered from the chill in the air, but at least it wasn't from the demons who plagued her dreams. It wasn't much, but it gave her a small respite.

She stepped back into her room and pulled the balcony doors closed behind her, locking out the beauty and returning to her profession. She was ready to take on the day —and the boy.

It took longer than she liked to hunt down Ethel in the backyard. She stood beating a rug and throwing dust and dirt into the cold morning air. Marion folded her arms to try to keep the frigid temperature at bay. For some reason, Ethel didn't seem at all phased by the weather. It was almost as if she gained more vigor in the colder months. The tall woman's cheeks were red against her pale skin, her thin lips almost devoid of color. Her short white hair was pinned up tight, and she wore a thin ivory scarf over her head and shoulders. Small wisps of white hair escaped like tendrils of spider webs from beneath the cloth.

Marion had no idea of Ethel's age, only that she had worked here for decades, toiling away in the shadowy parts of the manor. She handled the dirty side of the beautiful home, whether it be cleaning dishes or preparing baths. She had a few young women who worked beneath her, but Marion had been instructed to only approach Ethel with any questions that might crop up. The other servants were never to be disturbed.

"Ethel?" she called.

Ethel gave a short nod. "What can I do for you, Ms. Bowden?"

Marion clasped her hands together tightly, almost as if in prayer. The woman's discerning gaze caused Marion much anxiety. "I had one of my belongings in my room. I can't find it."

The old woman scoffed, folding her arms. "And you thought me or one of my women did something to it, do you? Start working here as a nanny, then get promoted to a governess, and now you think you can go around accusing people of theft?"

"That's not—I only wanted—"

Ethel gave a sour smile. "I can assure you that none of us took your things, ma'am." Her eyes narrowed, clearly insulted.

Marion swallowed the lump in her throat. "It was a small journal. I had it… it was beneath my mattress." She pursed her lips, her fingers blanching at how tightly she had them clamped together.

Ethel sighed and propped her carpet-beating stick against the wooden stool beside her. There, Marion saw a dozen more rugs, likely ready for cleaning. She tried to quell the guilt eating at her.

"So, let me get this straight, ma'am. You think me or one of my women went into your room, found your diary, and stole it. Now, what exactly would any of us do with that, dearie?"

Marion blinked in shock at the demeaning tone. "I don't know, but—"

Ethel waved a hand at her, fingers still partly bent as they had been when she held the stick earlier, like she couldn't extend them easily. "I assume you wrote words in that book, didn't you?"

"Yes, of course I did."

"Ah. That solves it. My women don't read. They don't know how. Not everyone has the benefit of an expensive education like you, ma'am. I'm the only maid under this roof who knows how to read, and I can assure you I didn't steal it."

"And Peter? He doesn't have access to my room, right?"

"Correct, ma'am." Ethel rubbed at her knuckles with a grimace as she spoke, slowly straightening out a few of her painful joints. "Even Barnaby doesn't have access to it. No need for a chef to go into bedrooms, especially that of a woman."

"No, I suppose not." Marion paused, wondering who the culprit could be. She looked up again to see Ethel staring hard at her with a sad expression on her face.

"How did you learn how to read?" Marion asked, trying for some lighter conversation.

"Me? My father taught me. He was a collector of books, if you can imagine that. Liked to think of himself as a researcher."

Marion furrowed her brows. "So why do you work as a maid now?"

"He died, ma'am. Shot and killed when I was eight. Work is work as long as it pays. Am I right?"

Marion bowed her head low. "I'm sorry. I didn't know."

Ethel sighed. "Will that be all, ma'am?"

"Yes," Marion whispered, realizing she prevented the woman from doing her work.

Ethel didn't wait for her to leave. She picked up her stick and returned to beating the rug without glancing back.

That hadn't gone at all like Marion imagined it would. And worse yet, she was no closer to figuring out what had happened to her diary, her dream logs.

Peter had never been a fan of piano lessons. He complained the entire time from the first moment he laid his small fingers upon the ivory keys. Marion suspected that he purposely messed up the songs, hoping he could skip out of lessons for a day, but Marion was far too resolute to permit that. His father, Dominic Rose, forbade him from playing any other instrument because Peter's mother, Alicia, was a renowned pianist. Before she got ill, she had toured the countryside playing for various nobles and occasionally for churches. Dominic wanted Peter to reach those same heights, but Marion suspected Alicia wouldn't have approved of such measures.

Marion knew better than to press for information regarding Alicia's death. All she knew was that after she passed, both father and son changed. Dominic began going on long, undefined business trips. Peter began harboring a pit of rage within him. But Marion understood she wasn't allowed to ask questions. It was made clear early on that she was merely a nanny and didn't need to know another above her station. Of course, that was before she had been promoted to governess.

Peter slumped over the ivory keys, his brows scrunched in consternation. A batch of brown hair fell from behind his ear, hitting his cheek and highlighting the fury in his gaze. It seemed the boy was always angry about something. Marion couldn't keep up with the indignations from one day to another, even though it was her job to do so. She had never known a child to have such an ill temper, and it had only gotten worse when Marion was tasked with teaching the child instead of merely watching him.

Being his nanny had been a difficult enough task. Being his governess was, at times, impossible. But losing his mother two years ago at the tender age of seven had to be difficult. He never spoke of her, and Marion knew little about her other than the occasional mentions from Dominic.

There were times she was frightened of Peter. At age nine, he was getting stronger and would likely surpass her in height in a few years, but it was the quickness of his temper that kept her up at night. Maybe by the time he was older, Mr. Rose would find a true governess to watch the boy.

"Do you remember where center C is, Peter?" she asked in what she hoped sounded like a kind and patient voice.

"Yes, I do!" Peter spat, but his hand placement said otherwise. He kept shifting his hands up and down the keys, hitting the wrong key each time.

Marion gave a heavy sigh.

"I know it!" Peter said, urgency and panic coloring his voice.

"Peter, if you knew it, you would have found it already and been able to start playing the song."

He stared up at the sheet music, then down at his fingers. He didn't respond, but curled his fingers over the keys more, dropping more hair into his eyes so that she couldn't see his face.

"We've been over this countless times. If you don't practice or even care to touch the piano outside of our lessons, you won't ever be able to play your father's favorite songs. He'll be very disappointed to find you have made no progress."

Peter slammed his hands down on the keys, blasting discord as he turned to her. A strangely familiar darkness tinged his gaze. It made her think of her dream logs. Marion leaned back in her chair, instinctively moving away from him, suddenly eager to put as much distance between herself and the boy as possible.

"I don't give a damn what he says about my playing. I hate it! You know I hate playing this thing, but you make me do it anyway!"

Marion swallowed a lump of panic. "There's no need to raise your voice," she whispered, fear taking the fangs out of her words. "Just because Mr. Rose is away on business doesn't mean you can talk to me like that."

He glowered at her. "Is that right?"

She nodded, no longer able to form words. Where had this terror come from? She had dealt with unruly children before. Hell, she had raised her younger brothers as a teen and her mother had called them little devils. Why did she suddenly have the urge to run away from a child?

Peter lunged at her, knocking her chair backward. She landed hard on the wooden floor. He was on top of her, kneeing her in the stomach as cold, clammy hands wrapped around her throat.

He was just a boy! How in heaven was he so strong and she so very weak? She tried to pull his hands off her throat, but they held on like a vise. She could barely breathe, could barely spit out any words.

"Pet—" she gurgled. "Pleees."

He clutched her throat tighter.

Any small amount of air was lost. Her eyes went wide as her mouth opened, gaping like a fish on land. Her lungs burned. All she could see were Peter's dark eyes and his bared teeth. There was no remorse on his face, no regret. All she saw was rage.

Little devils.

He looked at her like she wasn't human. Like she had been nothing more than a nuisance to him in the two years she had known him, cared for him, fed him, and taught him. She tried to kick him off as panic settled in, tried to pull his hands free, but he was latched on too tight, and she was too weak.

Her vision faded as her lungs ached and her body went numb. She couldn't fight back. She couldn't resist anymore.

Darkness took her completely.

2

TADPOLES

Marion woke up coughing. Something constricted her throat, preventing her from breathing.

She touched her neck instinctively, but there were no hands there. It was nighttime. She was back in her bed, dressed in her nightgown.

She pawed at her neck, feeling for any tenderness, anything that would prove it was real, but she felt nothing. Already the dream threatened to dissipate.

"No!" she cried, crawling out of bed and rushing to the mirror attached to her elaborately carved dresser. Her hands shook as she struck a match and lit the large oil lantern and the two silver candelabras that sat on either side of her mirror. Golden light filled the room, and she peered at her own reflection emerging from the gloom.

Mousy brown hair clung to her neck and shoulders. Her pale skin looked sallow, and her eyes were sunken. The nightmares had sapped her youth from her face, pulled the brightness from her eyes. Ignoring the pit of worry in her stomach, she pulled her hair back and checked her neck from the front to the back. There were no bruises. No discoloration. Not even handprints.

She turned around and dropped her nightgown to her waist, checking her back. She remembered her shoulders hitting something hard, maybe wooden. But now she saw nothing, just her own ashen skin.

Returning to the bed, she sat on the edge and reached to where her journal used to be, as if hoping it had magically reappeared. But the space was still empty between the box spring and mattress. She put a hand to her mouth. A sob pulled at her, but she bit it down in frustration.

"Another nightmare," her voice hitched. "But it had felt so real this time." She dragged her fingertips over the places where she expected bruises and the phantom feeling of small fingers clutched around her neck came back to her in a distant haze. It wasn't just a dream this time. "It was real. Wasn't it?" That was all she could remember. The details fell away from her, as if swept out by the tide. She dropped a hand to her throat, trying to recall who had attacked her, who the hands belonged to, but already it faded. The face was a blurry mass of shadows and light.

She gripped the sides of her head and bent over, tears slipping down her cheeks.

"Not again, please," she begged to the empty room. "I have to remember this!"

Outside, the birds were singing. The sun would rise soon. She longed for that beauty, that consistency, that calm. If nothing in her life could be relied upon, at least she had her sunrise.

She pulled on her slippers and bathrobe and stepped outside onto the balcony, breathing in the crisp air. Out here, her terror faded. Her nightmares fled. Out on her balcony, she didn't fear her own mind. She simply existed with all her flaws and imperfections. She could be herself. The sun put on her golden display each morning regardless of who was there to watch, and Marion was simply happy to be part of it.

She stayed outside until her cheeks were frozen, and her hands were shoved down into her pockets for warmth.

"You're going to be okay," she told herself. "It was just a bad dream, that's all."

With that resolution, she stepped back inside to get ready to face the day. And to face Peter.

The warm sun had chased away the morning chill and given way to a lovely day. Marion decided it was perfect weather for a picnic. Peter seemed just as excited.

They chose a patch of grass near the pond where it was warm but still had a light breeze off the water. The flowers were just starting to bloom on the dogwood trees above their heads. They provided the perfect shade from the midday sun. Along the stone wall of Rose Manor, red and pink roses were blooming, filling the air with their soft scent. She took a deep breath and let her worries leave her.

Marion made them simple pimento cheese sandwiches, Peter's favorite. He spent most of his time running around and chasing the ducks and rabbits. Really, any animal he spotted was in danger of a chase. But Marion let him. She didn't mind as long as he didn't hurt them. That she never condoned.

He had balked at her rules at first, but that was Peter's

nature. He pushed against any rule she gave him. After two years, he had warmed up to the concept, and even helped when he spotted an animal in distress. She watched him move an inchworm from a rock into the grass at one point. Once, he even got a rake to move a garter snake away from the carriage house to keep it from being trampled. He had grown immensely in the years she had watched out for him. Marion liked to think that his newfound love of animals was her influence.

"Peter, come get a sandwich. I don't like you getting near those swans. I promise they won't run away like the ducks will. They'll fight back."

He hesitated briefly before running back around the pond to flop down on the picnic blanket. He grabbed a sand-wich in each hand, still breathing hard.

"Easy now, don't choke," she said with a grin. "Slow down and chew."

He did as he was told until he had polished off both sand-wiches. "There's an old log on the far side with some tadpoles. I want you to see them! They're see through! All eyes and wiggly bodies."

It was good to see him excited about something. Getting outside always seemed to cheer him up. And he wanted to share with her! That had to be a good sign, a sign that he was opening up to her finally. If he was comfortable asking her to see his latest animal discovery, maybe they had indeed grown closer over these past two years.

"Come on, you've got to see! There are so many, I couldn't count them all." He was already on his feet, ready to take off again.

Marion sighed. "Fine, I'm coming." She stood and dusted

the dirt off the back of her dress. She considered bringing her parasol but decided against it. A parasol was too formal for chasing frogs and tadpoles around old logs. So she lifted her skirts and headed off after him.

Through the tall grasses and across the gnarled tree roots, the path was more treacherous than she liked. She should have worn boots instead of the small heels that she had chosen for their picnic.

"Peter, how far away is this log?" she asked, breathless.

"Over there, see?" He ran ahead and leaped onto an old log with the ease and surety only a child possessed. It was in a shadowy end of the pond and a bundle of dragonflies flew away at his landing. The log had clearly been there a long time based on the fungi that had discolored the sides. It looked on the verge of collapse.

Peter leaned down to point into the water, brown hair falling into his face. But something else caught her eye. Something fell forward from around his throat and caught a beam of sunlight, flashing white.

Marion felt her heart skip a beat.

A whistle made of silver hung on a thin chain around his neck. It was a small, tarnished piece that had clearly seen better days, but looked more appropriate on a hunt to call dogs, not on a little boy's neck. Why did he even have one?

"Where did you get that?" she asked, pointing a gloved hand to the whistle around his throat. The longer she stared at it, the faster her heart pounded. Sweat broke out across her back and her stomach flip-flopped the longer she looked at it. Why in the world did a tiny whistle that hung around a child's neck fill her with such dread?

Peter pushed his fringe out of his eyes, noticed what she

was pointing at, and his eyes went wide. That was a guilty look, like he wasn't supposed to show her. With a quick motion, he tucked it back into the collar of his shirt. "Oh… that's for my dog." His gaze darkened as he pursed his lips. "Not anymore. But I used to have one before you came to live with us."

With a careful step up, Marion climbed onto the old log to reach him. "I didn't know that. Your father never mentioned you had a dog. Maybe I could ask him to get you another one. That would cheer you up, right? There's certainly plenty of land for one to run around here."

Peter fidgeted beside her, not looking at her. He seemed nervous, uncomfortable, but she wasn't entirely sure why. "I'm not allowed to have pets anymore."

Alarm bells went off in Marion's mind, but she had to know. She had to find out what made Peter so apprehensive. And the whistle. That wasn't for a dog. It couldn't be, he could barely look at her. She had to press for more information.

"That is not a dog whistle," she stated. "It's too short."

He furrowed his brows, giving that dark expression again. "You ask too many questions."

"Do I?" she asked, brushing off dirt and grass from her skirts.

"You shouldn't. It'll get you in trouble," Peter muttered.

"With your father?"

He nodded.

She glanced down into the murky pond, unable to see any movement. The water was too dark. She folded her arms and turned to him. "I don't see the tadpoles at all. Was that one of your lies?"

"No. You're just too far away!" he cried, rushing forward.

Marion barely had the chance to gasp as he shoved her hard in the stomach. All the air was forced out of her lungs, and she stumbled backward. Her arms pinwheeled as she lost her balance. Her heels slid off the old log, the soles too smooth to have any grip, and she fell into the icy water.

She bobbed for a few moments, trying to get her bearings. Trying to wrap her head around what had happened. Her body was frozen, from the punch to the gut and the icy temperature, and she couldn't get her limbs to move. She sank under the surface, her eyes wide as she stared up through the murky water. Dozens of tadpoles darted across her line of vision, moving far faster than she could. Peter stared down at her, his cheeks dimpled and his mouth wide. She heard the muffled sound of his laughter from beneath the water, mocking her.

Marion knew how to swim. She knew she could get to the surface. She just had to force her body to move. Only her determination allowed her to push the shock aside and slowly her arms obeyed her again. She paddled against the thick pond water that felt more like sludge. Something prevented her from moving upwards.

She looked to see thick tendrils of vegetation wrapped around her ankles, around her calves, and black heels. Waterweed and hydrilla had interlocked like ropes around her, tangling and twisting the more she struggled to break free of them. There didn't seem to be any end to the leaves. She tried to gesture to Peter to help her, to stop this prank and pull her out, but Peter merely waved at her.

Her eyes began to close as the small amount of air remaining in her lungs left her and rose rapidly to the surface in small, desperate bubbles.

Marion sank into the leafy mass that pulled her into its twisted embrace.

The last thing she saw was Peter's smirk through the murky pond water, distorted and dim in the depths of the cold, stagnant water.

3

FLOATING

om sat beside her at the small, square dining table. Their tiny kitchen doubled as a living room. There were only two bedrooms in their house, located on opposite sides of the kitchen. Marion's used to be a closet and pantry before they expanded on it a little and gave her a full room of her own.

Marion never really appreciated the work that took. Or how much it showed their love for her.

The dining table was really just a slab of wood with uneven legs and a few deep grooves. Mom was darning a pair of Dad's pants. He kept getting holes in the knees and she had to pull out the old patch and put in a fresh one every two or three months. Mom would cut patches out of old clothes to use. Nothing ever went to waste. Her hands worked swiftly with the needle and thread, even if they shook a little more than they used to. Her long brown hair hung a little too long in her blue eyes. She didn't look up from her work as she spoke.

"Are you watching me, or are you studying?"

Marion leaned back in her wooden chair, her back aching. "I'm tired of studying. I want to go outside to play."

"You ought to be studying. You need that education."

Marion huffed, getting up from her seat and stretching. Her long cotton dress, that she had worn for years, was a little too short for her now. It had its own patches and loose strings. "You and Dad didn't have to study this long. You went straight to work and never looked back."

Mom looked up from her sewing, her bright blue eyes piercing. There was no humor in her gaze, no playful indulgence. "No. We didn't have a choice. We had to work. It was either that or die. One day, this kind of labor will be the death of us, but you don't have to share our future."

"Mom, don't talk like that!"

Suddenly Marion felt her mother's callused hand cradling her cheek like she used to do when she was a child, the metal thimble scraping against her chin.

"You need to solve this. You need to escape. Use your mind and your studies."

Marion floated up. Her eyes went wide as her feet left the ground. With desperation, she reached for her mom but couldn't grasp her. She tried to scream, but only bubbles emerged from her throat.

Mom had tears in her eyes as she looked up at her. "Please, baby. That boy is killing you."

4

DOGWOODS

Air rushed into her lungs.

Marion coughed herself awake, flailing against the covers as she fell out of bed and hit the hard wooden floor of her bedroom.

She looked at the tangle of sheets around her, pulling in desperate breaths. She could still taste the pond water, algae, waterweed, and hydrilla. Slowly, she extracted herself from the sheets, noting how she was again dressed in her night-gown. Her hair felt dry, as though freshly washed. Not the hair of a woman drowned in a pond.

She pressed the palms of her hands against her eyes. "It felt so real this time," she whispered to the empty room. "I thought I had died!"

Tears fell and Marion lay on the floor, huddled under the covers. She sniffled and wiped her cheeks, realizing with a slow sense of urgency that the floor wasn't cold. It was warm.

She flattened her hand against the wood and confirmed

her suspicions. She remembered her mother speaking to her in a dream, "Use your mind..." Sunlight peeked beneath the doors of her balcony.

Marion climbed to her feet and padded over to the balcony, no longer bothering with her bathrobe or slippers. She pulled open the doors to a warm morning. The dogwoods had lost all their flowers. She gasped.

Yesterday at the pond, they had just started blooming.

She made note of the plants she could see. The roses which had blossomed into a cacophony of colors along the walls of the manor. The trees along the edge of the property were now full of greenery. It was no longer early spring, but mid spring.

"My mind might lie to me, but the sun never lies." She put her hand to the side of her head. "But how long have I been asleep?" She shook herself, remembering how she floated in the dream with her mom. She might not remember the nightmare, but she remembered her mother holding her cheek.

The nightmares weren't just dreams. Mom had practically told her as much. It was far worse.

The real question is, how long have I been dying? The thought made her shudder.

She needed a way to track her observations, or at least her suspicions. Without her journal, she had no proof, only observations and her own mental gymnastics. A dream with Mom wasn't enough. She needed paper, something to write with, but she didn't trust bringing back a journal. Ethel had likely been the one to steal it despite all her bravado. But Marion was running out of time. Already she could feel the threads disappearing again. She needed to get her thoughts out of her head before she forgot it all again.

She fluttered around the room. Carved into the floorboards? Too obvious and she didn't need to let on that she knew anything. She didn't trust anyone in the manor.

Finally, she settled on the soft wooden lining of the undergarment drawer of her dresser. She pulled out a hairpin and carved in the following words: mid spring, pond, drowned.

She paused, remembering her mother's words. Then wrote: Peter.

He was the only person around her all the time. He always lost his temper. She always got uncomfortable around him. It all added up.

She dragged a hand through her hair. It was difficult to imagine this could have happened to her, but she couldn't explain the lost days any other way. If she really was being killed over and over again, she needed to find out why.

She needed to stop it.

Peter didn't behave as if she had been gone, let alone for days or weeks. Overall, he was a skilled liar about it, but she saw the signs of restlessness. It was clear Peter had had no one to take care of him since her disappearance. His shoes had layers of mud on them, and a dark smudge of grime caked his cheek.

Marion chose arithmetic for the day's lessons. She didn't have a good reason other than being angry at Peter. He hated the subject even more than he did the piano. But also, she wanted to try his patience. She had reason now to believe he was trying to kill her—her mother had told as much.

The classroom was on the third floor of Rose Manor, at the top of the stairs, in an open space that used to be a studio once upon a time. Alicia Rose, had a practice piano she kept there. It still stood in the corner of the room, but it was covered with a sheet, like a sentry. As years passed, Marion watched dust mound atop it.

Dominic Rose had given the room to Marion to use as her classroom, which was quite generous. She asked once if Peter could use Alicia's practice piano, explaining it made her nervous for him to practice on the grand piano downstairs. But Dominic got emotional. She swore tears sprang to his eyes. He didn't give a proper answer, and Marion never brought it up again.

The studio was large, with unfinished walls and three double doors that opened to a wraparound balcony. It smelled of the chestnut wood it was built with, especially when the balcony doors hadn't been opened in a few days to air out the room. At one point, Marion could imagine how incredible it must have been to sit and listen to Alicia play with the doors all open, looking out over the gardens and the pond below.

But that would have been years ago.

Peter was less than pleased to be stuck indoors for lessons, especially when he learned they were tackling arithmetic. He groaned for a solid ten minutes, complaining it was too pretty of a day to be trapped inside. That didn't deter Marion. She started in on several chapters of practice problems, which would surely take up the entire day.

They had been working on Peter's multiplication tables for many hours and Peter's patience wore thin. Marion hoped to wear him down. Maybe then she could get some information out of him and finally figure out what was happening to her.

"Can't we take a break and go outside?" Peter asked, dropping his head into his hands. "I'm tired of numbers. My head hurts. And my hand is cramping."

She smiled at him. "I'm tired of hearing you talk back to me."

He looked up at her, eyes wide. He was taken off guard.

Good. Maybe that would help give her the advantage for once. She needed to confront him directly. She swallowed her nerves, closed her teacher's guide, and put down the chalk.

"Did you enjoy drowning me, Peter?"

His jaw dropped. "You…remember that?"

Victory. He'd confirmed her fears were true.

She nodded. "I remember more than you think." She took a step toward him, her back to the blackboard.

Peter shot to his feet, kicking his chair back so quickly it made a loud squeak across the wooden floor. She wondered if he might run, but he just stood there, looking around the room. "I want to look outside," he said, sounding calm despite his obvious fear. "I'm going to open the doors and get some light."

Marion permitted it. She followed as he went to the first set of doors and opened them wide to the balcony. He was stalling, but that was fine. She wasn't in a rush. She took her time keeping pace with him as he moved to the second pair of doors.

"I need to know why? Why did you do it?" Marion's voice shook as she remembered him shoving her into the pond. "You drowned me. You admit it. Yet you dare pretend as if nothing happened? And somehow, I still live."

He kept his gaze on her as he opened the second pair of doors, hurrying to the final set. As he turned, silver flashed at his throat.

Marion gasped and pointed at it. "The silver whistle. That's part of it, isn't it? You're always wearing it around your neck."

He flinched.

"So it is!" She cried. "Tell me: why do I always wake up in my room? How long have you been killing me? Answer me, Peter!"

He opened the last set of doors and stepped out onto the wraparound balcony. Below them, she spotted the dirt road that led to the house, the path Dominic Rose's horse and carriage would take as he made his way home from his business travels. Worry etched Peter's face, and he pursed his lips.

"Your father won't be back for some time yet. You know this. He won't rescue you." Marion stepped out onto the balcony and dropped a hand to his shoulder.

The boy flinched away from her, but she didn't remove her hand.

"I'm not mad at you; I just want answers," she said, trying to calm herself down. "I want to know what you're doing to me and why. You're the only one who can help me."

He didn't meet her gaze. Instead, he looked out over the grounds as the sun began to set in the distance, lighting up the ripples in the pond with brilliant reds and oranges.

"You're right. I don't know how it all works. I'm not allowed to know." Peter sniffled and wiped his nose on his sleeve.

He shifted under the weight of her hand, pulling away

from her. She let him. How much was Dominic involved in all of this? Or was this just another of Peter's many lies?

He glanced at her with dark eyes, scowling. "But even if I did know, I sure as hell wouldn't tell you."

With a snarl, he turned and shoved her hard in the stomach. Just like he had at the pond. She fell backward, tripping over a great stone flowerpot, its contents long dead. Her lower back hit the stone railing hard, and she gasped.

But that didn't stop him. He climbed the flowerpot, moving far too quickly, then his arms were around her shoulders, fingers gripping painfully into her skin.

"Don't—" she hissed, trying to catch her breath.

He grabbed her around the throat and shoved her hard over the railing.

"Peter!" she cried, too late.

She fell backward. Wind whipped her hair out of hairpins, her skirts flew around her like water, and tears sprung to her eyes. The sky streaked orange and red as Peter's laughter rang in her ears.

The ground rushed up to meet her and the impact made her cry out.

A gurgling groan caught in the back of her throat. She couldn't take in more air to breathe. There was too much blood. Her limbs wouldn't work. She could only stare up at the top balcony, at the small boy standing there.

His laughter rang against the manor walls, against the roses whose thorns scraped against the stones. It rang out across the murky pond and across the painted sky.

A part of Marion hoped someone would come, maybe Ethel. Either to save her or put her out of her misery. Surely someone had to hear his laughter. Someone had to hear her cry.

But no one came.

As her vision faded and her body bled out onto the grass, Marion could have sworn Peter waved at her.

5

SPIDERWEBS

Marion gasped as her eyes shot open. She flung her hands out in front of her, arms tangling in blankets. She sat up with a start, taking in deep breaths and expecting to still be rattled with pain, blood spilling out of her, blood filling her throat and dimming her eyes. But once again, she sat in her bedroom. She freed her arms from the sheets and examined her body. Whole limbs and unmarred skin met her inspection. She looked like she had merely fallen asleep. Again. But her mind knew better. She knew better.

Marion climbed to her feet and yanked open the undergarments drawer on her dresser. She pushed clothes aside and scratched beneath her previous note: Pushed off balcony. Shattered. PETER.

She shuddered at the statement, but it was important to remember it, in its gruesome detail. She couldn't fall back into complacency again.

Haphazardly, she pulled on clothes, yanking her arms through sleeves and buttoning up her blouse and vest in uneven patterns. Her hands shook as birds chirped cheerfully outside. By the time she was ready, the first rays of sunlight crept through the balcony window.

She didn't want to go out on that balcony. Not after what had happened.

No beautiful grounds would distract her from her fury. No sunrise could take away her determination. She clung to her rage like a lifeboat.

Heading for the door, she clenched her fists. She needed to find the boy. This time, she wouldn't let him best her. She would learn the truth of these incidents and finally be free of this torture.

Her hand gripped the elaborately carved door handle, but then she paused.

She had underestimated Peter before, and he had murdered her many times because of it. She couldn't face him without some kind of weapon. There had to be something she could use to protect herself.

She turned to the dresser and grabbed one of the small candelabras. It was heavy, made of silver or some kind of metal at least. She dropped it into a deep pocket on her skirt, feeling shame and horror wash over her.

"I won't use it," she promised herself. "But he doesn't have to know that."

Rose Manor was empty. It must have been a holiday and the rest of the staff had the day off. But someone was awake. She heard a repetitive sound, like a small drum beating.

The hair on the back of her neck stood up. What was it?

She followed the sound down the end of the hallway to the staircase. The pitch of the sound changed. It wasn't deep like a drum, but it took her a moment to recognize the sound. It was a small ball bouncing on one of the many hard-wood surfaces.

Peter.

She went downstairs and found him in the foyer, tossing a small rubber ball onto the ground and catching it repeatedly. She smelled him even from the archway that led into the room. His dirty, disheveled clothes indicated he hadn't had a proper bath in days.

He didn't look up at her as she entered the room. "Morning," he said in a flat tone.

"Peter," she whispered, settling down into an armchair. It was important that she didn't rattle him. She had been too forceful last time and backed him into a corner. This time, she needed to be smarter, more controlled. She sat with a straight back and folded her hands in her lap, trying to keep them from shaking.

"Your father wouldn't want you throwing that in the house," she said, indicating the rubber ball. "You'll break something. Or hurt yourself."

He glanced at her briefly, a pout tugging at his lips. "He's not here to be mad, is he?"

She watched him for several moments, allowing her silent disapproval and the repetitive noise of the ball to echo off the walls and up the stairwell. Marion channeled her patience into a physical force, keeping quiet as he continued bouncing the ball.

It clearly distressed him. He kept glancing at her, tossing the ball faster and faster. He nearly lost it a few times, but that didn't slow his pace. Finally, his hand slipped. The ball flew past his grip and struck him square on the cheekbone.

"Ow!" he cried, putting a hand up to his cheek as the small rubber ball tottered off beneath some furniture.

"I told you not to do that." Marion sighed.

Peter's eyes welled with tears, and she couldn't hold back the urge to comfort him. Yes, he had killed her many times—or at least she believed he had—but he was still a child and she, his caregiver. So caution be damned. She fetched a wet washcloth for him and pressed it against the blooming bruise.

Tears streaked his cheeks as she held the cloth to the injury. "You won't tell father, will you? I don't want to make him mad." He sniffled. "He'll know I was throwing the ball again."

"And how will you explain the bruise, then?" she asked.

He barked out a laugh that surprised her. "Oh, that's easy. I'll tell him you did it to me."

She froze, the wet washcloth pinched between her fingers. "You'll what?"

"I'll tell him you got mad and popped me." He grinned.

Marion leaned away from him, suddenly keenly aware of the weight of the silver candelabra in her skirts. But she couldn't correlate this crying, bruised child with the vile words that erupted from his mouth. She couldn't match his neediness with his cruel laughter or malicious smiles. She tossed the washcloth aside as laughter bubbled out of the boy.

"Why do you hate me, Peter?" she asked. "Why, after all I have done to help you, to teach you, do you continue to hurt me like this?"

His smile faded to disgust.

"I don't like you. I've never liked you. You're nothing like my mother. She was beautiful, she was funny. She didn't make me do anything I didn't want. She loved me despite everything." His eyes narrowed.

A coldness entered her veins. She knew that look. She had seen it enough times that it was etched into her nightmares. Her body was hard wired to be cowed by it. She reached for the candelabra and pulled it out like a gun, aiming it at the boy.

This time, she would have her answers. She would have her truth.

"Tell me what the silver whistle does!" she shouted.

Peter trembled, his fingers fumbling for it around his neck, holding it tight like a talisman. He pulled it out, a small, tarnished thing that looked almost as grimy as he did.

"What does it do?" she demanded, backing the boy up against a wall.

He bumped into it and glanced back, terror filling his eyes. "It…brings you back."

"From the dead?"

He nodded, tears bobbing back into his eyes as the bruise turned purple on his cheek. "But Father wouldn't bring mother back. He refused. I didn't want you. I wanted her!"

Marion ignored him and focused. She didn't know how long this threat would work or how long Peter would talk. She had to take advantage of the moment while she had it. "How does it work? What the hell did you and your father do to me?" Marion shouted.

"I—I don't know. All I know is it works!"

"You're lying," she hissed. "You're always lying to me. Answer me or so help me God, I will use this."

Peter swallowed, shaking his head. "Please, I can't tell you. He'll be so mad if I tell you."

Marion brought the candelabra back, lifted the heavy metal high above her head, but she never got the chance to bring it down.

A gunshot rang out.

The back of her head erupted with pain and Marion crumpled to the floor. As her vision faded, she spotted Peter's rubber ball beneath the loveseat, saddled up beside a dozen others. All but the newest was covered in spiderwebs, lost and long forgotten.

EPILOGUE
DUSTY TOYS

Peter leaped over the body of his governess and ran over to the tall, silver-haired man who stood in the doorway. The pistol in his hand still smoked from the gunshot, and his face was frozen in a look of disgust.

"Father!" Peter cried and wrapped his arms around the man. However, his father didn't return his hug.

"Did she hurt you?" Dominic Rose asked.

Peter backed away and pointed to the circular bruise on his cheekbone. "Yes. Right here. She struck me, father! I told you I need a new nanny. I told you this one was trash."

"Let me see." Dominic holstered his gun and crouched to take the boy's chin in his hand, turning his face side to side to examine the wound. "That looks pretty bad. It certainly won't heal quickly. What did she use?"

Peter's eyes darted to the side for a moment before he excitedly blurted out, "A silver candelabra! She even has it on her still. See?" He pointed to where it lay, still gripped in her hand.

Dominic nodded. "Must have hurt pretty bad, hmm?"

"Oh yes, terribly! I—"

Dominic grabbed hold of his son's shirt and pulled him close, cutting Peter off.

"Do you think I'm a fool? That's from one of your damn rubber balls, not a candelabra."

Peter stared wide-eyed at his father, his bottom lip trembling.

He let go of the boy, climbing back to his feet. "If she's attacking you, then she knows something she shouldn't. What does she know?" He pulled off his riding gloves and hat, placing them on a side table, his gaze averted from his son.

Peter sniffled, wiping his eyes. "Too much."

Dominic closed the door behind him and walked over to take in the grisly scene. He let out a long sigh and placed his hands on his hips. "Son, I left her in your care, and you in hers. All you had to do was keep out of trouble."

Peter narrowed his eyes. "You said she was mine. So I had fun with her."

Dominic glanced at him with a hard expression. "How many times have you killed her? Often enough to cause suspicion?"

Peter shuffled his feet, looking away from him. He opened his mouth to speak, but his father held a finger out at him.

"And don't you lie to me again. The next time you do, I won't be so kind."

His bottom lip trembled as he looked down at his dead governess. Peter shrugged. "I don't know. Five times, maybe more? I lost count after a while."

"Five times?" Dominic scoffed. "Jesus, Peter. Once is too much. Twice is overkill. You've been torturing this woman!"

Peter folded his arms. "You said she was mine! She was mine to take care of, so I took care of her. Besides, she kept making me do boring things like math and piano. I hated it. I wish you would bring me with you. Let me meet the other necromancers. Maybe they could help bring mother back since you couldn't."

Dominic bared his teeth. "I told you, don't ever mention your mother to me. It's too late for her and you know it. Two years? There's not much left of her, son."

Peter flinched.

"That you're even mentioning it tells me you should not be near any necromancers right now. Not yet, at least." He sighed, rubbing at the salt and pepper scruff on his cheek. "Maybe if you let Marion watch out for you like I directed her to do, you wouldn't be bored all the time. Maybe the problem is you, son, not the governesses."

Peter scoffed. "She's not my governess. She's my nanny. You never got me a proper governess!"

Dominic rubbed the bridge of his nose. "She's your governess, because I say she is. And you're not getting another one. You'll just torture the next one like you did her." He held out a hand. "Now give me the damn whistle."

"But Father!"

"Now."

Peter whimpered, tears filling his eyes, but he pulled off the necklace and dropped it into his father's palm. Dominic checked it before nodding.

"She's just going to be angry with me again," Peter said. "She's always angry with me."

"Is she? Or are you the one who's always angry, Peter?"

The boy looked away from him.

"As for her memories, that's going to be a problem. I'll have to bind her again, which is a long, messy process. I wouldn't have to go through it all if you just learned to mind your toys." Dominic sighed, dragging a hand through his silver hair. "And no more whistles for you. If you kill her again, you're getting locked in your bedroom for a week. With whoever is *my* latest project."

Peter went a shade paler.

Dominic smirked. "You loved it so much last time, didn't you?"

"No sir," Peter shuddered.

Dominic nodded to him before raising the whistle to his lips. It emitted a sad, airy sound, more like a broken party favor than a musical instrument.

The blood which had pooled around Marion's body flowed back toward her corpse, even the smallest drop pulled up from the floorboards and soaked back into her. The splatter of brains and blood on the wall crawled like insects down the paneling and across the floor, back to her body. Once all the blood had returned, the back of her skull began knitting together again. The entire process took mere minutes and soon Marion Bowden took in a deep, rattling breath. Slowly, she crawled up to all fours before flinging herself up to a standing position. The front of her head was still a bloody mess. Larger than the entry hole in the back of her skull, the exit wound took longer to stitch together.

Peter cringed and took a step back.

Soon Marion's body was whole again. She stood, breathing softly, her eyes closed in a deep, dreamlike state.

Without a word or a glance, she padded across the floor with barely a sound and climbed the stairs to the second floor.

"Barnaby found her in the pond," Dominic said. "Said she was tangled in the weeds under water. Told me how he had to wade in to fetch her body because she was stuck." He rubbed at the stubble on his cheek. "She kept trying to walk out of the weeds down there and would get more stuck. He had to use a damn knife to cut her loose. Apparently, she had been missing for over a month and you didn't tell anybody. You're lucky he likes to take strolls around the pond."

Peter shrugged.

Dominic narrowed his eyes. "I don't give you toys just for you to go abuse them. This work is messy and difficult. I need you to show me some respect, son."

Peter slumped, shoving his grimy hands into his pockets. "Sorry, Father. I don't mean to disrespect your work. I guess I didn't think about it like that."

Dominic gave a heavy sigh and put a hand on his son's back. "Well, an apology is a start, at least. Let me get cleaned up so I can bind her again. It's going to take a lot of work. I'll have to get it done before dawn."

Peter watched as his governess climbed the stairs without a sound, not tripping once even though her eyes were closed.

"Father, why does she always go back to her bedroom when she resuscitates?"

Dominic sat down in the armchair to take off his riding boots and the rest of his guns. "Because that's where I first killed her, son. Every time she comes back, she yearns for her place of rest. I've taken that from her to make sure you have a decent education. You need some kind of companion while I'm away. I've stolen her eternal peace. It's the worst thing you can do to a person. Which is why I need you to grow up and stop killing her." He ruffled his son's hair. "Am I being clear?"

Peter pursed his lips and nodded. "Yes, sir. I'll do better next time. I promise."

"You better. Cause your dear old dad is tired of cleaning up your messes."

ABOUT MARLENA FRANK

Marlena Frank has always been fascinated by monsters, and now gets to write about them. She is the author of young adult fantasy and horror novels, short stories, novellas, and series. Many of her books have hit the Amazon bestseller charts, including her debut novel, *Stolen,* and her first short story collection, *The Impostor and Other Dark Tales.* In 2022, she will be kicking off her young adult dark fantasy series, *The Wolves of Kanta,* featuring mad scientists, hunters, and werewolves.

Although she was born in Tennessee, Marlena has spent most of her life in Georgia. She lives with her sister and two spoiled adopted cats. She currently serves as the Vice President of the Atlanta Chapter of the Horror Writers Association and is an avid member of the Atlanta cosplay community.

She is an INFJ, a tea drinker, and a wildlife enthusiast.

CONNECT WITH MARLENA

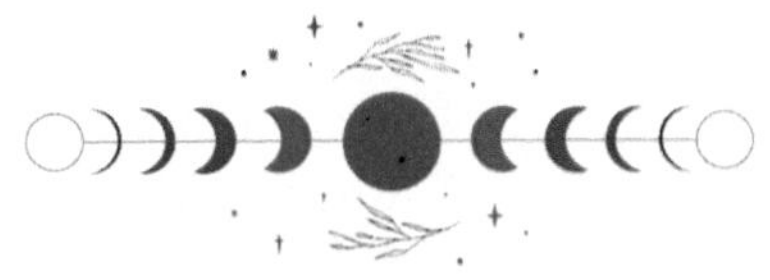

marlenafrank.com

instagram.com/authorlenafrank

facebook.com/MarlenaFrankAuthor

twitter.com/MarlenaFrank

MORE FROM MARLENA

The Wolves of Kanta Series

The She-Wolf of Kanta

The Blood of Kanta

The Hunters of Kanta

The Fury of Kanta

The Howl of Kanta

The Stolen Series

Stolen

Broken

Chosen

Standalones

The Impostor and Other Dark Tales

Anthologies

Emporium of Superstition

When You Hear Them Scream

By C. Vonzale Lewis

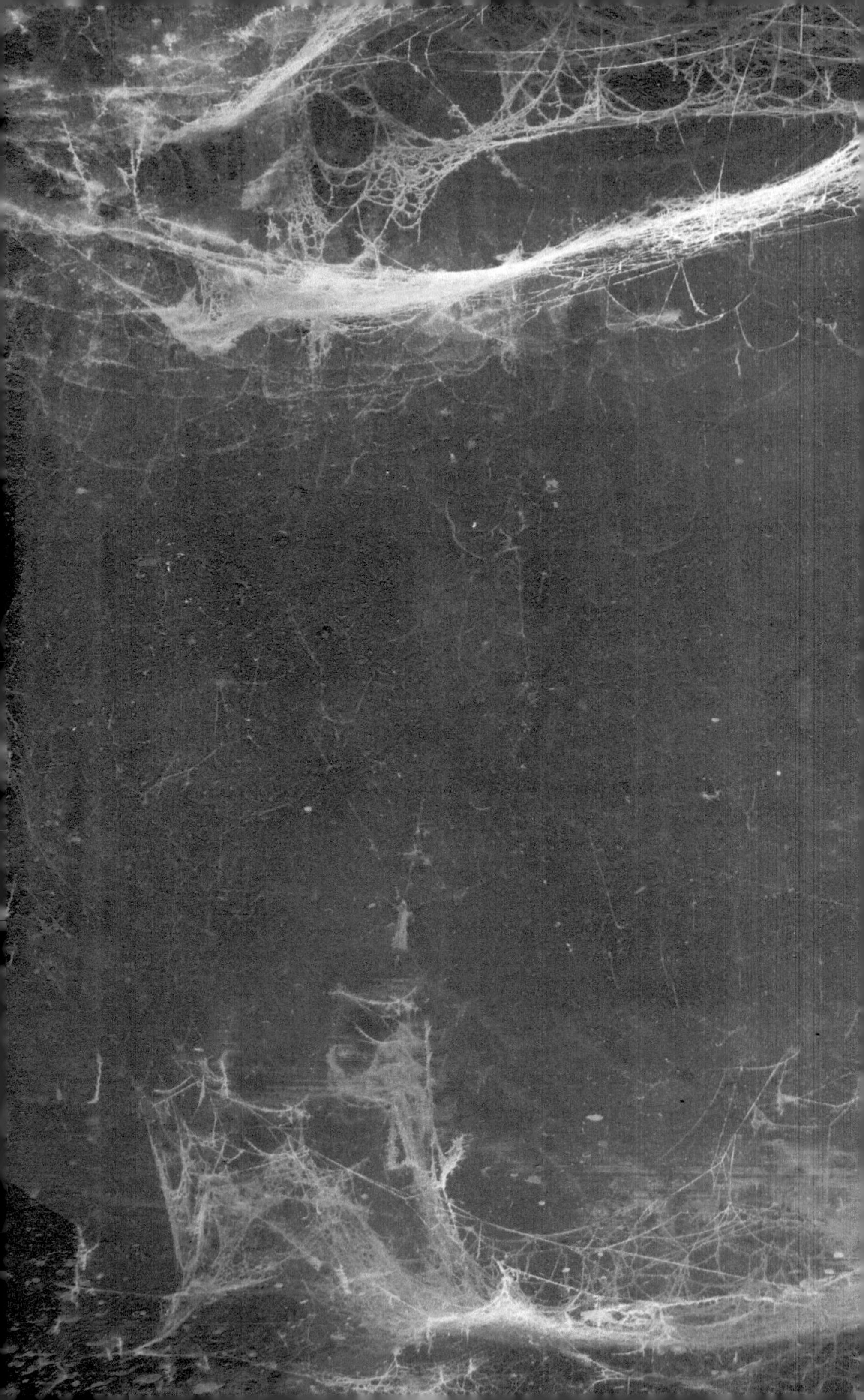

1

The stillness surrounding Pagonis House seemed unnatural. Even the air had an emptiness to it that made Samuel Bowden uneasy. It was as if all life had been sucked into a void, leaving a blot of nothingness in the middle of the land. But in that abyss stood a sprawling Victorian home with peacocks engraved into its burgundy wood.

Samuel's horse, Pete, neighed. The gelding jerked his head, agitated, and backed away from the house. Samuel climbed down. He held on to the reins and ran his hand absently over Pete's side to calm him while he studied the dark red mansion.

Word in town was it was home to a cult that worshiped the Greek goddess Hera.

Of course, Samuel had grown up hearing stories of when the settlers had invaded his people's homeland. Bringing their sickness and strange rituals. Forcing his people into Christianity.

But this place. This place held something much darker. He could feel its evil seeping out onto the land. Tainting the very air he breathed.

He'd told his good friend, Bass, that he'd hunt down the illusive Minos Kalakos since he was heading west anyway. The man had been accused of kidnapping some colored children from down south. And it would give him great pleasure to bring the man and all who aided him to justice. He only hoped he would find the children as well. Be good to return them to their families.

Samuel pulled his hat off and ran a cloth over his forehead. The previous year, snow had ravaged this area; now it was the sun's turn to bake the land. He let out a sigh, eyes still on that stain of a house. He'd been out here for a while and was somewhat surprised no one had come to a window or even opened the door.

He tore his gaze away and took in the surrounding yard. Tall alder trees had been planted in a patchwork pattern around the house. Grass, a dark luscious green, blanketed the yard, with splashes of color coming from the flowerbeds. It seemed almost unreal.

Thump! Samuel's gaze shot back to the house. There, in an upstairs room, one of the curtains had moved. He took a step forward, then paused. The hairs on the back of his neck rose. Sweat broke out along his hairline.

Pete reared up, striking at the air as if he could push back the wrongness.

Samuel started to worry about what he was walking into.

After giving Pete one last reassuring rub, he made his way

to the door. His boots thumped on the hardwood. He raised his hand to knock, then stopped. A strange metallic clock, with a demonic peacock engraved in its center, had been affixed to the door. Before he could examine it further and puzzle out its meaning, a child's scream tore through the air.

He tried the doorknob.

Unlocked.

When he pushed it open, a gust of stale, frigid air rushed out.

The stench of rot swirled around him when he stepped inside.

"Hello," he called out.

No one answered.

Another step inside. The floorboards groaned with his weight.

A large winding stairway sat directly in front of him. And on it, a little girl stood, her mouth open in a silent scream.

She stepped down and reached for him.

He started forward only to stop when a tall man with black curly hair appeared behind the little girl, holding an axe over his shoulder.

Minos Kalakos.

He pulled his revolver. "Minos Kalakos. By order of the martial service, I'm placing you under arrest."

The man's dark eyes swam with madness. "You shouldn't have come here, lawman."

A woman appeared on the landing wearing a white linen dress. "Thirteen souls to power the clock," she said in a voice seeming to come from everywhere. She extended her hand, and the little girl went to her.

Minos raised the axe.

A grinding of gears sounded, shaking the very foundation.

Samuel aimed his gun and fired.

2

I stared at the two open suitcases on my bed, my mind a chaotic jumble of anger, frustration, and sadness. My life had changed in a matter of hours. One minute, I had a clear path outlined for my summer, getting myself ready for a two-month live-in night nanny job at Pagonis Manor; the next, I was staring at an empty keepsake box that used to contain my emergency cash.

Now? Now I was cramming all my belongings into a suitcase and gripping a pair of scissors in my hand and thinking how they would cut nicely through my roommate's belongings.

Just when had I picked them up, anyway?

I pushed a breath out of my nose. Letting the frustration and anger seep from my pores. Then, with a herculean dose of willpower, I set the scissors down and studied the piles of clothes scattered all over the furniture in my tiny room. No matter what I did, all my things were not going to fit. I'd lived in this apartment with my so-called best friend, Janelle, for two years, accumulating more than I really needed.

I *could* leave it all behind. But it was mine. And I fought for what was mine. I glanced at the scissors again and smiled. Instead of cutting her shit into tiny strips, I'd take her suitcases. She owed me anyway. I started for her room only to stop short at the *Indiana Jones* ring tone coming from my phone.

My mother.

I loved my mother. But getting her to cut conversations short took divine intervention, and even then, she'd have a few more points to add. So, I made a mental note to call her later and went to get Janelle's suitcases. Once I finished packing my stuff, I left her a little receipt next to her stupid apology letter I'd found in my box. A letter dated a week ago.

As far as I was concerned, she'd better be happy I didn't cut her crap into tiny ribbons.

An hour later, I loaded up my car and looked up at the apartment I'd shared with her for the past two years. So many memories. So many good times. I'd always believed we'd grow old together. Not necessarily living together always, but at least living in the same vicinity if not the same neighborhood. Our kids were supposed to become best friends. Much, much later in life, of course—I definitely wasn't ready for a husband and kids. But still. Janelle had been a constant in my life for fifteen years. And in a single act of pure greed, she'd destroyed our friendship. What bothered me the most, though, was if she had asked, I would have gladly given her the money.

Now I had to move. And once my summer job was over, find another apartment, because I was sure all the dorms had been taken by now for the next school semester. I'd still try. But I didn't hold out much hope.

I glanced at the time on my phone. It was just after ten in the morning.

When Hermoine Kalakos and I discussed the job over the phone a few days ago, she hadn't been real forthcoming about my actual duties other than keeping watch at night. But what she had stressed repeatedly was that I be there at 5 p.m. sharp. Her insistence on the time had started to border on maniacal and had me, however briefly, reconsidering taking the job.

Punctuality was understandable. But the way in which she kept stressing the exact time had me wondering if there was some great import behind the hour.

Despite that, I had reassured her I'd be there on time, and now, sitting here with all my things in my car, I was hoping that she wouldn't mind me arriving early.

I pulled away from the curb and joined the rush hour traffic to make my way to Pagonis Manor.

3

The houses in the Forest Hill neighborhood were upscale, and I was surprised they actually had a children's home in the area. It reminded me more of a middle-aged community where people settled right after retirement—more posh than playground.

But looks could be deceiving. According to The Pagonis Society's website, they'd been operating the children's home in this area for well over a hundred years.

I checked the time again. Not even noon yet. So still way too early.

I rolled down my window and glanced at the house.

A weird sort of stillness surrounded Pagonis Manor. Like someone had stopped and left this tall burgundy structure sitting in the middle of a void. Waiting. An eerie picture, complete with the cool morning fog rolling around its base and obscuring the rich green earth. I shook my head at the thought. Houses didn't move. Yet . . . they did give off an energy of movement. And this one had none.

I tried to pinpoint the strange feeling. No, not feeling.

Impression? Don't get me wrong, the house was beautiful—a tall, gothic structure with complex rooflines and patterned shingles. Even the horseshoe opening was eye-catching. The picture in the brochure really didn't do it justice.

I rested my head on the back of the seat and continued to stare at the tall home while this . . . sensation twisted my gut into knots. Why had I suddenly become so apprehensive?

I couldn't figure it out.

But something about this old Victorian home had every nerve in my body standing on end, a faint warning bell. It could've been the effect of the fog. I didn't know.

As I started to turn away, I caught a strange design out of the corner of my eye. From my periphery, inside the grooves of the burgundy wood, a large clock covered most of the surface of the house. Resting inside that clock was an animal . . . a peacock. One with madness in its eyes.

Shocked, I jerked around and lost the image. I sat there for a while, moving my head side to side, but no matter what position I put it in, I couldn't see the design anymore.

Had I imagined it?

And why the hell was I still sitting in the car?

"Get out of the car, Imani," I said aloud, then sighed. I should have eaten before I came. Or at least drank some coffee to clear my head.

I pushed open the door and stepped out into the chilly air. San Francisco in the morning had a crispness in the air that I was still getting used to. My brother and I grew up in Oklahoma, just outside the Cherokee Nation where my father lived for most of his life. The humidity had baked into our bones, and foolishly, we both believed we could handle the cool weather.

We were wrong.

The fog rolled away from the path, exposing the red brick walkway. I considered the strangeness of it. It seemed as if a curtain had been pulled back to reveal the way forward. Unease settled in my gut. That wasn't how fog behaved.

When I got to the door, I paused. I'd seen the house in brochures before. But never this close. The dark wood looked almost . . . alive. Like the burgundy paint wasn't really paint at all. More like blood.

I glanced up at the wooden sign hanging over the horse-shoe entrance.

Σπίτι Αιώνιο

Greek. I snapped a picture of the sign and climbed the porch steps. I would look up the words later. Hopefully, they had Wi-Fi. If not, I'd have to go to the library or my brother's restaurant to use the internet.

I lifted my hand to knock, when an object that couldn't have been part of the building's original design stopped me. A large thirteen-hour clock with Roman numerals hung on the cherrywood door. At its center rested an ancient peacock with obsidian eyes swimming in a pool of redness. Those malevolent orbs seemed to pierce my very soul. Its beak arched into a sharp point, directing my eye toward a temple. Inside that sanctuary was a rendition of a human being with no discernable gender.

Roman pillars held runes carved into the surface. Animals floated inside infinity symbols.

A chill raced down my spine as I stared at the strange clock with its long hand resting between what should have been eleven and twelve o'clock. I touched the odd metal, and a charge of electricity bit into my fingers and shot up my arm. I stepped back, shaking my hand to ease the painful sensation.

I backed down the steps, sucking on my still throbbing fingers, and studied the house more closely. The dark color had hidden all the little intricate designs carved into the wood. They looked like whorls, or a language maybe. Something about it felt . . . ominous. Wrong, even.

A curtain on the top floor fluttered. I squinted to get a better look. Nothing. My gaze went to the gables, and I noticed several small marble statues of peacocks.

Omens, portents, and mythology were a common topic in our household growing up. My mother and father had spent their entire adult lives combing history to compile all the lost mysteries of ancient cultures. One of the things my father used to drill into us was the abundance of occurrences in relation to beauty and evil.

Like Lucifer, believed to be the most beautiful angel in heaven, some things in nature and in myth have worn a disguise of attractiveness. Meant to disarm prey, the most beautiful in nature could also be the deadliest.

In mythology, the peacock was the Greek goddess Hera's favorite bird. It was also a symbol of immortality. Not widely known, but in some texts, the bird represented trickery and evil. My mother had found these origins in an old text referencing the longevity of the soul. She wasn't able to make out more than a few passages in the ancient text she'd unearthed in a rare bookstore in Greece. But the gist was, people who wished for long life, or immortality, worshiped the peacock.

Was that what I saw here?

It couldn't be. This was supposed to be a children's home. Speaking of, I had been standing out here for a while, and aside from someone peeking out on the second floor, no one had come to the door. Not much for security.

Taking a reluctant step up, I made my way back to the

door and knocked. A short while later, a woman opened the door, and a blast of cold, stale air rushed out and slapped me in the face.

A tall, bronze-skinned woman stood in the doorway, her long black hair pulled into a que at the nape of her neck. She wore a simple white dress that reminded me of Peplos and a long gold chain with a peacock pendant on it. She stared at me out of cool brown eyes.

"Umm . . . hello, I'm Imani Nez Deschene. I'm looking for Ms. Hermoine Kalakos." I paused. "I start the night nanny job today?" I didn't mean to make the last statement a question, but the way she just stood there studying me had me wondering if I'd made a mistake.

"Yes," she said finally, wincing as if she were in pain. "I'm her sister, Collette. And I know who you are. Why are you here now?" There was a bit of a chill in her voice as she pronounced each word carefully, with a heavy accent.

"I . . . I thought I'd get moved in early. If that's okay?"

"No. It's not. I need you to return at five, as was discussed." She glanced behind me. "You can leave your things on the lawn, and I will have the caretaker put them in your room. Or you can return at the scheduled time, and I will have him move them then."

I stepped back. "I'll . . . come back later."

She smiled then. A warm smile that had me doing a double take. "Of course, thank you, Ms. Deschene," she said and shut the door.

I stood there for a minute, mind racing with questions. That was an odd exchange. And why wouldn't she allow me in the house? What was so significant about five? I glanced at that strange clock again. Had the hand moved? It looked closer to the eleven now. No, I had to be imagining it.

I scowled at the door for minute, running different scenarios through my mind. Trying to suss out the exchange in a way that made sense. When nothing immediately came to mind, I started for my car. Looked like I'd have to wait at my brother's restaurant after all.

It wasn't until I drove off that I realized . . . I hadn't seen any children.

4

My brother, Shiye, had moved to San Francisco four years before me to open a restaurant he named *Nez Deschene*. The menu was a fusion of Creole and Cherokee dishes with spice blends he created himself using the knowledge he got from our grandmothers.

My mother called us creative souls. I had the gift of story-telling, and he was a master in the kitchen. In my opinion, I didn't think anyone could hold a candle to his cooking.

Most restaurants took years to start making money, but my brother's creations had his place packed every evening.

I parked behind his restaurant and climbed out of my car. The rich aroma of spices floated in the air, mixing with the stench of old garbage and city exhaust. I let myself in the back door. Music blared from the front of the building, intermixing with loud voices and laughter.

Closing my eyes, I stood in the hallway and let the drumbeat take me. It reached into my soul and settled the turmoil swirling around my heart. I'd always been just a little too sensitive. Maybe that was why, despite my bravado earlier, I was having a hard time. Why I'd allowed a little rudeness from my new boss to trouble me so much.

My stomach rumbled, reminding me of one of the reasons I was here. I really needed to eat something.

The door to my brother's office stood open. I stepped inside to find a minefield. Every available surface was covered with ceramic bowls. He was mixing again. In his happy place. He used to tell me, *That is where the fusion lies, little sister, in the meld between the spices. But you must remember, every great meld starts with salt. The most potent spice on earth.*

His familiar footsteps sounded on the hard marble floor. I smiled just as he rounded the corner. My brother. Well over six feet tall, he wore his long black hair in a braid like our father, had deep hazel eyes like our mother, and wore a grin that was all him.

"I need a place to sit," I said, waving at all his concoctions.

He chuckled and shifted some stuff off his office chair. "Hello to you too, little sister. Thought you were starting work today?"

I sat down heavily on the chair. "I was. I am. I just have to be back *precisely* at 5 p.m. They wouldn't even let me move my stuff into my room."

He sat on the edge of his desk. "Did you consider accepting Janelle's apology?"

"Really, Shiye? Accept her apology?" I shook my head.

He hesitated, then said, "You always have before."

"What?"

He stared at me as if willing me to understand. Finally, he said, "Janelle has always been a terrible friend." He raised his hand to ward off my protest. "She has disappointed you. And honestly, none of us liked her." He stared at me out of eyes filled with love. "But we knew it was always difficult for you to make friends."

"It . . . wasn't?" I sighed, looking down at the floor. "Okay, maybe it was. But I don't remember her ever doing something like this to me."

He chuckled, a dark sound filled with disbelief. "No. She's done much worse."

We stared at each other for a minute. Had I been in a toxic friendship all along?

"I don't even think you'll mourn her," he said, tapping me on the nose like he used to when we were little. "It's what she represented."

I wanted to deny it. But the one thing my brother and I always swore to do was be honest with one another. No matter what.

"Now, what has you so upset about the job?"

I nodded, thankful for the change in subject. "They have this weird obsession with time." I pulled my phone out and showed him the pictures I took.

He studied the image for a minute. "Yeah. That is a bit creepy. But it was also common back then to build houses that way." He shrugged and handed back my phone.

I tapped it against my leg.

The idea of gauging an individual based on your first encounter came from my Grann Yvette and the summers we spent with her in the Louisiana Bayou. She and my grandpa had a great many dealings with their white neighbors. She had a saying: *Sa ou wè lè ou gade yo.* Translated: What you see when you look at them. She always asked us in Creole. For them, it was the only true way to tell a person's intentions. They could lie to your face. Even smile while doing it. And the most practiced of them could even make that smile reach their eyes.

"Don't think." I paused, studying his face. "*Ki sa ou wè lè ou gade* Hermoine Kalakos?"

"*Li te defann*," he said, then narrowed his eyes as if surprised by his answer.

"She empty?" I asked, clarifying.

"*Wi*," he said, rubbing his goatee.

An individual who was empty had no set personality. They were more like a chameleon, becoming whatever a person needed. Always hiding their true nature.

"Well," I said, "I guess you can say most rich people could fit into that mold. Especially those who spend an inordinate amount of time doing philanthropic work. Not everyone is that charitable."

Shiye cocked his head to the side. "That's all The Pagonis Society does. Care for the underprivileged." A defensive note in his tone told me I'd hit a nerve. While my parents had given him the start-up money to open *Nez Deschene*, The Pagonis Society had sent a lot of business his way.

He glanced at my phone. "That strange clock would suggest they *may* have an affiliation with a cult." He paused. "But I've never seen evidence of that. And if they were, you know Mom and Dad would have discovered it."

I nodded. "True." I smacked his leg. "Either way, I want to do a little research on them. So . . . feed me, dear brother of mine." I smiled at him.

He smiled back and stood. "That I can do. Will even infuse some of my latest creations into the food. You can guess the spices I used."

He was back in his happy place. I was glad. That crease between his eyes worried me. It meant he was second-guessing himself. And if I didn't nip it in the bud, he'd get lost in that cycle of self-doubt. I couldn't let my attitude and misgivings impact his own feelings.

Didn't mean I wasn't going to still do research, though.

First, I looked up the Greek translation of the words engraved on the sign. House Eternal. Odd. A search on those words came up with mostly book and song titles, and a few references to Dracula. Not helpful.

However, my search on The Pagonis Society turned up thirty-two pages of results. Most people, when searching for something online, read the first few entries and move on. I read all of it. Even when my eyes threatened to cross with the copious amounts of repeated information, I kept reading. It was like mining. If you only scratched the surface, you were bound to miss something.

According to most of the sites, The Pagonis Society was heavily involved in not just charitable endeavors but also funded political campaigns, historical societies all over the globe, and gave small business loans to minority groups. Nothing in what I found even hinted at them being a cult. I did, however, find images of the house covering the span of a hundred years. None inside, though. Thirteen children stood on the stoop with two steely-eyed matrons on either side of them. The older pictures showed un-smiling children, but the more recent images showed the children with huge grins on their faces.

I leaned in and studied the picture. One of the matrons had a strong resemblance to Collette. Could it have been a relative? Had their ancestors established the home for chil-dren and kept the business in the family? I kept digging but didn't find the connection, so I moved on.

While I was engrossed in reading, my brother set

down a steaming plate of sweet potato hash with bell peppers, sweet caramelized onions, and bacon with two fried eggs and mushroom garnish on top. A second plate of fry bread and a mug of tea followed. I inhaled the plethora of scents, sifting through the sweet, the spicy, and the salty.

He stood over me with a wide grin on his face. "Take a bite."

I cut into the stack of potatoes and egg and scooped some onto my fork. "I already smell cinnamon in there." I took a bite and melted back in my chair. "Dear god," I said around the food in my mouth. "This is good."

"Go ahead. Tell me what else you taste."

I waved my fork at him. "Go away so I can savor this in peace."

He rummaged on his desk and handed me a bottle. "Here. Take it with you and tell me later." I laughed and shook my head. He really did love to wow people with his spice infusions. After I shoved it in my pocket, he tapped my nose and walked out.

As I devoured the food, I clicked on the last page of results, and it was more of the same. But when I started to close the window, I noticed a novel listed among the references: *The Colored Lawmen of the American Frontier* by Mary Jean Alice Miller.

Curious what a book about colored lawman had to do with The Pagonis Society, I went in search of the book and found it had been out of print for over sixty years. But a PDF copy was available online. I polished off my tea and opened the document. Once I typed in "The Pagonis Society", the cursor jumped to page 278.

Bass Reeves spoke fondly of his good friend, Samuel Bowden, last heard of while searching for Pagonis House—presumed missing.

I quickly searched for Samuel Bowden and turned up a blurry black-and-white photograph of two lawmen standing next to horses.

Next, I searched for Pagonis House, and the search engine asked if I meant Pagonis Manor.

Could they be referring to the same house? I sat back in the chair, belly full, and pondered. Out of all the searching, only this brief mention of a missing person connected to Pagonis House.

So, what did it all mean?

5

Samuel woke from a nightmare, hands bound to the bedpost. The fever had broken, and now he lay in a bed smelling of sweat and dried blood. Why had they bandaged his wounds? Why keep him alive at all?

The door opened, and the one calling herself Hermoine strode in carrying a tray with fresh bandages and antiseptic on it. She smiled at him as if she weren't holding him captive. She was a devil in disguise, and Samuel didn't much care to be in the same room with her.

"They'll come looking for me," he told her, eyeing the tray she set on the bed. "Best you let me go . . . with the children."

"The children are dead, Marshal Bowden." She sat on the bed. "And they have come looking for you. I think we were convincing enough. I even gave the money we made from selling your horse as a reward for information that leads to your return."

She unwound his bandages and winced. "I really should

have redressed this sooner." She locked gazes with him. "Wouldn't want you dying on us."

After she dressed his wounds, her sister, Collette, came in with a bowl of soup and a chunk of bread. Of the two, he knew he could trust Collette more. She wore her evil like a cloak, not caring to disguise that meanness in her eyes.

He didn't want to eat their food or have them tend to him. But he also knew he needed to build his strength if he ever wanted to escape from this place alive. So he ate, and he planned.

A few days later, when he was able to stand on his own, their brother Minos—healed from the gunshot Samuel had put in his gut—came and got him. The large man escorted Samuel down a spiral staircase into the basement of the house.

When Samuel stepped into the large space, his hand flew to his side—reaching for the weapon they had already taken from him. His blood boiled with anger.

In the middle of that floor, resting on the wood, was a large rendition of the strange clock he'd seen on their front door. Its demon bird stared at him out of ruby eyes.

Thirteen children lay on the floor, each of their bodies angled at a different number on the clock. Ashen skin caved in, chests perfectly still. Every last one of them mere shells of what they once were.

Samuel surged forward, ready to strangle the smiling Hermoine, only to be yanked back by her brother.

"What have you done?" he yelled.

They didn't respond.

6

xcept for the mention of Samuel Bowden, I didn't readily have a legitimate reason to not return promptly at five. But I *did* have concerns. Ones that continued to play inside my head as I made my way to Forest Hill for the second time today. The only thing I couldn't figure out was why I was so fixated on it. Anger? I didn't like how I'd been treated by Ms. Kalakos. But that was no reason to suspect anything nefarious about the society. The woman was rude. Plain and simple.

So what the hell was my problem?

Trust your gut, my father would say.

My gut said there was something wrong. But my mind refused to accept it.

"Let it go, Imani. Let it go," I said and pulled to the curb in front of Pagonis Manor at 4:58 p.m.

I climbed out of the car and stopped dead in my tracks.

Voices carried on the cool breeze.

My gaze tracked the sound and found . . . children, milling around the side of the house. Not really playing, just moving as if on marionette strings. Freakish smiles were plastered on their faces. They turned when I got out of the car and stared at me out of dead eyes.

My hand went to my car door, fingernails digging into the plastic.

A grinding of gears sounded.

Laughter rang out.

And just like that, the children broke from those imaginary strings and ran around the yard as if just now coming to life.

I glanced up at the house. It no longer looked frozen in time.

The front door opened, and Collette Kalakos came bustling out the front door wearing a flowing white skirt and a turquoise top. Strands of her long hair feathered around her face. A large smile creased her mouth, and her eyes danced with pure joy. "Ms. Deschene! So happy to see you." She stopped in front of me and clamped her hands on my arms. "You don't need to stand outside. Please. Come in." She pulled me forward. "I will have Minos get your things. I want you to meet your charges first."

Reluctantly, I followed, mind buzzing with a slew of questions. One being, who the hell had this woman morphed into? And why did she act as if she were just now meeting me?

She moved past the children and started for the stairs.

I stopped. "Umm . . . shouldn't I meet the children?" I asked, waving my hand at the kids at play. Who, strangely, hadn't bothered to acknowledge us.

Collette shook her head. "No. No. They have already been assimilated. You will be in charge of two other children."

I cocked my head to the side. "Assimilated?"

She froze, eyes rounding slightly. "Oh. No. I mean . . ." She shook her head. "I mean they have been here a while and have taken nicely to the routine." She nodded as if trying to reassure herself this made sense.

It really didn't. Assimilation was indoctrination. Used in the past to strip children from their families and cultures and into the colonists' ways. My father had told me horror stories about his grandfather's time at the Indian boarding schools, where he was forced to learn English, convert to Christianity, and assimilate into society. Even my Haitian Creole grandparents did not escape the horrific practices of the past.

Anger rose inside of me. "Does The Pagonis Society practice indoctrination?"

She rushed forward, reaching for me. I stepped out of her grasp. Concern filled her eyes. "Oh, no. No. I misspoke. I truly apologize."

Did I believe her? I glanced at the children, who had stopped and were now staring at us. "Hello," I said to a boy nearest to us. "How are you?"

He smiled. "I'm fine, miss."

I shook my head and strode toward him, hand extended. "You don't have to call me that." I crouched and made eye contact with him. "My name is Imani. What's yours?"

"Nicholas, mi . . . Imani." His face lit up. "It's nice to meet you."

"Do you like it here, Nicholas?"

He bobbed his head up and down. "Oh, yes!"

Did I detect a false ring in his voice?

I studied him for a minute, then looked over at the other children. They didn't appear brainwashed. But what would that really look like? "Okay." I turned back to Collette. Her eyes were laser focused on Nicholas. I wouldn't be able to tell what was going on in such a brief exchange, especially under Collette's watchful gaze. "I think I'm ready to meet my . . . charges?"

Collette sighed heavily. "Yes. Thank you. Go and finish playing, Nicholas." She gave me a hesitant smile. "Please follow me."

I made my way up the stairs and glanced at the clock on the door as we passed. When I had come by earlier, it had read eleven o'clock. Now, it was twelve.

7

We stepped inside the house. A biting cold rushed at me and burrowed its way under my skin. I shivered and rubbed my bare arms against the worst of it. My teeth clattered. I should have put on my jacket. But the day had warmed a little, and I didn't think I'd need it indoors. Why would they keep the house so cold?

My gaze went to the spiral staircase in the center of the parlor. The design reminded me of a cyclone, climbing up into the unknown. Light arrowed down the middle, holding a storm of dust in its beam. Varying shades of turquoise and brown covered the walls. An enormous, ancient grandfather clock sat against the wall leading up the stairs. Embedded in the cherry wood were peacock feathers and striations of gold.

Collette started for the stairs, and I followed. The polished hardwood creaked beneath my feet. A subtle stench of decay and rot filled the air in front of me, and I stopped. I pulled in a deep breath, trying to piece together where the smell could be coming from, but it was gone. Only furniture polish, the strange scent of ozone, and burnt cinnamon filled the air.

Collette glanced over her shoulder, foot suspended between one step and the next. "Is something wrong?" she asked.

"Just admiring the details." I paused, curiosity brimming inside of me, ready to burst. "Why the two different names?"

She furrowed her brow in confusion.

"Pagonis Manor and House Eternal?"

She smiled. "You read Greek?"

"I had to look it up," I admitted.

"Yes, of course." She turned around fully, letting her hand rest on the banister. "Pagonis is also Greek. It is the name of our organization." She looked around and smiled. "House Eternal is the place we will all one day reside." She stared down at me. "Think of it as a prayer."

"I don't follow," I said, my own brow furrowing. *Were they a cult?*

She shook her head and continued up the stairs. "Please hurry, I'd like you to get settled as soon as possible. We do have a schedule to keep."

I wanted to protest, ask for more clarification. But my job didn't require me to know. We continued our trek up the stairs. As we climbed, the temperature dropped even more. Like we were walking into an artic zone. "Why is it so cold in here?"

"It helps preserve the house," she said, as if I should already have known that. Halfway to the top, my legs were screaming. How could a three-story house have so many stairs?

A man trudged down, meeting us as we rounded another bend. Tall, with curly dark hair that rested at his collar. He wore loose-fitting white linen pants and a turquoise shirt. A peacock pendant hung from a piece of braided rope around his neck. He smiled and dipped his chin in my direction. "Miss," he said in that same thick accent.

"Hello," I said, then glanced at Collette.

"Minos, this is Imani Nez Deschene. She will be with us for a few short months helping Molly and Troy assim— adjust to their new environment." She straightened her shirt and gave me a brief glance, then continued, "I believe she has her belongings with her. Please retrieve them from her car and bring them to her room."

It was so dang hard not to pounce on her obvious stumble with the word "assimilate". If I wanted to give her the benefit of the doubt, I could. Yet, a part of me also believed she knew exactly what she was saying.

This left me with a conundrum. I could leave. Refuse to participate in whatever they were up to. But what about the kids? Who would advocate for them? I could report it. But with what evidence? A misspoken word?

"Is everything alright, Ms. Deschene?" Minos asked, hand extended. I looked at both of them and realized my inner thoughts had made me miss something.

"Yes, of course. I apologize. What did you say?"

"May I have your keys?" He paused, dark eyes studying me. "For your car. So I can get your things."

I reached into my pocket and pulled out my keys, only to stop before handing them over. "I can help."

He took my keys. "No. It's my job."

Before I could protest further, he made his way down the stairs. Humming what sounded like a nursey rhyme along the way. A stray string of words carried up to me: "*. . . to* *power the clock.*" Maybe it wasn't so much a cult as people who were obsessed with time.

When we finally reached the top floor, I bent over and looked back the way we came. It didn't look like a long way up, but my thighs were screaming at me, and my breaths had grown shallow and labored. As I leaned against the banister, catching my breath, my gaze snagged on the spot directly in the middle of the floor. A faint image of that strange clock had been embedded in the wood. Those ruby, evil eyes of the peacock held me in its gaze.

Cold, tiny hands pushed at my back. I stumbled, catching myself at the last second. I whipped around, eyes narrowing as I stared at Collette. There was no way she could have touched me and moved away so quickly. Had I imagined the sensation?

"You should be careful so close to the edge," Collette said. "Many have fallen to their death standing right where you are."

I eased back, eyes glued to hers. Was she threatening me? Or warning me? Her gaze said it could be either. But her tone said it was the former.

She smiled. "I would never let you fall, of course."

"Of course," I said, face blank.

She jerked her head toward the hallway. "Come. We really do need to keep on schedule."

After a brief hesitation, I followed, still trying to puzzle out what just happened.

From the outside, the top floor looked like a bell tower. Instead of a round structure, our climb led us into a short hallway with four rooms. Along the right side sat a single door, slightly ajar. Collette led me into the room.

"This will be your room for the next two months."

Pale turquoise walls infused with gold filigree adornments greeted me. A single bed with plush pillows and more turquoise rested against the wall near the door. Directly across from it was a small desk with a window above it. Hardwood floors covered the entire space.

The room was a bit small, but at least the bed looked comfy. I might go a little insane staring at the varying shades of turquoise all over the place. But I only had to work here for two months.

I walked farther into the room and stopped. It was a bit warmer in here. Surprising given the frigid temperature circling the rest of the house. But that wasn't what had me puzzled. It was the smell, a strange sort of musty, floral scent at war with the stench of ozone after a storm. Yet the window was closed—and nailed shut. Strange.

Footsteps had me turning. Minos walked into the room carrying my suitcase and laptop bag. How the hell had he gotten up here so fast? He set my luggage near the desk and stood there, staring at the window. After a beat, he handed me my keys, then walked out of the room.

"Thanks," I called out belatedly.

"Yes," Collette said and eased the door closed. "I must give you a few instructions on their care. Do you wish to write them down?"

I hesitated, then pulled a notepad and pen from my purse. "Okay," I said, mind still on Minos's odd behavior. Why was he staring at the window? More importantly, why was it nailed shut?

"At 6:25 p.m. sharp, Molly and Troy will exit their rooms. At no time shall you enter their space, nor shall they enter yours." She paused, eyes on my notepad as if to be sure I was writing it down. "Since introductions will take some time, we will have to wait until you all arrive in the dining hall. Once they have eaten all of their food, it will be time for their baths." She opened the door and motioned for me to follow.

I stepped out into the hall, gaze lingering on the two doors opposite mine. Affixed to each door was a number— twelve and thirteen. A single long peacock feather, with the ocelli visible, ran down the length of the dark wood. I suppressed a chill and continued down the hall after Collette.

She motioned for me to enter a large bathroom. I almost let out an audible sigh at the absence of turquoise. Pale gold walls with intricate details painted on them covered the entire space. A large Roman bathtub sat on a dais in the middle of the floor. Clay pots filled with plants surrounded it. The air smelled of cardamon and mint, with just a hint of almond.

A long sink with three washbasins ran along the right wall, and two windows sat directly across from them, gold curtains framing them.

"This is really extravagant," I said.

Collette grinned. "Before the Romans introduced society to the bathhouses, we Greeks also bathed in luxury. A gift from the goddess Hera to her most loyal subjects."

What? I'd never heard that before. Hera was the goddess of motherhood, family, and marriage, not bathhouses. Did

The Pagonis Society pull from another pagan practice and superimpose it on their own worship of Hera?

"Umm . . . okay," I said, still puzzling through the answer and wondering if it really mattered anyway. "So, the children and I share this bathroom?"

"Yes, it is imperative they take baths in *this* tub using the oil from *this* jar." She pointed to a clay jar on a small table at the head of the tub. "You will have to supply your own bathing oil."

"You mean . . . soap?" I asked.

She furrowed her brow. "Yes, yes. Soap." She smiled. "At 7:30 sharp, they must bathe in warm water and the oil."

"What kind of oil is it? Bubble bath?"

"Bubble bath?" she asked, then paused. "No. It is oil. For cleansing."

This was getting a little . . . strange. Why so many odd rules? And what the hell was up with the oil? She signaled for me to follow her out. We went back into my room, and she shut the door again.

She sighed, clasping her hands in front of her. "I must warn you now," she said after a while. "The children still wish to return to their old lives and will demand to leave. We've had to lock the doors at night to prevent them from getting out of the house. They may attempt to run away. It was why we decided to hire a night nanny." She studied me. "It can be sad seeing them in distress, and you may even want to take them outside. But they cannot leave."

"Not even to play with the other children? Surely getting some fresh air wouldn't hurt."

Her eyes rounded. "Oh, but it will. I have a strict regime for a reason. I've been doing this sort of work for what seems like forever. If rules are not implemented and followed, then chaos ensues, and the children . . . they don't . . . thrive?"

Why would she phrase that as a question?

"Okay. So no going out. Got it."

"Do you need a stopwatch or timer to keep you on schedule?"

I shook my head slowly. "No. I think I can manage."

"Good. After they bathe, they may spend some time reading downstairs. We have a vast library. But they must be in their rooms at 9:30 sharp. Not a minute later. Once they are inside, they must stay until breakfast. I will take care of the schedule in the morning. You are only to keep watch during the night."

I finished jotting down notes and looked up at her. "Is there any reason I can't meet them now?"

Collette shook her head and opened the door. "Spend time, as I said, getting your space in order. If you need anything, just ask Minos. He is here to aid us." She walked out and shut the door.

I stared at it for a moment, willing the exchange to make sense. When it didn't, I looked at my notes. Nope. Still didn't make sense.

What I mostly got hung up on was why I couldn't meet the kids I was caring for. And why such an odd schedule. Warm bath in the oil at 7:30? What if they bathed in cold water? Or with bubble bath? How would that hurt their ability to *thrive*? And honestly, I didn't think that was the word she'd meant to use. No, we both knew what word she'd wanted to say.

Something was off. I could feel it deep in my bones.

8

Samuel held the worn Missing poster in his hand, staring at the man he used to be. Along with the deep creases on his skin, were the scars from the many attempts he'd made to get free of this place. And each time, that evil woman with a smile on her face and light in her eyes would bandage his wounds and tell him of the children she took.

Every twenty-five years they fed that clock the souls of the young so they could live forever.

On those days, when she wiped the blood from his skin, she'd offer to give him the gift of immortality. And every day, he refused. He didn't want their dark gift.

His wife, Olathe, had long passed. The Kalakos took pleasure in giving him updates of the life his family had lived without him. Even showed him photographs of his grandchildren.

One day, he would see them.

He opened the door to his room. They had long ceased locking him up. But they had nailed his window shut. Didn't matter. He had no plans to leave. Not without the children whose ghosts haunted these halls, forever trapped in this place.

A cool draft bit into his old bones. He shuffled out into the hall and stared at the two doors across from him. Twelve and thirteen. Two children slept in those rooms. Two children whose lives were being slowly drained. And every night, they would bathe in a preservative to keep them fresh. Until the last of their souls had died.

He placed a hand upon one of the doors, letting the cold infuse him with determination. Whether in spirit or body, he would find a way for him and the children to escape . . . the House Eternal.

9

At exactly 6:25, a pale-skinned little girl, no more than five years old, wearing a long white linen dress with a turquoise sash around her waist and two identical thin ponytails in her hair, stepped out of the door marked twelve. As if in sync, a slender, pale-skinned boy with short brown hair, wearing a pair of white linen pants and a white linen shirt with a turquoise belt, stepped out of the door marked thirteen.

Neither child looked at me.

Goosebumps broke out along my skin as I stared into their washed-out eyes—so filled with rage, as if they were in the midst of screaming.

I crouched down. "Hello, I'm Imani."

"We have to go eat now," the boy said, taking the little girl's hand.

Damnit.

"Do you want to go eat?" I asked. Maybe a choice in their routine was all they really needed.

They both stared at me. "Miss Collette makes us follow

her schedule. We don't get any time in the library if we don't," the little boy said, his face filling with fear.

I stood and reached for their hands. They didn't take mine. I shook it off and started forward. Their tiny footsteps followed.

Collette and I were going to need to have another little chat about assimilation.

Located at the back of the house, the dining hall had red walls with white-framed French doors, breaking up the color. A round wooden table sat in the center of the opulent space, surrounded by chairs covered in patterned cushions of light blue and green. Large planters hung from the wall, with plants spilling their foliage onto the floor. In the center of the table rested a large clay jar with grapes, still on their vines, encircling it.

The children I'd seen playing in the yard earlier sat, eyes forward, with gold-rimmed turquoise plates filled with cheese, bread, fruit, vegetables, and small slices of roasted chicken in front of them.

Collette and Minos sat at a tall bar table near the wall, observing the children, with their own plates of food.

My charges rushed to the table and took their seats. A woman bustled over and set a plate down in front of them. Collette motioned for me to join her and Minos.

The same woman handed me a plate of food, then left the room.

"Thank you for being on time," Collette said, a subtle note of relief in her tone.

A grinding of gears sounded. "You may all eat," she announced.

Collette took small bites of her food, her eyes fixed on the children. Minos filled three gold goblets with a dark, sweet-smelling wine. The crimson liquid settled inside the cup.

I didn't want to drink the wine. But the food did smell good. However, being micromanaged down to the very instant I could eat rubbed me the wrong way. So, when Minos and Collette had finished most of their food, I took my first bite. I had to admit, the combination of fruit and cheese and vegetables tasted pretty good. Couldn't hold a candle to my brother's cooking, though. The chicken could have used some salt.

After my hunger eased, I turned to Collette. "I'm a little concerned about the children," I said.

Minos glanced at me, goblet in hand, then looked away, tipping his cup back to drain the contents.

"Oh," Collette said, wiping her fingers. "What is the problem?"

I could have searched for a diplomatic way of broaching the subject, but Collette rubbed me the wrong way. And I wasn't about to beat around the bush trying to find a pretty word to dress up an ugly topic.

"They all seem to have been *assimilated* into a quite rigid schedule. They seem fearful to step out of line. Children need to feel loved and comforted. Not beaten into submission."

She pursed her lips, but didn't look at me. "What do you know of teaching children?" she asked, a chill in her voice.

"I know cruelty is not love," I said, matching her tone.

"Oh, you believe spoiling a child and letting them run wild is showing love?" She turned to me. "This society is filled with such offspring. They grow to adulthood and abandon their children. Rob the less fortunate. Rape and murder. Children with no discipline are not loved. They are disregarded. Their lives filled with no meaning. No purpose." She dipped her head toward the children eating. "They have purpose. They have meaning." She paused, studying me. "If this job is too much for you, you will tell me now so that we may find a suitable replacement. Time is important, and we cannot so easily stop the flow of it."

"You can't stop time, period," I said, my anger rising. "And no, Collette. I am able to do my job. I just wanted to point out what I observed."

She gave me a tight smile. "Thank you for your *observation*." She stood, gave me one last scathing look, and walked away.

Bitch.

The oil I'd been instructed to use in the children's baths smelled like burnt ozone and wet feathers. Of course, I'd rubbed some on my arm first to make sure nothing was wrong with it. When my skin didn't melt off or blister, I figured it was okay, however foul smelling. I mean, what was wrong with good old-fashioned, kid-friendly bubble bath?

"Do you need me to help you?" I asked.

"No. We have to do it on our own," Troy said as he undressed.

"Okay. What about you?" I asked Molly.

She shook her head.

They bathed together, each simply running the sponge on

their skin, over and over again, while they stared mutely at the water.

Again, I thought of cults and ritual practices, and again, I dismissed them. I glanced around the room, thought of the food and the décor, the Greek lettering on the door. Maybe it wasn't so much time and routine they were obsessed with. Maybe they simply wanted to teach the children about their culture. Could that be it?

No. Even if that were the case, it didn't explain the refusal to let them go outside, nor did it explain the obsession with time and schedules.

Once the children dressed, I followed them as they made their way to an enormous library on the second floor. We spent exactly one hour in that house of books. I would have normally enjoyed flipping through those old volumes, inhaling the scents of old paper and ink. But my mind kept screaming at me. I studied the children as they silently turned the pages of books too advanced for their age, all the while trying to find some semblance of life inside of them.

After the children had settled in their rooms, I stood in the doorway of my own, staring at the numbers affixed to their doors. Twelve and thirteen. I counted the other children I'd seen in my head—eleven.

I leaned against the doorjamb. How had the children come to be in this place? Simply asking them could induce trauma, and I doubted Collette would be very forthcoming since I'd ruffled her ridged bitch feathers at dinner.

I wasn't one of those people who equated withholding

information with being tantamount to lying. No one was really required to tell everything about themselves.

But in this case, like my assumptions about cults, I had to revisit my own definition of untruthfulness. Was Collette lying? She was certainly covering something up. In this case, my knowledge of the children I was to take care of had to be fully revealed. Anything withheld could harm them as well as me. And Collette didn't seem to care.

No. Her concern was with bath oils and time and . . . yes, assimilating them into her demented views on child-rearing.

My stomach rumbled.

I hadn't finished my dinner, and I really could've used a snack. Preferably one that was properly seasoned. I stepped back into my room and grabbed the bottle of infused salt my brother had given me. Maybe I'd take some time to figure out all the ingredients, and after my belly was full, I would soak in that enormous tub.

While I wanted to go and physically check on the children, Collette's warning to not enter their rooms blared in my head. So, I settled on listening outside their doors for a minute before I walked toward the stairs, only to stop when movement below startled me.

Easing toward the landing, I peered into the darkness. The center of the house was an abyss, its dark maw yawning at me, gazing into my soul. I tried to look away, but something in those murky depths ensnared me, rooting me in place.

A cold breeze blew across my skin.

Icy fingers trailed along my neck.

But still, I couldn't move.

Something cold trailed down my spine, as if it were tracing the vertebrae with its frigid finger.

I gasped, and the sensation stopped.

And still, I gazed into the abyss.

". . . if you gaze long into an abyss, the abyss also gazes into you." - Friedrich Nietzsche

The quote circled my head as I willed myself to look away. I spotted Collette, wearing a white peplos and gold band around her head. She descended into the abyss, and its jaws closed—the wood floor becoming solid again.

I stood there. Heart pounding. Adrenaline coursing through my body, creating a hum in my ears as I tried to orient myself. What the hell was that?

I glanced down the hall and was met with darkness.

A grinding of gears sounded, and the floor shook with a vibration that made me bite my tongue.

Blood welled in my mouth.

And a child's scream tore the air in half.

10

I rushed to the children's doors. The mystery of what I'd just witnessed would have to wait. Molly's door opened, and she stood in the doorway, mouth open. A few seconds later, the sound came from somewhere deep inside of her, a constant shriek filled with agony and loss. I stepped toward her, but the air surrounding the girl had changed. She pounded her fists at an invisible wall, dark eyes wild with terror.

Until, suddenly, she pitched forward into my arms. I gathered her shaking body, rubbing her back, trying my best to soothe her. Was it a nightmare? No, more than that. Why hadn't I been able to reach her? I glanced at her room.

A glossy shimmer rolled through the darkness.

I stared at that open doorway, waiting, until the burn in my eyes made me blink.

"I want to go home!" she yelled, pulling my attention back to her.

She flailed in my arms, then suddenly pushed away. Her wild eyes stared at me.

I didn't see it coming. But I should have.

Tiny fingernails raked across my face, my arms, as Molly scratched at me with all her strength. Pure madness fueled her movements. I tried to wrestle her arms together, tried to pull her back to me, but she was too strong. Too angry. Too scared.

"Please, Molly. Stop. I won't hurt you. Promise," I said in a soft tone.

The stench of blood filled the air. My blood. Mixing with a noxious scent of burnt ozone and roses.

A pain, so intense, rode every bit of my body and mind. But I did not lash out. Only tried over and over to still her gently.

Her scratches and slaps became kicks. I had to stop her. Had to get away. Why had no one come?

I scrambled backward; my back hit the wall, and tears streamed down my face.

"Molly, please stop," I said, infusing as much calm into my voice as I could. The urge to yell lodged itself in my throat as she delivered yet another painful kick to my leg.

Troy's door opened; a chilly fog rushed out. He stepped into the hallway and walked slowly toward me. "Take us outside," he whispered. "It hurts."

Molly stopped, fingers still arched into claws, and turned to him. Her little chest heaved. "Will it stop?" she asked him.

He nodded, eyes still on me. "Please. We don't belong here. They stole us."

"Stole you from who?" I asked, swallowing the lump in my throat. Slowly, carefully, favoring my right side, I eased up the wall. Every inch of my body ached. But it was nothing compared to the pain I saw in both their eyes.

Troy didn't answer my question. Just stared at me.

I licked my lips and nodded, my own chest heaving.

"You can tell me when you're ready." I opened my arms, and they both rushed into them. I gritted my teeth against the pain. I needed to clean the blood off me and bandage the cuts. But that could wait; the children needed to go outside. I didn't give a damn what Collette had said. Or what fucked up rules she tried to impose.

I took their chilly hands in mine and led them downstairs. When we reached the door, I let go long enough to try and open it, only to be met with resistance. Even after unlocking it, the door wouldn't move.

Troy tapped my arm and pointed up. I followed the line of wood and noted a small latch up high. I glanced around the room, trying to find something to stand on. *Crap.*

"Come on," I said, taking their hands again. "We'll try another door."

Our search grew frantic as every exit seemed barred to the outside. Then I remembered the French doors in the dining hall.

We climbed the stairs to the second floor. "Quiet," I whispered as we made our way to the dining hall.

Muted light filtered in through the glass, illuminating the room that, in that very moment, seemed straight out of a Greek painting. The scent of olives and grapes hung in the air, giving off an intoxicating perfume. I grabbed a chair, my gaze momentarily snagging on the deep cuts on my arm. They had stopped bleeding, the crimson smears coating my arms. I pushed the thought of Molly attacking me away and set the chair in front of the doors.

I climbed up; my fingers barely reached the gold latch. When I tried to move it, it wouldn't budge. It was as if it had been glued in place. I grunted with each failed effort until my entire body was covered in sweat, stinging the cuts on my skin.

Finally, heaving, I gave up and pressed my face to the cool glass. The walls seemed to be closing in on me. A cold hand touched my leg, and I jumped. The chair rocked, then tumbled over, and I hit the ground. Hard. Air rushed out of my mouth.

Maybe I should just break the glass, I thought. No. The noise would surely alert Collette or Minos.

Molly lay next to me, her slender arm circling my waist. "We need to get outside," she said in a small voice.

I lay there, patting her hand. "Why won't they let you outside?" I asked. Troy sat on the ground next to us and stared out the doors.

"Ms. Collette said we weren't ready. That we had to get assim . . ." He shook his head, eyes still glued to the moon and stars—the world he had been denied for some time.

Assimilated.

I surged to my feet, bringing Molly along with me. "We are going outside," I said through clenched teeth, then dragged the chair across the floors, hoping I left grooves in the polished wood.

We once again made our way to the front door. I slammed the chair down in front of it and climbed up. Just like the lock in the dining hall, this one, too, seemed to be glued in place.

"Fuck!" I yelled, letting my head rest against the wood.

"Just what do you think you're doing?" Collette's cool voice raked across my damaged skin. I wouldn't have been surprised if she made my cuts start bleeding again.

I didn't turn around. Just took my time climbing off the chair. "Taking the children outside." The kids rushed over to me. I turned then, easing them behind my back. "Now. If you could please unbar the door."

"Did I not make myself clear, Imani?"

I cocked my head. "You know, *Collette*, I would prefer if you called me Ms. Deschene. Now open the damn door."

Her eyes rounded for a brief second before narrowing in anger. "I do think you have overstepped our boundaries."

I shook my head. "No. I don't believe so."

"Just who the hell do you think you are? Coming in here—"

"I'm. The. Damn. Nanny. And my charges need some fresh air. Did you not hear Molly screaming? Or were you too busy in the basement?"

Her chin rose. "It is your job, *nanny*, to assist . . . when you hear them scream." She looked at the kids, then back at me. "And as for what I do in the basement, it is of no concern to you. Now, return them to their rooms, and I will forget all about this . . . transgression."

I started to reply, but she raised her hand, silencing me. "The children can go outside tomorrow." She paused, her face twisting, each crease seeming to move in slow motion. Finally, a frown touched her mouth, and sadness filled her eyes. "I understand they are frightened." She looked at my arms. "Do you need first aid?"

My brain stuttered, trying desperately to understand the abrupt change in both her tone and mood.

Li te defann.

Collette was an empty shell, morphing into the person she believed I needed. Someone who was empathetic and concerned. And I watched that painful transformation as if time itself had slowed and allowed me to watch.

She held her hands out. "Come along, children. You must return to your rooms." Her voice had a hypnotic quality to it.

The children moved around me and went to her as if being pulled. She took their hands and smiled down at them; the gesture even reached her eyes. "I will leave you to your devices, Ms. Deschene." She looked up at me. "If you need me to help you with your injuries, just let me know. I am truly sorry this unfortunate incident took place." She gave me a sad smile and walked away.

I stood there, mind still racing. I needed to get out of this house. I turned back to the door. Foolishly, I expected it to open with a mere thought from me. The floorboards creaked, and I turned to the sound. Minos walked into the room and over to the door.

"I can give you ten minutes outside," he said, wincing. "I understand the need to see the moon and the stars." His gaze found mine. "It is a powerful pull." He slid the bolt open, and the house groaned.

Cool night air rushed into the house. I pulled in a cleansing breath and stepped out of the House Eternal and into a moon-filled night. Each step felt like liberation. As if I'd spent months, even years cooped up inside. And I'd only been there a few short hours.

I turned to find Minos watching me from inside the doorway. His gaze held longing. Not for me. I knew what that gaze looked and felt like. No, this one was for something much deeper. Was he not allowed to go outside either? That couldn't be right. He was able to open the door, a grown man.

"You don't want to come out?" I asked, smiling at him.

He shook his head. "Ten minutes, please." Again, he winced as if he'd been hurt.

I turned away and pulled in another lungful of air. Since she hadn't fired me on the spot, I assumed I still had the job. The thing was, I didn't know if I really wanted it.

Something dark and sinister was at work here, crawling along the floors and, I feared, feeding on the children.

11

Bright rays of sunshine woke me, and someone knocked at my door. I eased up, feeling every one of the bruising wounds Molly had inflicted. Once I had returned to my room last night, I cleaned myself up and soaked in the tub for a while, but I didn't enjoy it. Nothing could stop the children's screams ringing inside my head.

I pulled on my sweatpants and opened the door. Hermoine Kalakos stood in the doorway, holding a first aid bag and wearing the most brilliant smile I'd ever seen. Her eyes, a deep green that bordered on black, held a warmth only found when standing in the sun. She practically radiated concern.

"I understand you had a rough night," she said, a small frown touching her mouth. "I would like to help you. If you want."

"I . . . of course. I can . . ."

She shook her head. "No. No. I can wait out here. Or in the bathroom. It's up to you. Whatever makes you most comfortable."

"I've already cleaned my cuts."

She nodded, smiling at me. "Of course. I know. But please, allow me to look at them. I would hate to have you get an infection."

"Let me get dressed. And . . . the bathroom?"

She grinned. "Yes. And then we can have breakfast and talk."

"Sure," I said, then shut the door.

I refused to make eye contact while Hermoine cleaned the scratches on my arm with antiseptic. I was at a loss as to what to say, being a little uncomfortable with her ministrations. It felt almost . . . predatory.

"I love the bathroom," I said, growing uncomfortable with the silence.

Hermoine paused and looked around. "Yes." She smiled. "Yes, we believe the children should have nice surroundings." She looked back at the cut on my arm. "Molly, it would seem, has a violent streak." She shook her head. "Sadly, this is not the first time we've seen this type of behavior from her."

"She was just scared," I said in a rush.

She didn't respond.

"Your sister said the bathroom was in homage to Hera," I said, filling the awkward silence once again. I really needed to pick a different topic. Why did this woman make me so nervous?

She made a non-committal sound and continued to clean my cuts.

When she was done, she rebandaged my wounds and

stood. "She's not in trouble. Not that we won't have a discussion with her about violence. No. We don't believe in striking children." She shook her head, biting her bottom lip. "That sort of thing would never happen here." There was so much conviction in her voice, I almost believed her. Almost.

"Then why keep them from going outside?" I shook my head. It sounded so trivial. But the way the kids had behaved . . . I couldn't just brush this aside.

Hermoine made a sucking sound with her teeth, shaking her head. "As much as I love the bathroom, I say we continue this discussion over breakfast. I really am famished." She winked at me and left the room.

I stared at the door and tried to see the exchange in the way Hermoine had presented it—a concerned employer tending the wounds of an employee. Yet there was something just a little off about the whole thing. And I couldn't put my finger on it.

Either way, I had to be cautious.

We sat in a small sunroom next to the kitchen. The table had been laid with fine white and turquoise linen with gold accents. An array of sweet-smelling cheeses, large strawberries and melon, croissants that looked like they'd been bathed in butter before they were baked in the oven to a golden brown, a ceramic bowl of yogurt, and a carafe of strong coffee sat in the center of it all.

I readied myself for what I assumed would be another half-truth like her sister Collette had given.

She poured me a cup of coffee. "We are cult of sorts." She

glanced at her watch. "Would you like the cook to fix you some eggs? We have a little time before your off hours."

"Umm, no. This is fine," I said, mind blown by her honesty. And I'd completely forgotten the emphasis on my leaving before 9 a.m.

"The croissants are decent enough." She leaned forward. "But nothing compared to your brother's. He is a master in the kitchen." She smiled and sat back, placing a white linen napkin on her lap. "Where was I?" she asked, taking a sip of her coffee. "Aww, yes. Giving you an inside look into our domain. Modern-day cults. And yes, some in the past have deserved the disdain of the public given all the foul, unclean acts their leaders practiced." She shook her head as if a fresh memory of such a cult had surfaced in her mind. "But when I say *we* are a cult, it in no way mirrors what I assume you understand the word to mean." She paused, studying me. "Eat something."

I took a sip of coffee, then placed the cup down softly and looked over at her. "Help me understand."

She smiled, nodding her head. "We have a very healthy respect for our ancestors and their way of life. Modern society . . . just . . ." Her lips thinned. "They do not respect the family. Nor the rearing of children." She waved her hand as if dismissing an ugly thought. "My sister. She, out of the two of us, studied the old ways the most." She paused. "We both have been unable to bear children." A single tear slid down her carefully made-up cheek. She dabbed at it and continued. "Some people don't realize how lucky they are. How blessed," she said in a whisper.

She reached over and touched my hand lightly. "You wouldn't believe the sheer number of children born into this world without people who truly love them."

"So you decided to love them all?" I said, picking up a croissant. I took a tentative bite, and the fluffy pastry practically melted in my mouth. "Thirteen at a time."

"That's all we're licensed for." She reached behind her and pulled two file folders from her bag. "These are the records for Molly and Troy." She set them on the table. I reached for them, and she placed a hand on top. "I have to warn you. What you will read in those files will haunt you. Despite the abuses they suffered, despite the uncertainty of whether they would get their next meal, these two children are programmed to run.

"My sister is trying." She chuckled. "She can be a bit . . . much. But she does care. And she is deeply sorry for what happened last night. I hope you stay, Ms. Deschene."

"You can call me Imani."

She smiled, and her eyes lit with joy. "Thank you, Imani."

We ate in silence. Which gave me the opportunity to realize she had told me everything and nothing. I even looked through the files she'd given me, and after the third instance of abuse, I closed it. She was right; it would give me nightmares.

After breakfast, I got dressed and looked for the kids. They were nowhere to be found. I'd even listened at the door. I only hoped Collette had kept her word and taken them outside. But if not, I would. I told Hermoine I would run a few errands during my off time, and she got Minos to open the door for me.

Like last night, he stood under the doorframe, waiting for me to exit with a pained look on his face. Why didn't he come outside? He'd retrieved my luggage the day before.

"I will return at five," I told him, and he visibly relaxed.

"Thank you," he muttered, then shut the door.

Were they really that worried I would quit? Or was it something else? And why did I have to leave by 9 a.m. and return at 5 p.m.? What did they do during those hours? When I got in my car, I glanced up at the house. It had gone still again, all the life suddenly grinding to a halt.

12

I carried a red shopping basket in my hand while I held my phone to my ear, waiting for my mother to answer. Not wanting to spend hours on the internet searching, once again, for any crumb about The Pagonis Society, I opted to go to a reliable source.

My mother answered on the third ring, just as I was dropping a bottle of unscented children's bubble bath in my basket.

"Imani Nez, why is this first time you are calling me after what happened between you and that girl?" She said *that girl* as if it were a dirty word.

Had my entire family really not liked Janelle?

"Hi, Mom. How are you?" I made my way down the tool isle. "I need some information." I threw a hammer, a crowbar, and a flathead screwdriver in my basket. I also added a knife, just in case. There was no telling how long the window had been nailed shut, and the thick coat of paint covering the nails would also pose a problem.

She sighed. "I'm doing okay. Your father is in a tiff about my cleaning."

"What are you worried about?" My mother always cleaned to the point of exhaustion when something bothered her.

"My children. They never let me help."

"We're not children anymore. We're adults. Remember?"

Another sigh, this one long and filled with suffering. "Wait till you have kids. Just wait. Now, what kind of information did you need?"

I gave her a rundown of what I'd found online, what I'd observed, and also sent her the pictures I took of the house while I grabbed a can of WD-40.

My mother grew silent, working through the information in her head. The sound of rustling papers told me she was also searching. Something I said must have jarred a memory.

With the window down, I went in search of some snacks for the kids. I couldn't begrudge the food they were being fed. It was healthy. Under-seasoned, but healthy. But throwing in a little sugar wouldn't hurt. So I grabbed a box of Twinkies and made my way to the checkout line, tossing a silly T-shirt in the basket as well to wrap my supplies in.

"House Eternal is the newest translation for an old idea involving the clock that began time itself," my mother said just as the cashier had started to ring me up.

My jaw dropped.

"Cash or card, ma'am?" the woman asked, concern on her face.

I mutely handed her too much cash, picked up my purchase, and left the store. My mother continued to talk.

"In this context, 'house' is another way of referring to the soul. Every living being is said to have one. Even animals.

And 'eternal' is self-explanatory. Immortality has always been assigned to the eternal duration of a life."

I got in my car and finally found my voice. "Was this with the information you found on the longevity of a soul and the worship of Hera?"

Raindrops drummed on my window. I started the car and turned on the wiper blades. The information my mother was giving me was disturbing, and I couldn't gaze out at the world through a haze of obscurity right now. It was too unsettling.

"No. That was the beginning of my search. I did find other references." She paused. "Her beloved peacock was one of the things I found. Similar to the one on that clock. A prehistoric bird that, like most animals from ancient times, evolved into what we see today. Before its evolution, it stood over seven feet tall and had no known predators."

"What was it called?" I said, chills breaking out along my arms.

"A phoenix." She paused again, probably because she realized my brain had gone into overload. "But what is most significant about its origins is the belief that it created time. And when it brought this to the beings with souls, it subjected them to death."

"Is there more?" I asked.

"No. Your father and I are still tracing the origins of this faith. But these images you sent help. Do you think The Pagonis Society would allow you to search their records?"

I didn't want to tell her I suspected The Pagonis Society of wrongdoing. At least, not without concrete proof. And what could that wrongdoing be in regard to this new information?

After thanking my mother and promising to ask for a

look at The Pagonis Society's records, I drove off, ready to throw a wrench in Collette Kalakos's schedule.

I arrived at Pagonis Manor at exactly 5 p.m. This time, there were no children out playing. Or simulating playing. I guessed the time for subterfuge was over. Not a problem. I grabbed my bundle and headed inside.

I had a little over an hour to work the nails out of the wood in my window. By the time I pried the window open, I was covered in sweat, and the entire inside of my mouth had teeth marks embedded in the flesh.

Like yesterday, the kids stepped out of their rooms at 6:25 p.m. Only this time, I crouched in front of them, and they made eye contact with me. "I know you are suffering, and I won't sit here and let that happen any longer. I have a plan," I whispered. "Do you trust me?"

They nodded slowly, a little light coming into their eyes.

"Good." I stood, took both their hands, and we made our way to dinner.

I only wished I could've added some of my brother's seasoning to our dinner. While I had stashed it away in my pocket, I doubted I'd get the chance to sprinkle some on my food without Collette noticing.

After giving the children a bath using a drop of the oil and a generous amount of the bubble bath, I gave them a Twinkie each, and we did our hour in the library.

At five minutes to ten, having already pried open the window completely, I stood in my doorway and waited.

A grinding of gears sounded, announcing it was now 10 p.m., and the children's doors opened. I put a single finger to my lips and motioned them over. They moved swiftly, eyes still registering pain, and ran into my room and straight for the window as if they were seeking the air. I helped them both up onto the desk and held them as they stuck their heads outside and inhaled deeply.

Dark spots appeared on their skin, spreading as if a pocket deep inside them, filled with brown liquid, had been punctured and was slowly leaking out underneath their skin. They dragged in breaths, their whole bodies expanding and contracting.

Molly's hair began to fill out, fluffing up, as if she might have worn an afro. Troy's hair also grew.

I pulled them inside and turned them toward me. "What's happening to you?" I asked, my eyes rounded.

"Life," Troy uttered and then turned his head toward my bedroom door.

A second later, it banged open, and an enraged Collette stood in the doorway with Minos looming behind her.

"What have you done?" she shrieked, rushing forward. She grabbed my arm and flung me sideways. I stumbled onto my bed. Before I could stop her, she wrenched both of the children's arms up into a bruising grip and stormed out of my room. "Lock her inside!" she yelled over her shoulder.

I surged to my feet, only to be coldcocked by Minos.

"You should have obeyed the rules," I heard him say before the world went black.

13

I came to with a melody playing in my head. I sat up slowly, massaging my sore jaw, and blinked a few times to clear the blurriness from my eyes. I was still in my room. Window shut again, and most likely nailed shut, and the bedroom door closed. They'd even turned off the lights.

I eased up and walked over to confirm, yes, they had locked me in. But not for long.

I'd stashed my bundle of tools under my bead and the pocketknife in my tampon box. While the tools were gone, the knife was still there.

"Here's hoping the lock is as old as this damn house," I said, ramming the blade into the old-fashioned keyhole, A pop sounded, and I pulled the door open.

A strange, dark melody floated into my room. Children were singing.

On careful footsteps, I eased out of my room and down the hall. When I peered over the railing, a few words of the song became clear.

13 souls
13 souls
Drain them slow
Drain them slow
13 souls
13 souls
Lay them out
Lay them out
13 souls
13 souls
Power the clock
Power the clock

My blood ran cold as every single piece of this strange puzzle became clear. They were killing the children. Silence be damned, I raced down the stairs, only taking care not to stumble over my rushing feet.

When I reached the bottom, I found the cavern leading to the lower level open, its dark maw once again staring into my soul. I gave it the finger and entered.

The children's dark, twisted rhyme pierced my ears, growing louder with each step. Intertwined in it were raised voices, arguing.

Ahead of me, taking up most of the basement floor, was a life-sized replica of the clock I'd seen affixed to the front door, with all the children lying prone as if they were the hands of the clock. Eleven children, pale and ashen, their mouths moving as they continued to sing that morbid song. And poor Molly and Troy, bodies trembling and unable to move, lay with their hands resting on their stomachs.

I needed to get them out of here.

"How shall I explain your death?" Hermoine asked,

strolling toward me, Collette and Minos behind her. He held a sharp-looking axe over his shoulder and a promise of death in his eyes.

I cocked my head, truly perplexed by the audacity of her asking me that question. "I see no point in helping you concoct a lie for something that will never happen."

She laughed, a quick response that held so much disdain. "You believe you will make it out of this? Alive?"

I shrugged. "Yes."

She shook her head. "Do you know how hard it is to erase the past?" She sat on a chair made of ivory and gold and stared down at the clock. "We never tried to hide who we were until we set foot on these shores." She smiled, a wicked little grin that created a fire in her eyes.

"Oh, they balked at our sacrificing of children to the time clock to fuel our immortality. Told us we couldn't take their sons and daughters." Her lips thinned. "And to appease these . . . things that were beneath us, we took the ones they didn't desire."

Adrenaline and rage flooded my body. I wanted to claw the bitch's eyes out. But I'd let her finish her little speech. It would give me time to work through my plan. So, I slid my hand in my pocket and touched the bottle of spice I'd slipped in there earlier.

"But when the slaves were freed, and the Natives gained some semblance of their former lives, we could no longer use them as a source. And here is where all my efforts went. Each thread, each tiny change. So much painstaking time to reinvent ourselves so that we could hide in plain sight. Using individuals like your brother. Like we had planned to use you. To sing our praises. Give testimony to our good deeds."

She stopped, suddenly standing and balling her hands into fists. "While we took their children from them."

We stared at each other while I slowly, slowly unscrewed the top on my bottle of seasoning.

"Molly and Troy will need to start the process again. Right now, they have too much life in them. Oh, don't get your hopes up. They died twenty years ago when they first set foot in this house. But the time clock is a fickle master; it drains them slowly. By letting them touch the air outside, you reinfused life into them. Now they straddle the space between."

She took a step toward me, and I stood my ground. "So again, I ask, how shall I explain your death?"

I chuckled and pulled the open jar from my pocket. "I, too, am a student of history. But I get the impression you already knew that. Probably studied every bit of my and my brother's life." I paused, thinking. "And those files." I watched her closely. "Those fabricated files you showed me about abuse." I shook my head, disgusted. "You really did have me believing you cared. The tears were a nice touch too.

"Two points, and we can debate my demise. The first: you should have learned in your long life that villains who wish to give long, elaborate speeches often end up giving the hero a chance to survive."

She gave me a half grin. Minos moved forward, and she stalled him with a single gesture. "You fancy yourself a hero?"

"Heroine," I said and poured some of the contents into my hand. The smell of cardamon and cinnamon filled the space. "Second point: there is one spice in great abundance that is said to ward off evil. It's so commonplace in movies and folklore that no one ever doubted its potency."

"Cinnamon?" she asked, staring at the brown flecks in my hand.

"No"—I tossed the contents over the entire clock—"salt, you long-winded bitch!"

The reaction was so sudden, I didn't have time to brace myself. A sharp whining rang out, gears grinding as wisps of smoke rose off the ground. Hermoine, Collette, and Minos screamed, clutching at their chests.

The children stopped singing. Their mouths remained open, dead eyes staring at the ceiling. I rushed over and scooped Molly into my arms, grabbed Troy's hand, and ran, only sparing a brief glance behind me to confirm they weren't following us. No. They were too busy dying.

Up the stairs we went as the house shook. A large energy wave pounded at me; invisible hands slid across my skin, trying to gain purchase. I muscled my way out of their ghostly grip and kept running. When we got to the first floor, I remembered the lock. Not wanting to waste any time, I set a still trembling Molly down, pulled off my shirt, wrapped it around my arm, and then smashed it against the side window.

Shards of glass rained down. I pushed the large pieces away, and just before I stepped through, a strong hand landed on my shoulder and yanked me backward. I landed on the hard floor and slid till I hit the bottom step.

"You should have followed the rules!" Minos yelled, his face wrinkled and emaciated. He lifted his axe, then tilted to the side and fell.

"And you"—I stood—"should finish dying."

I stepped around him and started for the window. A shrieking Hermoine came running toward me, her withered hands stretched out. I braced myself. And when she was close, I kicked her in the stomach. When she landed on the ground, I went to my knees and whispered in her ear, "Consider this my resignation, you twisted fuck."

I scrambled up, looked around, and once I was sure Collette would not come crawling out of the abyss, I rushed outside and fell on the wet grass. The children stood in the yard, their faces turned up to the moon. Spots of color dotted their skin.

. . . they straddle the space between.

Two children. Stolen. And for twenty years, their souls had been feasted on.

I lay on my back and opened my arms. They both lay down beside me, and I hugged them to me. Now that the fight was over, the adrenaline rush had left me bone-tired. "How about we get up in a minute," I said. They nodded.

Movement at the door caught my eyes. I tensed, ready to fight again. But I had no need. The ghost of Samuel Bowden stepped out into the night, leading the souls of all the brown children stolen throughout time.

He led them. One by one.

Finally escaping the House Eternal.

ABOUT C. VONZALE LEWIS

My name is Carla Vonzale Lewis and I like my martinis shaken . . . never stirred.

Carla was born in Georgia, but please don't mistake her for a Georgia peach. She's more like a prickly pear. Speaking of being born, someone asked her recently if she remembered her birth. And she had to say, "Yes, I do remember that handsy doctor pulling me out into the cold. Right Bastard!!!"

Despite being born in the South, she grew up in California. Every once in a great while, she gets to experience all four seasons. But mostly, it's just heat.

When not writing, Carla enjoys reading, binge watching shows on Netflix, and trying to convince her husband that getting a dog is a wonderful idea.

And one day, she will discover how many licks it actually takes to get to the center of a Tootsie Pop.

CONNECT WITH C. VONZALE

cvonzalelewis.com

facebook.com/CVLauthor

instagram.com/carlavlewis

pinterest.com/carlamc30/boards

bookbub.com/profile/c-vonzale-lewis

MORE FROM C. VONZALE LEWIS

Blood and Sacrifice Chronicles

Lineage

Zealot

Tribe

Anthologies

Masks

Love on Main

Flicker

Link by Link

Beyond the Cogs

Emporium of Superstition

This Fresh Hell

A Little Blood and a Broken Cage

By Jessica Cranberry

1

"If life is but a stage, the show isn't over when the great curtains fall."

Beyond and Further Still, Sofia Brewer

Mags sipped at the café's signature bloody mary and read the line over again. The concept of a world beyond this one quickened the pace of her heart and sometimes brought tears to her eyes. It was nothing revolutionary—an old idea, really. But it was a thought brought to the forefront of Mags's life the day her older brother had disappeared after leaving a high school party. No longer could she trail him from room to room or poke her fingers under his bedroom door when he needed to be alone. No, they'd been separated for years now, and likely for good after the Butler County PD had towed his truck up from the bottom of Mirror Pond.

Yet some, like the famed psychic and author of the book Mags read, believed only a veil kept them apart.

How . . . meager, she thought.

"What the fuck are you reading?" her best friend's voice barked over the heads of patrons enjoying a rare "patio weather" day this early in March.

Mags closed the book and set it aside. Stacy would never understand. In fact, Mags figured the whole pretext of this specific get-together was probably geared toward talking her out of what she had planned this summer.

"I went ahead and ordered for you." Mags changed the subject, indicating the tall drink with paprika and garlic salt lining the rim.

"Thanks." Stacy sloughed off her coat but kept her woolly infinity scarf tightly coiled around her neck. She pulled the kabob from her drink, slid the first stuffed olive off the stick, and popped it into her mouth. "But you're not getting off that easy." She spoke and chewed at the same time, her words coming full and thick around the mashed bits of green olive flesh. "That book is complete trash." She swallowed, her gaze lingering on the psychic's taut, filtered image.

"I know you disapprove." Mags sighed and took another drink. The spicy, acidic tomato flavor lingered on her tongue.

"Disapprove? She's a charlatan, Magnolia! I don't know how you can't see that. She takes hardworking, grieving folks and puts them on TV to tell them, what? Their loved one is at peace? Puh-lease. Anyone could do what she does, but you know why they don't?"

Mags didn't even bother with an answer. When Stacy got going like this, it was useless to try and make a counterpoint.

"Because *they* are not lying, capitalist assholes. That's why. Plus, she misquotes Shakespeare on the first page."

Stacy slid the rectangle of cured bacon off her kabob. "God, this is so good," she said, talking while chewing again.

"Are you done?" Mags asked.

"Never." Stacy shrugged. "But I'll take a break for this drink."

Mags took the chance to explain. She didn't need her best friend's approval, but she did want her to understand. "It's temporary. I'll only be gone a few months," she began.

Stacy rolled her eyes, her cheeks collapsing as she sucked on the straw.

"It's a good opportunity."

"Bullshit."

"It's a lot of money and a free place to live. No expenses. All I have to do is entertain a little kid."

"You hate kids."

"No, I don't!" Mags could feel herself getting heated, defensive. "I have zero problems with little people."

"You're doing this for the wrong reasons, and we both know it." Stacy sighed and sat back in her seat, her drink only half finished. She nibbled her bottom lip and looked sideways at Mags. "You think she'll have a message from—"

"Stacy, don't. I—"

Stacy held up her hand. "You think Hawthorne's gonna contact you through her." She tapped the front cover of the book, right in the center of Sofia Brewer's smooth forehead.

Mags brushed her friend's hand away, lingering over the imprint from her fingernail. Then she picked up the book and stuffed it into her bag.

"He's gone, sis. Don't throw away what you've got going on here just for some half-assed communication from beyond the grave. It's not gonna happen."

"And what exactly would I be throwing away here?" Mags asked. "My shift supervisor position in fast food? A boyfriend I hardly even like?"

"You've got . . ." But Stacy couldn't even complete the thought.

"Nothing," Mags finished for her.

"Me?"

Mags heaved a sigh. "I'm not leaving you."

Stacy rolled her eyes.

"You can come visit."

"I'm not driving back to East Buttfuck to stay in that creepy castle."

Mags laughed. "Oh, come on. It'll be fun."

"I don't know if you remember, but they hate people like me out there." She indicated her brown skin, purple hair, and the rainbow flag pinned to her scarf. "I don't plan to end up dead in a ditch somewhere because I didn't smile at the right farmer."

Mags sighed again, knowing her friend was serious. Neither one of them trusted country folk, and that had come from living among them for eighteen torturous years. As soon as they'd graduated, they'd packed up and headed for the city. Although people on the coasts wouldn't really consider Columbus, Ohio a city, when you came from a place where they cheered about having "pigs and nuclear power" at high school football games, Columbus could feel as big and free a place as San Francisco.

"Well, her assistant said I'd only be nannying through the summer, while the kid is out of school and Sofia works on production for some new podcast. I'll be back before you know it."

"Summer's the best season in the city. COM-FEST!"

"Hasn't been what it used to be in years," Mags replied. "I'm doing this, Stacy. You can't talk me out of it."

"Fine. Fine. But you're gonna get your hopes slashed up there; she's a fake. Don't say I didn't warn you."

"I could never."

2

"The soul is eternal, journeying from one state of being to the next."

Beyond and Further Still, Sofia Brewer

The road wound through and around the minor sloping hills of southwestern Ohio. Mags's car, an older model she'd bought used from her dad's cousin, took the turns about as well as could be expected—a bit haltingly. The steering wheel shook in her grip, as if the car were having second thoughts about driving to a castle everyone knew to be haunted.

Stop, Mags thought. *It's just the power steering going out.* She struggled through another turn, the muscles in her biceps straining against the pull. *Well, car, you can just die when we get there.* Sofia's assistant had assured her at their last interview that a fancy-ass rich person's car with a driver came along with the nanny job. They'd take Mags wherever she needed to go with the kid.

The kid.

Mags didn't hate children. It was just that everything about them made her teeth hurt. They were screechy, spasmodic little things, and none of their behavior fell into neat, predictable patterns—which was the only thing Mags's brain truly craved. Patterns and, well, silence. Suddenly, her best friend's misgivings didn't seem so uncalled for.

As secluded and rundown as the roads were in this part of the state, they were familiar to Mags. She'd grown up not far from the estate where she'd be working this summer. She rolled down her window as she entered the woods. The smell of pine and moss mixed with the dotted white blossoms of climbing hydrangea. The woods, dark but never in a threatening way, had been home to many of her and Hawthorne's early childhood adventures. They'd spent hours out there, alone except for their dog, Utah. Utah's nose and sense of direction had been the only things that had gotten them home on more than one occasion.

It wasn't until Hawthorne's freshman year of high school that the siblings stopped playing in the woods together. By then, Hawthorne preferred the company of his friends to a twelve-year-old Mags and an aging boxer dog. But none of those so-called friends came to their family's aid when Hawthorne had gone missing his senior year. No, they'd gone silent instead.

But now she had an opportunity to get close with a famous psychic, someone who pulled the curtain back and glimpsed life beyond. If anyone could tell Mags what happened to Hawthorne, it would be this woman. So she'd deal with entertaining a kid for eight hours a day. She'd give up the carefully patterned, silent portions of her life for the chaos of someone else's childhood. And she'd do it at the notorious Fault Hill Castle.

As she exited the forest, the dark spires of Fault Hill Castle appeared. The castle had sat vacant, falling into disrepair in the 1950s, until some historical committee or another took it on as a project in the late '70s. Throughout Mags's childhood, it had been used by the community to host seasonal craft fairs and a haunted house on Halloween. But a more macabre reputation shadowed the castle's distant past.

In the 1800s, Fault Hill had functioned as a boarding school for young delinquent boys. Yet no one ever saw the children once they went in. It was as if the castle just chewed them up and swallowed. Few townsfolk cared—they were "troublemakers" after all. When the headmistress was found dead by a truckdriver delivering food and supplies, the time of the castle functioning as a school came to an end. Nobody had lived there since—until now.

Mags put her blinker on and turned onto the gravel drive. Rocks popped and turned under her tires as she pulled to a stop in front of a large iron gate. A rusty padlock and chain hung uselessly near the latch, and Mags looked around for some kind of clue as to what to do. There was no intercom, no guard. Finally, she opened her car door and stepped toward the gate. Examining the simple latch, Mags lifted it and pushed the heavy iron door open. The hinges let out a great groan—a warning, she imagined, and quickly pushed the stupid thought aside. This was exactly what she'd wanted; an old creaking gate wasn't going to stop her.

Mags got back into her car and drove the paved switchbacks that wound up Fault Hill. In the heat of the day, the pungent smell of newly laid asphalt wafted through Mags's open window. The architectural splendor of the castle came into full view. The red brick building boasted many floors and towered over the sloping hillside. The spires seen from a distance as black and sharp were even more so close up. Mags counted five of them, wondering which ones would be living spaces and which ones, if any, had been left alone.

Mags had yet to speak to the famous psychic or the child she'd be managing for the next three months, so she'd expected to meet Sofia Brewer upon arrival. But at the castle entrance, in tight jeans and a staggering set of heels, stood Kendra Tims, Sofia's assistant. She wore a pink satin camisole under a light cardigan. Her collar and shoulder bones looked like steel rods propping up a living, breathing doll.

"Magnolia! You made it!" Kendra moved from her perch near the doorway to the front steps. "And almost on time!" she added.

Mags waved, noting the creased wrinkle of Kendra's brow and frantic energy. She rolled up her window, turned off the engine, and checked her phone. It was three minutes past the agreed-upon meeting time. Mags shot Stacy a quick text: *Made it!* But seconds later, she received an error message in return: *Emergency Calls Only.*

Shit, no service.

Mags opened the driver-side door to greet Kendra, who was still making her way, precariously in those heels, down the steps of the castle. But before Mags could even issue a hello, Kendra's ankle turned grotesquely. The small woman crumpled and fell. Her head smacked the stone steps with a sickening *thud.* Kendra's body went limp, a marionette whose strings had just been cut, as she toppled down the remaining steps.

"Oh my god!" Mags ran over and crouched next to Kendra at the bottom of the stairs. "Are you okay?" Yet Mags wasn't sure how to help Kendra. Move her? What if she had a neck or spine injury? Kendra had fallen and rolled—she surveyed the steps, logging the smudges of crimson on the brick—a good ten feet. Kendra's long blond hair, streaked red with blood, covered her face, preventing Mags from surveying damage. Hell, she wasn't even sure if the woman had survived. Mags took a breath, swallowing back a gagging sensation, and pinched strands of Kendra's blood-matted hair in her fingers. She peeled back the wet hair, ignoring how the red stained her own hands.

"Kendra?" Mags whispered her name like a prayer. *Please don't be dead. Please don't be dead on my first day.* She reached for Kendra's arm, and her flesh felt warm to the touch—a good sign.

And like a gust of wind, Kendra lurched and screamed, "Fuck!" The cursed howl drew itself out, twisting and winding its way across the grounds—a lament. She fell silent and stared at the horizon, drips of deep scarlet pulsing steadily from a gash on her forehead.

"Okay, okay," Mags reassured herself more than Kendra. "You're awake. Do you think you can walk?"

Kendra blinked several times. She touched her fingers to her head, and they came away slicked with blood.

"It's not that bad," Mags rambled, lying. "Head injuries are just like that. They bleed a lot. Let me see what I've got in my—"

"Leave her." A smoky, velvet voice Mags recognized from television came from the castle entrance. Mags looked up, and at the top of the steps stood Sofia Brewer.

Her presence alone commanded Mags to get to her feet instantly. "Ms. Brewer," she stammered, "I-I don't know what happened." But of course, she did know. What she'd witnessed, Kendra's fall, unfolded like a stop-motion film in her mind's eye: the wobbling pinprick of a heel; the sickening snap and crunch as her ankle turned; the smack of Kendra's forehead on brick. Mags fought back a wave of nausea.

"I've warned her many times about her . . . heels. My man will take care of it." Sofia turned to go back into the house, then stopped and added, "Well, come on, then."

"We're just gonna leave . . ." But the words died in Mags's mouth. This was her boss, the person with all the power. She looked down at Kendra, who still hadn't really registered Mags's presence since the fall. *It's fine. Just a cut and a sprained ankle. Of course Sofia has someone who can take Kendra to a hospital and get her fixed up.* What could Mags even do? She rifled through her bag and pulled out a pack of tissues.

"Here," she said, handing them to the injured woman. At least this time, Kendra met her gaze. She took the packet and pulled some out, then dabbed at her forehead.

"I-I'm sorry. I have to . . ." This felt so wrong. Leaving someone hurt out here, alone? But Sofia Brewer had just given an order. Mags shouldered her bag and stepped away from Kendra.

"Wait," Kendra murmured, trying to pull something from her pocket. "Take this with you."

"Oh no—you shouldn't—you're hurt. Just be still. Someone's coming to take you to a doctor."

Kendra snorted, though the effort of it caused a grimace. "You're going . . ." But she didn't finish the thought. Instead, she pulled an antique compact from her jean pocket. The tarnished metal, still warm from being tucked away, fit perfectly into Mags's palm. The slight heft of the object felt good in her hand. She examined the lid: a creamy teal enamel with the design of a blossoming flower in the middle done in mother of pearl. Automatically, she opened the clasp and found the mirror still intact, although a collection of dark black spots ringed the edge, along with an old puff, stained beige. Mags closed the compact—*click.*

"The girl needs that," Kendra stated, craning her neck toward Mags. Her face was a mess of smudged makeup and trickling red. A false eyelash had come loose in the wet gore, and Kendra looked even more doll-like with one grotesque blinking eye. "Don't let the bitch break you."

Mags couldn't think of a reply that made much sense. Why would Kendra say such a thing? Surely she was just out of it, concussed even, from her fall. That had to be it.

"Uh, okay then. Thanks, I guess!" She held up the compact, then dropped it into her purse. Making her way up the castle steps, she looked back at Kendra, wondering what she'd meant, but the woman only stared toward the horizon, waiting for help.

3

The lack of grandeur surprised Mags as she stepped across the castle's threshold. Its outer appearance obscured its institutionalized past. Inside revealed the castle's original purposes. The entrance hall was large, with a refurbished reception desk running along the back wall. Behind the desk were rows of wooden cubbies. The area smelled of wet cement.

People bustled around another section of the lobby where a kind of set had been erected. Long tables with a vast array of fruit and snacks cordoned off the area. Conversational tones echoed around the room, interrupted every few seconds by the *click-swish* of a camera shutter. The excitement and newness of the scene did a good job of tamping down Mags's misgivings over what had just happened to Kendra. Lights on stands with umbrellas—Mags didn't know their proper name—spotlighted a row of antique-looking students' desks.

Mags's vision wavered, as if she'd opened her eyes under water. Children sat there at the desks. Some had their legs twisted around the wrought iron; others lifted the surface top—searching. She thought they were boys, but it was difficult to be sure with their shaved heads and nondescript tunics. Dark half-circles stained the skin under their eyes. All at once, they noticed her, and their mouths opened—slowly, widely—and showed only a shadowy blackness. No chittering, squirrel-like laughter as children ought to have. No pearly teeth puncturing smiles like jack-o-lanterns. They were voiceless, lost to history and trauma.

They were hollowed out. Mags shook her head, and the thought, disturbing and intrusive, disappeared along with the image of the boys. *What* was *that?*

When she returned to herself, she saw that Sofia eyed her carefully. A makeup artist stood in front of her, blotting her forehead with a tissue.

"Where'd you go just now?" Sofia asked with the air of someone who never needed to introduce themselves. She waved the man fixing her powder away. He shrugged and walked toward the snack table.

"I just thought I saw something out of the corner of my eye," Mags said. "It startled me. That's all."

"Nonsense." Sofia stepped closer and grabbed Mags's forearm, her perfume overpowering Mags's sensory input. *Gardenia.* Sofia was at least twenty years older than Mags, but it showed only on the back of her hands, where ropy blue veins twisted over bone. Her eyes were a gold-green hazel color that shimmered and changed depending on the light, a disarming effect. Mags stood there awkwardly, letting the older woman complete what felt like some kind of examination on her with those ever-changing x-ray eyes. "Tell me what you saw."

Mags explained about the boys.

"And have you ever experienced a vision like that before?"

"No, ma'am."

Sofia grimaced. "You can use my name." She crossed to the set, where the desks stood under the lights. "Right here?"

"Yes, ma—Sofia."

"Ready for more, Sofia?" a man behind the camera asked. "We've had a good go today, but if you think we haven't gotten what's needed, we can keep on." He twiddled some knobs on top of the camera.

"No, no. I'm done today." She strode off set, back toward Mags.

Mags didn't know what to do, so she started apologizing. "I'm sorry. It was probably nothing. I'm just reeling over being here and meeting you, and then watching Kendra's fall. My head is in a really weird space."

Sofia waved away Mags's excuses for the vision. "The veil is worn thin here. Too much suffering in one place will do that. You've only seen a bit of the castle's past. And that's part of what we're here for!" Sofia gave the reception area another once-over and seemed to mentally be tallying something. "Alice, let's add a night-vision camera here . . . right above the desks." A young woman with purple hair took notes on a clipboard as Sofia spoke. "Ok, with that settled, let me show you to the living quarters. And then you can meet my daughter. You just missed her. We finished the photoshoot right before you got here."

"Photoshoot?" Mags repeated absentmindedly. Clearly that was what she'd walked in on.

"Promo," Sofia answered.

"And your daughter? Is she into that kind of thing?" Mags asked, wondering if she'd be stuck playing model and fashion show with the girl the rest of the summer.

"Not really, no. I wouldn't say she likes them. But we do what we must."

Mags wasn't sure what that meant but drew in a breath of relief at the idea that they could skip hanging out for the marketing stuff if the kid wasn't into it.

Sofia led Mags up a curving staircase and talked as she went.

"The castle has been repaired enough to be considered structurally sound, but you'll find that very little has been altered. Throughout the years, most have found the castle a little . . . resistant to change."

"What do you mean?" Mags interrupted.

"Oh, it's mostly rumors, you know. The usual blather about mysterious illnesses. Construction workers disappearing. A couple deaths by suicide. Nothing that can't be explained, really. But you know how stories get started. Soon it's the castle's fault instead of asbestos." She almost sounded as if she didn't believe in the supernatural.

"So you *don't* think—"

"Oh, don't get me wrong. This place is absolutely haunted. But acting as if the building itself is some kind of sentient being?" She gave a derisive snort.

Confusion beset Mags. Belief in an afterlife was well and good, but a malevolent castle was too much? Something to be scoffed at? Why would someone like Sofia Brewer draw such a distinction? But she didn't have time to ask because

Sofia had just unlocked a set of French doors and ushered Mags into an updated living space.

"These are the old headmistresses' quarters. They've been kept in quite good condition. We only had to apply some minor cosmetic touches."

Mags stepped toward the center of the room, her sneakers squeaking on the creamy marble floor. *Minor touches?* The room was exquisite. A plush seating area was staged with oversized gray couches and white fur rugs. One whole wall boasted an expansive set of floor-to-ceiling windows that looked out over the grounds and the forest beyond. The verdant green of the treetops and the cerulean sky became all the color the room needed. A large spherical light fixture with an art deco fan design imprinted into the glass hung over a long table littered with scripts, a boom mic, and a fancy camera.

"I thought you were just working on a podcast." Mags gestured at the table, considering how many of the podcasts she listened to were filmed in closets or over Zoom.

"We are. The film aspect is mostly for promotional purposes. I'll have to do the rounds eventually, and we'll need clips for social media. At least that's what they tell me." Sofia moved to the kitchen area, which was open to the rest of the space. "Would you like something to drink?" Sofia opened the refrigerator and selected a bottle of champagne.

"Uh, sure." Mags pulled out a cushioned barstool and sat at the counter. She couldn't help but run her hands over the smooth, luxurious white stone, like a frozen pond. "This place is amazing."

"Thank you." Sofia placed a flute of golden sparkling wine in front of Mags. "We've been working on it for the better part of six years."

"Oh! So this was all planned?"

Sofia's brow crinkled softly, questioning. "Of course it was planned."

"I mean, the media"—and this included all aspects of Sofia's social media—"kinda made it seem like this move was an impulse buy or something."

"Oh, that. Don't believe everything you see on the internet."

"I don't," Mags whispered before taking a sip of her drink. Sofia Brewer had a way about her that made Mags feel small, like a child constantly being reprimanded for having sweets before dinner.

"Now tell me about yourself." Sofia made commands, Mags noted, and hardly anything else.

"I grew up around here. Went to college in Columbus. And now I'm back."

"That's a very abridged version of your life, Magnolia."

"Mags. Everyone calls me Mags." She never knew how to answer big questions like "tell me about yourself". How much did the person asking really want to know? Mags always bet on very little, understanding that most people weren't listening. "It's not such a unique story."

"Sounds like it could be one of those sappy holiday movies."

"A little light on the romance aspect, but pretty much."

"And now you're back." Sofia narrowed her eyes, seeming to not fully buy into Mags's short narrative. But Mags wouldn't give the woman anything else to go on; Sofia was the psychic after all.

"And what about your brother?"

Mags choked on her drink, coughing and sputtering the expensive wine all over the counter.

Sofia slapped her palm on the counter and laughed manically, a witch who'd just gotten her way. She grabbed some paper towels and handed a wad to Mags, who, eyes watering, went to clean up after herself. "You didn't think you could hide it, did you? It's practically town lore."

Mags's heartbeat sounded in her ears, and the whole of the room turned a bright red. The words coming out of her boss's mouth were barely audible, all except for *town lore*. That part she'd made out easily.

Sofia located a rose-gold laptop and flipped it open. She turned the screen toward Mags and clicked on a file titled TREWIN, Mags's surname. The file opened to a list of documents. Sofia selected one, and a copy of a news article filled the screen. The headline read "After-Party from Hell: Local Teen Disappeared." Hawthorne's handsome face, the school picture they'd used for his missing posters, smiled back at her. Mags couldn't breathe.

"Oh, honey." Sofia pouted, looking at Mags's expression. "I'm sorry. Background checks can be a real bitch, but I had to do my due diligence. You had zero experience working with children!"

A cold spring of defiance filled Mags's stomach. She'd wanted her new boss to discover Hawthorne, to give her some clue about what had happened to him, but not this way. Not via an internet search.

"Don't look at me that way." Sofia's head tilted to the side. "This is a mutually beneficial situation, and you know it. Why else would you have taken the job but to be close to me and my abilities? You want information about what's happened to your brother."

"That's"—Mags swallowed her indignance and took a calming breath—"true."

"And so, we will provide it."

"What?"

"You'll find out what happened to your brother." Sofia snapped her fingers and gulped down the rest of her sparkling wine. "Easy." She stifled a hiccup. "But first, it's time for you to meet my sweet Persimmon."

4

"We're all born with the ability to see and feel into the beyond. We turn it off, because we must, but children still speak of it at times."

Beyond and Further Still, Sofia Brewer

Mags felt as if a thick fog pressed against her every step forward. What she'd hoped for was going to happen! Sofia Brewer herself had all but promised she'd give Mags the information she wanted about her brother. Mags suppressed the urge to run back to the kitchen, grab Sofia Brewer by the arms, and shake the knowledge out of her. Instead, she carefully set her prickling need aside and found the girl's bedroom door. Mags knocked, the sound seeming far-off and distant. There was no answer. She turned the knob and walked in, the way Sofia Brewer had instructed.

"Just go in. She ignores . . . everything. In her own head all the

time." The woman had made some vaguely insulting hand gesture, and with that, the conversation was over. Well, if anyone understood being in their own head, it was Mags.

The girl, with her silky brown hair flowing down her back, sat on the floor in the middle of an aggressively gendered bedroom. An array of dolls splayed out before her, she appeared to be fully immersed in play. Mags watched her from the threshold. The girl couldn't have been more than eight, and memories of being that age bloomed in Mags's mind: Hawthorne swinging from a rope over the creek; Hawthorne climbing a tree ahead of her. Always ahead of her. Mags shook off her memories and walked into the room.

"Hi! You must be Persimmon."

The girl startled, a shiver that started around her shoulders and traveled down her spine, then she sat very, very still.

Mags moved closer, waiting for a response. A "hello", a "who the hell are you", a scream; any kind of response would do, but Persimmon Brewer seemed frozen. *I've scared her,* Mags thought. "I'm sorry. I didn't mean to interrupt—"

"Yes, you did," said the girl, her face still turned away from Mags. "My name is Persi."

"You're right. I guess I did mean to interrupt. I'm Mags, by the way. Magnolia, really, but that's always felt pretty extra." Mags sat next to Persi, making sure to leave a good amount of personal space between them. "Your mom's hired me to look after you this summer."

"That's *not* why she hired you."

Mags felt as though she'd been pinched. What did the girl know about it? "Okay." Mags tried another tack. She picked up one of the dolls Persi had been playing with and started braiding its hair. "What's her name?"

"Julia."

"And what's her favorite thing?" Mags fully expected the girl to say "cookies" or "unicorns".

"Her best friend's husband, Tom."

Laughter bubbled up and out of Mags before she could squelch it. "Really?"

"It's not funny. Her best friend is pregnant with Tom's baby. And she knows what they're doing behind her back." Persi indicated another doll, lying on her side. A wad of tissue poked out from under her dress, posing as a makeshift pregnant belly.

"That's some really sordid stuff."

"Julia's a whore. And she's going to die." The girl's words had grown icy, as if she really were familiar with the pain of a cheating spouse.

A spike of surprise shot up from Mags's midsection. She gingerly set Julia back down and tried to play it cool. "I'll leave her hair messy then. Maybe Tom will leave her alone."

"It doesn't matter. They both will die. She's"—Persimmon picked up the pregnant doll—"already decided."

"Well . . ." Mags attempted to hide how shocked she felt by the grim display. *It's nothing.* She and Hawthorne had imagined and played through all kinds of wildly fucked-up narratives in their day.

Persimmon went about stripping the pregnant doll. She picked out an impractical sparkling ballgown and tiny plastic shoes and redressed her.

"So, what's her name?" Mags asked. "The soon-to-be mom?"

"Sofia."

"Oh . . . like your mom?"

"Yes." Persi finally looked at Mags, their gazes meeting

over the jumbled graveyard of plastic doll parts scattered across the carpet. *"Just* like her."

A jolt, as if she'd just wiped a socket with a wet rag, coursed through Mags. But before Mags could even register what it might mean, Persi asked, "Who is he?"

"He?" Mags could hardly keep up with this little girl.

"The one who follows you. Who is he?" Persi asked, almost to herself, her gaze veering over Mag's shoulder.

Mags turned, but nothing was there except a bubble-gum-pink wall filled with framed illustrations of Peter Rabbit.

"He's . . ." Persi's voice trailed off for a beat and then she added, "He looks like you. Long hair, brown like yours. I think if he smiled, he'd look even more like you. But he's not smiling."

Mags was too stunned to speak. She looked around the room. *Was this a joke?* Some kind of elaborate prank?

The girl's eyes roamed back and forth, a spiraling dance in their sockets. Mags would have given anything to see what she saw. "What is it?" Mags could barely breathe.

"His name is Hawthorne," Persi whispered.

Mags's eyes flooded with tears. To hear his name spoken by someone else, someone who should've had no idea of his existence. This strange girl. This absolute treasure.

"He's"—the girl smiled—"funny."

"He was! So funny!" Joy bubbled throughout Mags. She could almost hear Hawthorne's laughter or the goofy way he would act out things that had happened at school each evening, not stopping until he got their dad to crack a smile.

"Is." Persi's gaze flicked from the middle distance to Mags. "He still exists, just not here."

"Oh, right. Yes. I'm sorry," Mags apologized to

Hawthorne, to Persi, to the air, which here in this castle seemed like some kind of portal.

"He's sad." Persi added, "I think he misses you."

Mags reached out, grasping Persimmon's hand—so small, so fragile. Mags didn't understand how or why Persimmon had such an ability, but she recognized it as a heavy weight for an eight-year-old. Being able to see beyond the veil, just like her mother, would've left Persi with a kind of distorted childhood—a lack of one, really, even as she'd sat here playing with dolls. Death would have never been some far-off, abstract idea for her. Instead, it would have been ever-present, following Persi around, warping her perspective of this world, of this life.

Persimmon Brewer never had a chance at being innocent.

A blinding sear of pain erupted behind Mags's eyes. She let go of the girl and pressed her palms to her sockets. Behind her closed eyelids, she saw nothing but static—black, white, a burst of red. The ache throbbed with the beat of her heart.

"Headache?" Persi asked from some distance Mags could not pinpoint due to the pain.

Mags nodded. "A bad one," she said, but her words sounded garbled to her own ears. She managed to squint at the girl. "I get them sometimes."

"Mommy does too." And Mags could have sworn she saw a devious little smile grace Persi's features. But the pain in her head gave a violent pulse, and she couldn't be sure.

"I know where Mommy keeps her pills. Do you want some?"

"No. I'm sure I brought something. Just hand me my purse, please."

The girl practically skipped across the room to where

Mags had dropped her purse by the door. But Mags's vision blurred around the edges. Little black lightning bolts filled her line of sight. She'd had migraines before, but she usually had a little warning when one was coming on.

Persi stood before her, handing Mags her bag. Mags rifled through her things, searching for the clacking bottle, while the girl flitted off to do . . . whatever. From somewhere, Mags heard water rushing from a tap, and Persi came back carrying a tumbler filled to the brim, some of the water splashing onto the carpet as she walked on tiptoes back to where Mags sat on the floor.

"Thanks," Mags heard herself mutter just before the lid to the Excedrin came off with a *pop*.

Persi skipped around the room, her cape of long hair trailing and whipping behind her.

Mags gulped some water and shuffled to her feet. She made a mental note to tell Sofia to find a better hiding place for her pills and watched as Persi spun in circles until she got too dizzy and fell over laughing, again and again.

Tap-tap-tap. The knock on the door stopped Persi's spinning. The girl swayed on her feet.

"Hello?" Another soft, quick rap, and the door opened enough for a woman with purple hair—Alice, Mags thought she remembered—to stick her head through. "There you are! Sofia's asking for you both." The woman left as quickly as she came.

Persi looked up at Mags, a note of resignation playing in her eyes.

"Dinner?" Mags suggested.

Persi shook her head and whispered, "Not just dinner." Her little shoulders slumped, and she moved toward the door, her dragging feet leaving trails in the carpet.

Mags needed a moment before joining the others. The headache had not subsided. She rested her palm on her stomach and breathed deeply, counting the beats of her inhalation and exhalation. Who knew what kind of dusty-ass shit floated through the castle air? It probably *was* asbestos that had caused her headache.

Beyond a set of bay windows, the sun began to set. Orange swatches of color painted the horizon. To even look at the color, to perceive it, seared her brain, so she homed in on the trees, how their silhouettes, black shadow branches, cracked the sky.

"Damn it, Persimmon Rose!"

The sharp, hissing tone snapped Mags out of her reverie, and she rushed out of the girl's room and toward the living area.

"How could you be so careless?" Sofia stood over her daughter, questioning her. She gripped Persi by the elbow and shook her a little. "I asked you a question, young lady."

Mags absorbed the scene: a shattered glass, the puddle of red liquid on the floor, a scared girl, and a group of adults doing absolutely nothing.

"No worries!" Mags chimed in, the pain in her skull dulling a bit. "I've got this."

She reached for a roll of paper towels and began mopping up the fruit punch around the Brewers' feet. Sofia let go of Persi with the tiniest of shoves. Mags noted Persi's now-hardened features—no fear, only hate. Mags swallowed her own panic; she wanted to stay in control, to exude calm. But she'd never seen someone grab a child that way.

Don't let the bitch break you. Kendra's final warning rang in Mags's ears. She pressed her fingers to her temples, fruit punch dripping down her wrists. This place made her feel unstable, unhinged, as if she'd wandered off the beaten path to follow a blackened crack in the sky.

"Can one of you bring a broom?" she yelled, directing the question to all the adults sitting around the long table. Purple-haired Alice scrambled out of her seat and came back carrying a broom and dustbin.

"Thank you," Mags spit out gratitude.

Sofia huffed and paced back toward the group, her kitten heels clacking along the cement. Persi sank into one of the big couches, crossing her arms and staring angrily out the floor-to-ceiling windows, which were slowly becoming like mirrors as the sky darkened.

Along the kitchen counter, a spread had been set up: sourdough bread, an array of lunch meat, a slab of congealed potato salad in a tray. Conversation erupted around the dining table as if nothing had just happened, which dialed up the pain pounding behind Mags's eyes.

Sofia sidled beside Mags, carrying a wine glass. "Care for some?"

"No." After what she'd just witnessed, she could hardly speak to the woman.

"Drink helps." A satisfied grin crossed Sofia's painted red lips, and she tapped her forehead. "Trust me."

Why would I? She kept the question to herself, but she couldn't deny a kind of dirty laundry list had started to form around her boss.

"Just water."

"Suit yourself."

Alice handed Mags a bottled water, and the seal crackled as she twisted the cap off. She sat on the couch and listened to Sofia's crew chatter about the plan for recording their podcast. Eventually, she started to zone out as her headache subsided. It wasn't gone, but the sharp edge of it had eroded.

"Magnolia, are you ready?" Sofia asked.

"Oh. Yeah. Does Persi have a bedtime routine?" She'd assumed that was why they'd brought her and Persi out here, to eat and then go over Persi's routines and expectations while they all worked in other parts of the castle throughout the night.

"Haven't you heard anything?" asked Alice.

"Uh, not really."

Everyone at the table gawked at her. Mags couldn't maintain eye contact as they stared. She took inventory instead: piles of spiral-bound scripts, legal pads, schedules, plates with half-eaten sandwiches, and coffee mugs littered the table's surface.

An overweight guy huffed a snide little laugh. "I don't think there'll be time for any *bedtime routines* tonight." He laughed.

An embarrassed resentment bubbled inside of Mags. *What is going on here?*

"I'm—but that's—" she stammered and then gained purchase, "—what I was hired for."

"The hell you were," said that same sniggering, sarcastic loser from the other end of the table.

"I'm sorry, who *are* you?" Mags asked.

"Ignore him." Alice glared at the guy, then adjusted her glasses and addressed Mags. "We're going to need you to come with us. For the podcast."

"What? Why?"

Mags watched the crew at the table exchange looks.

"Because Persi's the star now!" Sofia exclaimed, rushing to stake a claim over the awkward pause. Wine sloshed against the sides of her glass, nearly over the top. Mags couldn't tell if she was drunk. If not, she was well on her way.

"And where Persi goes, you go," Sofia added. The woman's fury over Persi's spilled juice had simmered to a dull sarcastic tone, but Mags recognized the danger there too.

"It's all right, Ms. Mags." Persi's tiny hand encircled Mags's wrist and pulled her toward the main doors of the apartment; beyond them loomed the rest of the castle. "We might as well get this over with," the girl said, and in her other hand, she twisted a strand of her hair around her index finger, then stuck the end in her mouth and chewed.

"You shouldn't be a part of what they're doing . . ." *You're too young. It's too scary.* But her words dried up in her mouth. They carried no conviction because she'd just seen Persi's abilities in action. Hawthorne had come through the veil, and this could be a real chance at finding out what happened to him. Sure, it felt wrong. Maybe a little icky. But Persi would be fine. What real harm could be done? This was the family business after all.

Just chill, sis. She could almost hear her brother attempting to calm her nerves as they all left the living quarters and headed into a different part of Fault Hill Castle.

Persi led the way, her fingers lightly tugging at Mags's wrist. Every now and again, she'd look back and give a reassuring glance. But Mags didn't feel comforted. A sense of dread bloomed in her chest, like an ink blot on a page, the deeper they went into the castle.

From the headmistresses' quarters, the group walked through a maze of hallways. They passed room after room: some contained a series of metal bed frames, springs rusted and poking at strange angles; others had still-dusty chalk-boards lining the walls. A large room with a lot of glass-front cabinets could have been a place for medical care.

On they went, twisting through and around the castle's many halls. Their footsteps and the errant nervous whisper were the only sounds. Sofia's team carried supplies: their laptops, a mic, headphones, a cooler filled with cans of sparkling water. A few of them snapped photos for Sofia's social media accounts along the way. At some point, it occurred to Mags that they were going down—underground.

Their footsteps clopped along a set of narrow wooden stairs. The air changed from dusty and dry to humid and mildewy. The dark encompassed them the farther they went, a curtain of black shadow that they were to pass through. As they moved forward, a tingling fear rose through Mags's core. It expanded like a yeast dough, spreading up her esophagus, sticking in the back of her throat. She could taste it—a stale beer, a rubbery, gooey ball of phlegm. Some of the group brought out their phone flashlights, and camping lanterns flicked on. It did little to calm Mags, but she still felt grateful for the light.

Alice maneuvered around Persi and Mags. "Just a sec, we do have electricity down here." She flicked a switch, but the flashlights and lanterns stayed on—a couple random over-head bulbs were barely enough to navigate the castle's immense basement.

Persi let go of Mags's wrist and skipped away from her the moment the lights came on. Mags took a breath, held it until it hurt a little, and blew it out through her mouth. Then she took stock.

Some of the walls had been repaired, smoothed by concrete and weight-bearing posts, while others were barely more than stacked stone, stringy root systems growing through cracks.

A placard marked one area as a "playroom", and Mags pictured a bunch of kids running around in the dank space, screaming wildly. She half expected to see the boys with their gaping mouths, the ones she'd seen as soon as she entered the castle, but they weren't here now. Along the back wall was a kind of divot or sloping ramp in the floor. Brackish water collected in the deep end, and Mags couldn't make sense of why a pool would be down here.

Her curiosity overrode her fear, and she asked, "What's with that?"

"Ah, the plunge pool," Sofia's voice rasped throughout the dim space. "Not a well-known detail! They dipped new boys in lye to make sure they were pest-free upon admittance."

"Jesus," Mags whispered.

"Perfectly safe, if you get the portions right," said Sofia. "But they didn't always. No, people have died down here—horrifically. Several of them, including the last headmistress."

"That can't be real," Mags said, mustering as much disbelief as she could. She couldn't be standing mere feet from where children had been maimed, even killed, over many decades. "There would have been reports. News. If something like that was happening here, people would have known."

"For certain, many people knew what went on here. You underestimate what wealth can hide, Magnolia."

Mags felt the sharp tip of the truth Sofia spoke. But money couldn't always conceal the horror of the castle's past; it existed. It happened. And like a handful of pebbles thrown across a pond's surface, there would always be ripples.

"How do you know all this?" Mags asked.

"The boys told me."

Mags startled at Persi's voice. The girl had snuck up behind her. "Don't do that!" Mags yelled involuntarily.

"Sorry," the girl said quietly, her gaze locked on her feet.

"It's okay. You just scared me," Mags said, then added, "You see the boys?"

"Oh yes," Persi said. She looked at Mags. "They've seen you too."

Mags tried so hard to control her face, tried not to react to what Persi had just said. "Oh," she managed to squeak.

Persi curled her forefinger, motioning for Mags to come closer. Mags obliged, and the girl whispered, "Don't worry. It's Mommy they don't like."

Mags swallowed her panic, the girl's breath still wafting against her earlobe. She slowly stood up, and Persi held her forefinger to her lips. A secret, then. The boys, the ones she'd seen upon arrival, with their inky gaping mouths and blackened eye sockets, the ones who'd apparently lived tortured lives and stayed behind to haunt the castle, were communicating with this little girl.

Persi smiled. "It's okay, Mags. They don't hurt me like the others."

"The others?" Her words came out like a crackling whisper; the inside of her mouth had been dried out by fear.

"You'll see." Persi skipped away, toward a crew member who stood near what Mags now recognized as a sound booth.

A prism of plexiglass, surrounded by light stands and worktables, had been erected in an area marked by a sign that read "showers".

"Come on," Persi called to her. But Mags hesitated. *Sure,* she'd signed a contract and committed to this job for the summer, but she hadn't expected all these extras. Sofia's book had made dealing with the afterlife, the supernatural, out to be something . . . peaceful, something natural. This felt like the opposite of that.

"He's waiting. It's his turn," said Persi. Maybe she sensed Mags's anxiety, her fear, her desire to get the fuck out and never look back, because she added, "Hawthorne."

His name was enough to unlock Mags. Their fondest memories rushed through her, and she found herself pacing toward Persi and the sound booth, her desire to find out what happened to her brother greater than her trepidation surrounding the boys and the castle's dark past.

Egg-crate padding lined the interior walls. Inside the room, the decor was sparse, with only a small circular table and three chairs. Three sets of headphones and three micro-phones had been set up on the table. Wires, tangled like vines, ran in every direction.

"Why are there three mics?"

"For recording," Sofia said.

"I figured," said Mags, letting annoyance dose her tone. "Will the ghost . . . or spirit, whatever, speak?" Her question sounded dumb even to her ears.

Sofia paused and tilted her head before answering. "In a way."

Hawthorne. "Where do you want me?" She hoped to be allowed to stay in the room, to be permitted to speak with her brother if he came through again, but also felt uneasy about that being exactly what Sofia desired as well.

"Right there is fine." Sofia indicated a seat at the table.

"But I'm just the babysitter . . ."

"Oh, don't look so surprised. It was in all the contracts. You're to participate in the podcast."

"How? I'm not very good at . . . public speaking. Or being the center of attention."

"Too late for that, dear. As you heard, it's your brother's turn, and we want an honest take from you. No script, no prep, just authenticity."

Alice handed Mags a set of headphones, and anxiety flooded her chest, a whole damn sea of it rising at high tide. But she focused on her brother. She squeezed the puffy foam earpiece of her headphones and pictured Hawthorne's smile; she heard his laugh that always came easy. This was about him. She could do this.

Someone snapped their picture. Mags's pulse matched the sporadic flash. *Ka-chick, ka-chick, ka-chick.* Her heart lodged itself in her esophagus, and its frenzied beat fluttered and spasmed. Neither Sofia nor Persi seemed to notice. Someone closed the door to the booth, and the lights overhead flickered.

"Ignore it, dear. It's how spirits often respond to Persi's presence." Sofia spoke as if what was happening was as banal as the weather, a spring rain versus a freak storm.

Mags wished she'd accepted that glass of wine.

5

"Those seeking answers on our side of the veil are not always prepared for the cost of a supernatural truth."
Beyond and Further Still Sofia Brewer

Sofia, Persi, and Mags settled into their seats. Alice paced around the small room, making minor adjustments before closing the door and leaving the three of them alone in the sound booth.

"Okay, let's get started. Roll the previously recorded narration for Magnolia. She needs to hear it to get her settled into the story—"

Irritation pricked Mags. That's all this was to them. A narrative. A money maker. It meant so much more to Mags.

Sofia snapped her fingers, and the tape rolled.

Eight years ago, my life changed drastically. Sofia's prerecorded voice filled the small booth. *I was pregnant, and my husband had been killed in a horrible accident.*

Accident. Mags remembered Persi's doll play from earlier. Had it really been an accident?

I was a famed psychic; *how could I truly grieve in a normal way when I'd been telling people their loved ones were still out there?*

That, at least, rang true.

I never told anyone, but my abilities, *my connection with the spirit world had been lost to me as well.*

Wait, what?

But I kept working, thinking I knew enough to fake it. It was a dark time, and I'm not proud of my actions. But I did what I thought I had to, like anyone else would have.

Mags couldn't help herself; she snorted. "So you're a fraud," she added, not backing down.

Sofia licked her lips and gave Mags a scolding look, obviously not appreciating the commentary. "*I* may be, but she's not." Sofia kept her words clipped and tight while gesturing at her daughter.

Mags looked to Persi, who sat with her eyes clenched shut. Had it not been for what she'd experienced with the girl earlier, she would have thought this whole experiment was for show.

"Come on, Persi. You don't have to do this. They don't need us for this . . . confessional." She placed her hand on Persi's shoulder, and the girl flinched as if she'd been stung.

"Persi stays," Sofia said.

"You're paying me to take care of her. Whatever you've got going on here is not appropriate for a child."

Persi's nails dug into the leather upholstery of the armrest. Her eyelids fluttered, little lashes like moth wings flying too close to a flame.

"It is what it is. This doesn't work without her."

"So you're using her."

Now it was Sofia's turn to scoff. "Just listen." She made a

twirling motion with her finger, and her voice emerged from the speakers once more.

A small-town police officer—a fan, really—contacted me through my website. A local teenager had disappeared, the biggest mystery the town had seen in decades.

Mags's blood ran cold—not Hawthorne's story.

Now, I'd been hired by the police force before. I'd worked a couple homicides and missing persons across the country. His request wasn't totally out of the norm. But I was very pregnant and really shouldn't have been traveling. Then he told me the boy's last known whereabouts . . .

Yes, Hawthorne's story. Mags couldn't breathe.

The castle. Fault Hill Castle. A place with a very dark and storied past.

"That's not true," Mags interrupted. "He went to a party. People saw him, and then he just left."

"And came here." Sofia handed Mags a piece of paper, a kind of report with hard-to-read, sloppy cursive writing coursing over thin lines.

"What is this?"

"Notes taken from"—Sofia leaned over and tapped the top of the paper; her red lacquered nail gleamed under the fluorescent light—"Detective Shaw."

"But I've never seen this. I don't think my parents have ever seen this."

"That's unlikely. But there's more." She made a clicking noise, like one might call a dog with, a little sucking *tuh-tick*, and the narration came through the speakers once more.

The town was within driving distance from my Indianapolis estate, and I needed the income. I figured I could come and look at the files. At the very least, I could make an educated guess as to what had happened to the missing boy. He had probably run away, and I said as much upon arrival.

Obtaining access to the castle, parts that no one had been able to tour in decades, that was a bonus. It intrigued me. Anyone who grew up within the tri-state area, like I had, knew about Fault Hill. I'm only a little ashamed to say I thought it might help me get my powers back, that being on the grounds might spark something for me. And it did—in its way.

"Th-the police hired you"—Mags's head felt as if she were underwater—"and you knew whatever you told them wouldn't be real? That you'd just be guessing?"

"Yes. It was an unfortunate situation," Sofia confirmed. She took a sip of water, and her lipstick painted the rim of the glass. "I mean, I hoped that wouldn't be the case. I really did, and still *do*, want to help. I just—couldn't. Everything was blocked to me at the time."

"Why didn't I know about any of this?"

Sofia shrugged. "I'm sure your parents were made aware. Some people don't like bringing a psychic into the fold. Maybe they were embarrassed. I don't know."

Mags stood and paced the tiny room. She'd only taken a few steps away from the table when she asked, "But the whole town would have known you were here. Someone would have seen you—you're famous! It would've gotten around."

Sofia sniffed and folded her hands together. "Mags, I really don't know how you've gotten to be this age still believing that there aren't certain things that can be kept secret or hidden. Money and shame and silence have always gone a long way in this world."

"What does that mean?"

"This would be cute if you were younger, really. I believe

your brother stumbled upon something here, something about the castle's history, and it took him. Now can we continue? Or are you suddenly not interested in what happened to Hawthorne?"

Mags swallowed her questions and disbelief; she sat back down to listen.

The investigation was at a standstill. They had the young man at the castle before he died, a security camera had picked the detail up, but by all appearances, he'd been alone. Why had he come? What had he found?

I thought it would be easy, that if I came here, toured the building, dug into the history, the answers would come. Instead, as soon as I set foot inside this place, I went into labor. The pain came quick and seared through my whole body. I collapsed in the lobby. It was nothing like what my doctors had prepared me for—hours of being uncomfortable, gradually increasing contractions. No. It was as if something or someone had reached their hand up inside me, gripped, and twisted. The baby's head was right there, ready to come. Detective Shaw was supposed to have followed me in his car, but he hadn't yet arrived, and seconds felt like hours in the blurry constraints of the moment.

Mags sat quietly listening. The story of Persimmon's birth had taken on an unnatural quality, as if the castle itself or whomever/whatever haunted it had ripped Persi from the womb. Mags looked at the girl, who'd calmed in the moments it took to relay this bit of her story.

Eventually, although I have little memory of it, Detective Shaw did come and helped deliver the baby. He called for an ambulance, and that was that. Our lives moved forward. The story of Persimmon's birth became an afterthought, until she started to talk.

Goosebumps broke out over Mags's forearms. She felt

like she might know what came next. After all, even she'd seen their gaping mouths and black eyes.

She spoke of boys and a bad lady with a mirror. It sounded like a fairy tale. Something she'd picked up in a book. I didn't take it seriously, thought nothing of it. Until one day, we sat down for breakfast, and she said, "I want to go back to the castle."

I'd never told her about Fault Hill. I wanted to leave the feeling of her being ripped out of me behind. Pretend it hadn't really happened that way. But she already knew the truth.

She's the true psychic now. The narration stopped. Above the door, a small bulb turned on, glowing red; they were recording now.

"And you're, what? Telling the whole world you're a fake? Why?"

"I'm securing her future." Sofia gestured toward her daughter. "She has more potential than I ever did."

"More potential to make money," Mags countered.

Sofia rolled her lips together slowly, calculating a response.

Maybe Mags had finally struck a nerve. Nothing about this strange day had felt as though locking in a future career path for Persi was the priority. No, this was a way to extract a resource while it was still under Sofia's control.

"People will see this for what it really is," Mags added.

Sofia regained her composure. "Many fans will remain loyal. We're building a legacy."

"And what about the castle? The way you tell it, something here tore Persi out of you. You're messing with some kind of power here. Why would you come back here at all?"

"She told me to."

Crack, like a branch breaking over a knee, but no, not wood—bone. The sound sickened Mags.

Snap. Crunch.

Mags thought of a mortar and pestle, of seeds and herbs being ground into a pulp. She looked toward the girl, whose complexion had gone waxy. The fingers on her right hand pointed upward and were splayed apart, all at different and impossible angles.

"What's happening to her?" Mags cried. She stood and crouched near Persi's chair, unsure of what to do, how to help.

"The cost of doing business with the dead," Sofia said offhandedly, as if hearing her own daughter's bones break and twist were commonplace.

Mags watched Persi's jaw clench and grind; her features, as twisted and strained as her fingers, flushed a deep shade of pink.

"You're hurting her!" Mags yelled.

"I'm not doing a damn thing," Sofia said.

"But you are! You're using her for your own gain!"

"And yours, dear. Or are you giving up on Hawthorne completely?"

The sound of her brother's name in Sofia's mouth made Mags woozy with rage, but it also smacked of the truth. She had wanted this, and it seemed they were so close. Mags watched, horrified, as the fingers on Persi's left hand bent backward—*pop*.

"Don't do this! I don't need to know what happened to him!"

At that, Sofia finally looked up from her script. A smile played at the corners of her mouth. "Come on, now. You know as well as I *that's* not true."

Mags looked to Persi, who sat ramrod straight in her chair. Her eyelids began to flutter, exposing the whites of her eyes intermittently.

"It is! I quit! Just stop this!"

Persi's head fell forward, as if some unseen person had shoved her. The flush that had painted her cheeks earlier had dissipated, leaving her skin a ghastly pale. Her breathing became shallow; the quick pulsing *rish-rush* of it filled the small room. All the lights went out, and the encompassing dark fell over Mags like a velvet cape.

"Magpie?" The voice was not Hawthorne's, even though it was the nickname he'd always used for her. "Magpie, are you here?"

Mags reached for the voice that was so clearly not Hawthorne's. A small, ice-cold hand met her in the span of darkness, the fingers all wrong, all splayed in different directions.

Mags gripped the girl's forearm. "Persi, you don't have to do this!"

"Oh Magpie, I can see-ee youuu."

The words lingered in the air, reading almost like a threat. "Hawthorne?" she whispered and searched for him, but the room was bathed in black. Mags sensed the girl's face nearby, could feel her breath on her cheek, but her eyes registered nothing but the darkness surrounding them. She was blind here in this place.

"Magpie, it's cold down here."

"Hawthorne, what happened to you?" Mags swiped her cheeks, wet with her tears. It was him. Her brother. The only other person in the world who'd understood her as a child, before school, before friends, before influence. He knew who she was at her core.

"There was a party."

"Yes, but you never came home. Where did you go?"

"There were trees and water . . ."

"Were you in the woods? Did you have an accident?"

"A lady. I was just messing around. Trying to tell the story of the castle. Maybe start a MeTube channel with the footage. But the lady didn't want that. She had to stay in the dark, Magpie. Everything has to stay in the dark."

"What does that mean though?"

"She's coming!" Persi's voice broke, a squawk of a warning.

Mags felt as though her heart had stopped, the fear was so great. *Who was coming?*

"Get out, Magpie! Fly!"

Suddenly, the blinding fluorescent tube lighting filled the room. Mags blinked, letting the scene come to her in pieces. She sat bent, nearly under the table. Persi lay on her side nearby, limp and seemingly broken. She swiped the girl's hair from her face. Persi's skin felt tacky and had gone an alarming shade of yellow.

"Somebody get in here!" Mags gripped the girl's hand, checking her fingers. They bent at their normal angles now but were bruised and swollen. "She needs help!"

"Nonsense."

Mags had almost forgotten Sofia sat there too.

"She'll be fine." Sofia pulled a cigarette out of what looked like a coin purse. She clicked a lighter and stuck the cigarette between her pouting lips. The cigarette lit as she inhaled, and then she blew the smoke around the sound room. "I always was."

"So this is just the *cost*?"

"Not always. But sometimes."

"Why do it then? This is horrific." Mags looked back to the frail girl, who started to stir.

Sofia smirked. "It's a gift, Magpie."

Mags's jaw ticked at the use of her nickname. This was like no gift Mags had ever received or wanted. She realized that now. Whatever had happened to Hawthorne, it wasn't worth hurting this girl. He was gone, and sometimes that was just how stories ended. There wasn't always a neat and tidy wrap-up, a sense of closure for everyone, and Mags just had to be okay with that. Because this . . . this power, it was too much, too great, too hurtful for a child to bear alone. Especially while their mother turned it into a hustle.

6

"A ghost is a spirit that chooses to stay behind. They never cross the veil because they continue to feel they have the right to interfere, nothing more than a narcissistic tendency."

    Beyond and Further Still Sofia Brewer

Crew members rushed in. Mags checked Persi's vitals; she'd taken the first aid class required in her contract. The others swooped around Sofia, congratulating her on what a success the podcast was sure to be.

"Magnolia's dialogue needs some editing," Sofia said.

"Nothing that can't be cut and spliced," said an eager-looking producer.

"And we need more on *the lady*."

"Tom's doing the research. What about the victims? Should we look into finding who some of them were? Telling their stories?"

"You mean the residents? Eh, they were wards of the

state, probably poor as hell. Everyone's heard that sob story. No, what we really need is a deep dive into who the headmistress was. She's who the audience will really be interested in. A potential female serial killer hiding in plain sight; she's the star."

Mags still held Persi's hand, cool against her own flushed and heated skin.

"I want Persimmon channeling her next."

"Let's get her out of here," Mags suggested to anyone who might be listening. "I can carry her." The girl was not much more than skin and bones, couldn't weigh more than sixty pounds.

"I don't think that's the plan," said Alice. She gave a nod toward the others.

The conversation around Sofia had tumbled into listing the scenes that needed to be shot in the rest of the castle tonight . . . with Persi, all while the child lay unconscious on the floor.

A need to protect the girl from this spectacle rose in Mags. She had to do something, had to put a stop to what was going on here. But how? She couldn't think with all these people surrounding her.

"Screw their plan. They can't record a thing while she's out like this." Mags hefted Persi into her arms. She marched past these living, breathing ghouls, out of the sound booth, and back up through the castle.

She reached the living quarters and walked down the hall toward Persi's bedroom. Mags laid the girl in her bed and tucked a blanket up under her chin. Persi opened her eyes.

"Did he come through?" she asked, her voice hardly more than a whisper.

"He did." Mags sat on the pillowy mattress and swept

Persi's bangs from her forehead. She couldn't help but compare Persi's life to a fairy tale: a princess being used for her talent, spinning gold for a queen, trapped in a castle. The girl's skin was still waxy and unbelievably cool to the touch. Her teeth chattered, making a *click-clack*ing sound like dice.

"What did he say?" she managed to ask.

"He just called my name and said he could see me." Mags didn't really want to get into this now. Persi had carried enough of the burden.

Persi let out a sigh. "So not what you were hoping for."

"It was enough."

"No, we'll do it again." Persi turned onto her side, tucking her swollen hands under her cheek. "Just let me sleep a little first."

"How are your . . ." Mags swallowed the word *fingers* as the image of Persi's broken and bent appendages flashed through her mind.

"It's no big—" The girl yawned, a long and moaning sound. "—deal. Looks worse than it feels. The bones, they don't actually break."

"Persi, this has to stop. It's not right."

"It will." Persi chuckled, a huffing kind of shuffling sound. "The boys will help me. Kendra made sure of it." She sounded much older than she should have, too certain for an eight-year-old.

Kendra? "Your mom's assistant?"

Persi nodded, her hair matting in knots and tangles against her pillow. "She found the mirror. It'll all be over soon."

"The compact?" Mags asked.

"Yes. Will you bring it to me? It's in the dollhouse."

"Of course." Mags paced to the dollhouse and looked for

the mirror. She knew she had to make a plan, had to stop what was happening to Persi. But could she? How could a mortal, barely functioning young adult fight against all the supernatural shit she'd just witnessed in the basement?

Her gaze landed on a little tableau Persi must have set up in the dollhouse. The mirror was open, and a doll, the pregnant one named after Persi's mother, stood in front of it. For a moment, Mags caught another glimpse of the boys, their gaping mouths yawning out toward the doll, but it was only the black spots on the aged mirror, the backing being scraped away or mirror rot. Mags clicked the mirror shut and took it to Persi.

The girl's fingers peeked out from under the blanket, and she reached for the antique. "It was just something from a fairy tale she told me."

"I love fairy tales. Wanna share it?" Mags sat in a wing-back chair nearby.

Persi's gaze met Mags's. The girl smiled meekly and drew in a deep breath. Maybe this was too much for her. *She should be resting*, Mags thought. But Persi continued, telling the story of a girl who found herself in the woods. When she came upon a lake, she spotted a fish caught in a net. She untangled the net and let it go free. The scales left in her hand turned into a mirror.

"When she gets trapped by a witch, the girl uses the mirror to escape."

"How'd she do that?"

"Calls upon the souls inside it."

Mags swallowed. Something about the detail had made the hair on her arms stand on end.

Persi's sweet features, the little bit of kid magic she'd shown when she shared the story, dropped, seemingly with disappointment. "Don't worry. Fairy tales aren't real." She flicked the compact open and closed. *Click. Clack. Click. Clack. Click. Clack.*

"So the compact is like a symbol, a kind of charm?"

Persi nodded. Her skin had returned to its normal tan color. Little splotches of pink topped her cheeks.

"I'm glad Kendra remembered to give it to me before she left. So you can have it."

Mags didn't know how to ask her next question. Had Kendra been determined to help Persi? Or had she just helped the girl dream of escape—something far off in the distant future?

"Was there a plan?" Mags asked.

"For what?"

"To . . . get you out of here . . . to stop your grown-ups from using you for—that stuff."

Persi shrugged and let the compact drop back onto the comforter. "Can I sleep now?"

"Oh god, yes. I'm sorry." She stood and gave Persi another good tucking in, then grabbed the compact and her phone and sat in the window seat, looking out over the woods.

A breeze blew over the trees, their tops moving in a kind of slow hypnotic sway under the moonlight. What the fuck could Mags do here? Call Child Protective Services? And say what? *A famous psychic is using her daughter's body as a conduit to further her career! No, I swear! It's real! And grotesque!*

Even on the off chance someone believed Mags, it would be weeks before they'd come and investigate. Who knew what Persi would've been put through at that point? Plus, Persi was well taken care of on the surface. She had a rich, famous, white parent. Filing a report with CPS seemed unlikely to change anything at all. But Mags couldn't get the popping sound out of her head, the girl's bones snapping and grinding together as she took on Hawthorne's spirit.

Mags needed to feel grounded again. She needed to talk to Stacy, needed some of her best friend's direct common sense because this place made her feel nuts. When she checked her phone, there was only the slightest nub of a bar —definitely not enough to make a call or even a text.

She set her phone on the bench beside her and clicked open the compact. She thought of Persi's story and considered the idea of souls trapped in the little mirror. She fought the urge to dismiss the idea as some childish dream. She'd witnessed Persi's abilities all day. Maybe there were spirits trapped in the compact, and maybe they could help. Hell, somebody had to do something; why not a compact full of collected souls? All the adults, the crew, had stood around and listened while Persi channeled Hawthorne, her body splayed out over the carpet of that grim sound booth. Sure, some of them were probably horrified—Mags had felt that way, but she'd also let it continue. She'd set the child's pain aside for her own gain, just like every other person nearby.

Mags sighed. The situation felt hopeless, and she wasn't that much closer to figuring out what had happened to Hawthorne. What had he been doing at the castle that night? What had he discovered? Mags's thoughts twirled and twisted around Hawthorne and Persi. At some point, she realized she'd absentmindedly been opening and closing the compact. *Click. Clack. Click. Clack. Click. Clack.* Her shoulders slumped, and she rested her head against the wall, the stretch feeling glorious in her neck. Her eyelids drooped, the adrenaline of the day draining out of her, and when she closed her eyes, she saw the usual static.

7

"No one alive should want to see a ghost's work completed."
Beyond and Further Still, Sofia Brewer

Mags woke to the sound of screaming. Her heart racing, she jolted upright, not fully remembering she was still in the castle. The screaming rang continuously, a profound wailing that perforated every inch of the living space. Mags jumped up, her body cramped and out of sync from sleeping in the window seat, and stumbled to the door. A stream of crew ran back and forth.

"Somebody call 9-1-1!"

"They're on the phone with them right now!"

"What happened?"

The question was met with silence, save for the screaming that hadn't stopped. Mags watched their eyes, all wide and unbelieving, some already wet with tears.

"What are we supposed to do?"

"I don't know! I don't know!"

"We can't just wait for the ambulance! There has to be something we can do!"

"Fucking Google it; I don't know."

Mags watched breathlessly as Alice stopped in front of her and pulled out her phone.

"What's going on?" Mags asked.

Alice didn't answer. Her thumbs worked frantically over the tiny keyboard: how to treat lye burns.

"Lye?" All Mags knew about lye she'd seen in the movie *Fight Club*.

"Yeah, she fucking bathed in it."

"What? Who?" Mags asked.

"Sofia. Who else?" Alice's eyes never left her phone as she scanned an article from the CDC. "I think we need saline. Who the fuck has that amount of saline?"

Mags stepped back, away from the action. Her brain seemed to glitch, not fully functioning as she took in the information. Her hand, though, subconsciously reached for Persi's doorknob. *Get to the girl. Keep her safe in her room. Don't let her see.* Those three thoughts repeated through Mags's mind like a mantra.

She closed the door, leaving the chaos of the hallway.

"Who's there?" a little voice squeaked in the dark. "Mags, it's you, right?"

A rainbow nightlight flashed through the array of colors, creating a frenzied, pulsing vibe in the girl's room.

"It's me. Something's happened. I don't know a lot of details, but an ambulance has been called for your mother." Mags led with as much of the truth as she could. She left out the lye bath, a whole body covered in burns.

What had Sofia been thinking? But then another thought, a

darker one: *Had she even known?* The implication to that question was that someone put lye in her bath, where she'd use it. She remembered the girl's murmured response from earlier: *The boys will help me.*

Suddenly, the room felt very small. The nightlight flashed red, then faded to orange, then yellow. Mags stared at the girl, who'd sat up in bed.

"Persi, did—"

"I didn't do *anything,*" the girl whined. "It wasn't me, Mags." Persi threw back the covers and crawled to the end of her bed, her body sprawling on spindly limbs. The nightlight flashed blue, green, purple.

"But what you said . . . earlier." Mags could barely swallow. Her mouth had dried out; she thought of the lye desiccating Sofia's skin. The screams still sounded from the main bedroom. When would the ambulance come? When would help arrive?

"I didn't mean it! I swear!" Persi cried. "It was the boys!"

Mags shook her head, confused. Nothing made sense here. None of it.

"The boys!" Persi cried again. "I know you saw them when you got here. They said you saw them. They . . . didn't like how she treated me. They tricked her."

"You're telling me a bunch of ghosts hurt your mom?" Mags asked.

Persi's shoulders slumped. "It doesn't matter. You don't believe me."

But Mags did believe her. She'd seen the boys and their cavernous mouths, and how she'd felt like she could walk right into their darkness. Mysteries lived there, between the blackness of their loose jaws, answers to all kinds of questions. They'd whispered that they knew what happened to her brother, that he was right there with them.

Mags crossed the room and turned on a reading lamp next to Persi's bed, stopping the incessant rainbow strobe. Persi's face was wet with tears.

"I didn't know," she whimpered. "I didn't know what they were going to do."

Mags sat next to her and put her arm around the child, gathering her up and drawing her near.

"Shh, it's okay. It's going to be fine," she lied, like every other adult. Nothing was going to be okay. Nothing had ever really been fine.

The girl cried softly, her tears wetting Mags's T-shirt. At some point, Mags heard authoritative voices in the hall and realized help had come. She heard the *bang-clang* of a gurney and pictured them wheeling a ruined Sofia Brewer out of the castle. She checked Persi; the girl had gone back to sleep.

8

"A human life is but one chapter."
Beyond and Further Still Sofia Brewer

The summer plan had come to a crashing halt. Most of the crew had been sent home. Production of the podcast ceased while Sofia Brewer lingered in an ICU downtown. Persi hadn't wanted to visit her, and Alice had begged Mags stay and care for the girl while she dealt with everything else.

Mags walked the grounds. Except for the checkerboard effect in the grass made by some meticulous landscaper, the lawn was bare. No native plants. Not a weed in sight. Persi'd run ahead and lingered near the edge of the woods.

She'd been watching the girl carefully, looking for signs of trauma or grief or even fear. She'd spoken with Alice about Persi probably needing to see a therapist, but the suggestion had been met only with *yeah-yeah, sure-sures*.

Mags spread a blanket over the grass and set about unpacking their lunch from her backpack. She pulled out a bag of pretzels, two peanut butter and jelly sandwiches wrapped in foil, a carton of strawberries, and their water bottles.

"Persi! Come have lunch!"

The girl turned and ran toward Mags. Her long braids whipped behind her. She wore a princess costume over a pair of striped leggings. Her feet were bare and stained a yellowish green from the grass. She looked . . . free. Like a child should look.

Persi bounded to the blanket and plopped down. She opened her water bottle and gulped a fourth of it quickly. She caught her breath, and Mags took note of how her face gleamed with a light layer of sweat.

"What have you been playing?"

"Oh, nothing."

This was a noted change in Persi. Since the accident, she'd become a little less forthright.

"Are the boys here today?" Mags asked, trying to draw more of the truth out. It was like a game of hide and seek they'd been playing with each other since Sofia's accident. Mags dug for more information about what had really happened; Persi kept their secret.

"They're always here. The mirror makes sure of that."

"How'd they do it, Persi?" The question was a risk, one Mags had been putting off, but if Alice had no plans to set up therapy any time soon, someone needed to talk it out with the girl.

"I don't know." Persi took a bite of her sandwich and chewed. Then, out of nowhere, except maybe in an attempt to steer the conversation away from the boys, she said, "I can tell you what happened to your brother." Persi's gaze met Mags's.

"No. I saw what doing that did to you. What's dead is gone. The end."

"It makes him sad when you say things like that."

Mags swallowed. She bit her lower lip. She didn't want to make her brother upset.

"I have more information than I came here with, and that's all I needed." Mags had already made up her mind about her next steps. As soon as she could get away from here, she planned to ransack Hawthorne's old room, even though their mother had closed it up like a tomb. Whatever he was doing or researching about this old place, there had to be evidence of it somewhere.

"Do you want to know more now?" Persi set her half-eaten sandwich aside and twirled the end of her braid around her index finger, the skin purpling under the tourniquet.

Of course she did, but Mags shook her head, even though refusing made her stomach collapse. She tossed her sandwich back onto the foil. Having Persi do her thing could be so much easier than sifting through all of her brother's old stuff. He'd always been on the verge of being a hoarder. Mags blew out a breath, her cheeks going slack. *Do I dare?*

Mags nodded ever so slightly, guilt stealing her voice. Pulled between Persi's traumatic offering and her own desperation, she chose herself. She was a hypocrite. A failure. A sister grieving.

"There was an argument at the party. He was telling someone what he'd found out about the castle. A girl. Someone he liked. I see rain. Wait—was that her name?"

"I-I don't know. Maybe?" Mags's thoughts whirred

through a collection of faces and then landed on a pretty girl from Hawthorne's class. *She'd been in drama with him,* she thought. "I think so. Yeah. There was a Rain Winters in his class." The name came to her suddenly. "Did they leave together? Was she here with him?"

Persi's head tilted, and she looked up toward the deep blue sky. "I don't see her in the truck with him. He left the party. And he was annoyed she wouldn't come. He liked her, wanted to impress her. But she didn't want to trespass or get in trouble. He wanted people to know the castle's true history, about the boys. He'd stumbled upon some records for a project and was tracing them back, trying to find their families. The Winters family had a relative connected to the castle." The whole while Persi spoke, her eyes rolled from side to side, a scene playing out that Mags didn't have access to. "*She* didn't like that."

"Who? Rain?"

"No, the headmistress. She waited for Hawthorne at the gate, had sent the deer that had him veer his truck toward the pond at the bottom of the property. And when he trudged up Fault Hill, she held her mirror open for him."

Persi swallowed, her skin gone a sickening shade of gray-white. Mags prayed her bones didn't snap this time, that Persi could just tell the story without the awful price.

But that's not really how these things go.

Crack. One finger on Persi's right hand had wrenched upward.

"Persi! Stop! I don't want—"

"I'm with them now, Magpie." *Snap*—another finger. "And the boys can't be rid of how she's trapped them." *Crunch.* Persi's knuckles bent at odd angles. "But you can."

"What? Me? How?"

Persi's shoulders hunched forward. She pressed her lips into a line and rubbed her fingers back into position. Her eyes didn't meet Mags's. Instead, she stared into the middle distance.

"What can *I* do?" Mags shivered, even in the heat of June.

"Break this." Persi reached into her back pocket and pulled out the antique compact they'd traded back and forth. She handed it to Mags.

"It's that easy?" Mags asked.

Persi shrugged, coming back to herself. She picked up a strawberry and bit into the red, seedy flesh.

Mags held the weighty compact in the palm of her hand. To finally know some of what had happened to her brother felt different—less fulfilling—than she'd expected. It didn't bring a sense of closure; it brought a restrained type of futile anger. The big answer was just that her brother had been sucked up by an evil that kept him voiceless and inconsequential, along with all the other boys in the mirror.

"They got revenge on the headmistress eventually, right? She drowned. And your mother. What happened to her . . . they're not totally powerless in the mirror."

"Not powerless, true. But also not at peace."

"Why me?" She was so insignificant, couldn't change a single thing about the whole wide world. "Why not . . . anyone else? Why not you?"

"I can't." Persi scratched at a scab until it peeled away, and a bead of red bubbled up on her arm. "Because I used them."

Sofia's screams were still fresh in Mags's mind. Persi had asked the boys for help, to set her free from her mother's ambitions and abuse, and . . . well, look at what they'd done— horrible things.

She opened the compact—*click*. It seemed so . . . trivial.

Innocuous, really. But then as she looked upon the mirror, taking in her reflection, the rot along the edges began to swirl and move. Faces emerged in the glass, the same terrible, sagging, sad faces she'd seen when she first arrived. Among them was one she recognized. His skin had turned sallow, and his eyes were gone. The joy, his easy confidence, had been stripped from him. She only saw torture painted among what was left of his features, trapped behind the rotting mirror.

Mags pressed her thumbs to the glass and wrenched the hinge until—*crack*. She felt a pinch of pain; the sharp edge of the broken mirror had pierced the pad of her thumb. She withdrew her hand—blood already trailing, dripping onto the mirror's surface—and stuck her thumb in her mouth.

Thank you. The words came as a whisper of wind against Mags's ear. She turned to see who'd spoken, but they were already gone.

"That's it?" Mags asked, her words garbled around her hurt thumb.

"Sometimes all it takes is a little blood and a broken cage." Persi's gaze flicked toward Mags. What did Mags see there? An innocent? Someone who'd been used and abused for her power her whole life? Malevolence? Just a girl.

ABOUT JESSICA CRANBERRY

Jessica Cranberry lives in the Sierra Nevada foothills with her family and spends days striking a balance between parenthood, teaching, editing/proofreading, and writing—suspense novels and eclectic short stories mostly. When she's not doing those things, she's reading, attempting to garden, or hiking around town. Her novel, *IN THE TRAP*, was published in the spring of 2022 with book two scheduled for release in 2023.

CONNECT WITH JESSICA

jessicacranberry.com

bookbub.com/authors/jessica-cranberry

MORE FROM JESSICA

In the Trap

Amid the Haze

Anthologies

Emporium of Superstition

That Thing In The House With The Arched Roof

By Katya de Becerra

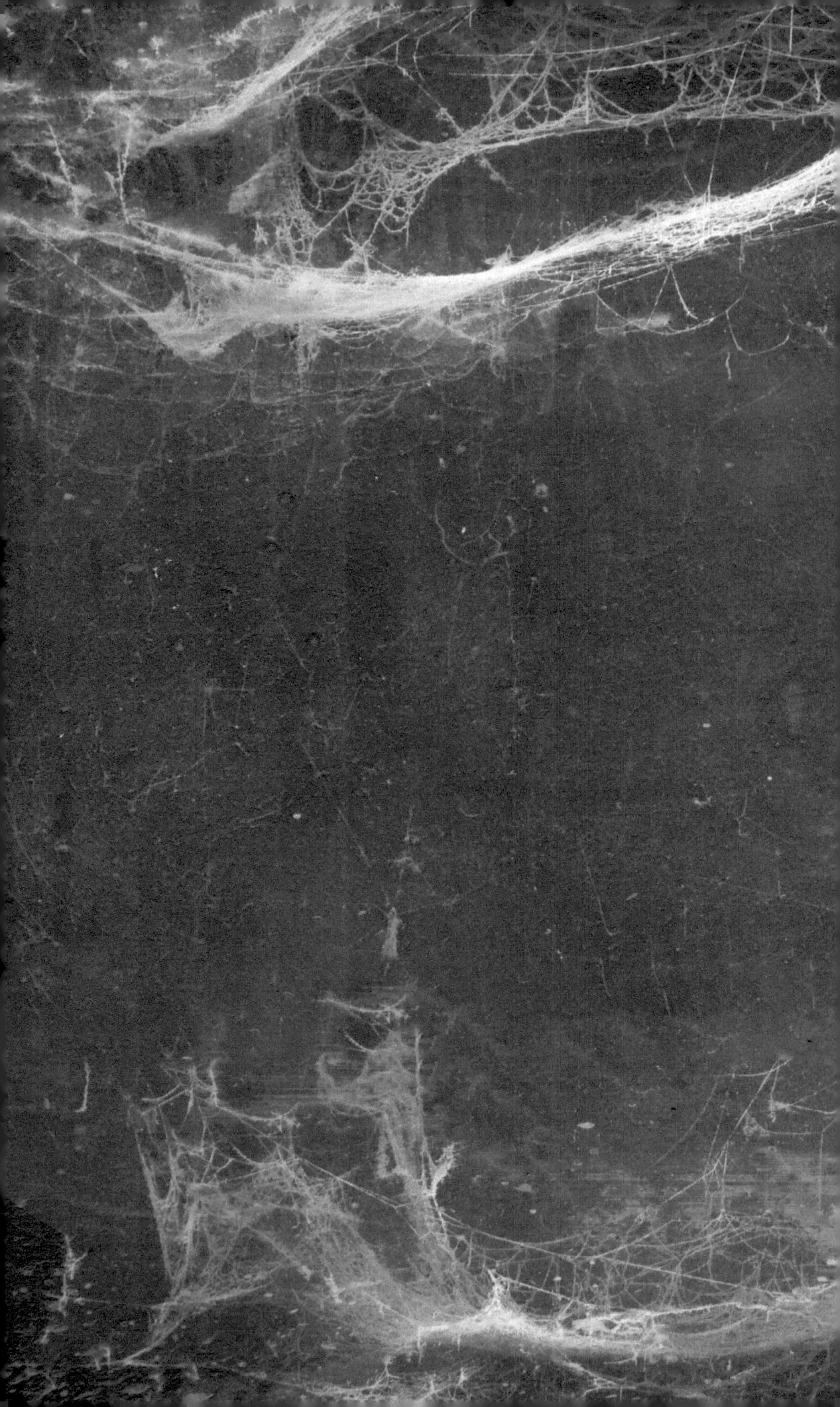

1

Clara Finnigan, the witch of Santa Solana and the woman who raised me, is laid to rest today at the Reminiscence Cemetery.

Cousin Maribelle and I trail after the pallbearers into the family crypt, where we watch them slide Aunt Clara's coffin into its niche in the wall. There she will rest next to my parents and other kin, generations of Finnigans nestled together, shivering in their stone beds. My name, too, will one day be added to the wall: *Emma Finnigan*. There's comfort in this certainty, however morbid.

I follow Maribelle's lead and touch two fingers to my heart, then to Aunt Clara's name on the plaque. We leave the crypt in silence. The gloomy drizzle greets us outside, where a sizable crowd waits. Aunt Clara has touched many lives, and today, they all braved the rain to see her off to the next world.

I spot three unfamiliar faces among the windswept mourners. A tall, rail-thin man with two young children by his side. The newcomers are immediately obvious to a local's eye, even if it's a former local like me. But that's not the only thing that draws my attention. Something's off about the kids. I can't quite put my finger on it.

"That's the Cressons," Maribelle says, following the direction of my gaze. "Jonathan, the father. And the children, Leilani and Marty."

With her luminous complexion and a lion's mane of red curls, Maribelle has the innocent appearance of a porcelain doll. But looks can be deceiving. Despite the veneer of fragility, her core is that of steel. She's a barracuda of a lawyer, a pillar of the community, and the sure-handed executor of Aunt Clara's estate. Even if there isn't much of a tangible estate to speak of.

As for my aunt's legacy as the town's witch, it'll require a proper review once the funeral is over.

Once upon a time, I was Aunt Clara's stalwart apprentice, her witchy sidekick. Orphaned and uprooted, I found new life in Santa Solana and, for a time, my purpose. Mom never talked about my heritage as a Finnigan, so it came as a shock when I learned we were all witches. Some, like Maribelle, were dormant, with only a suggestion of magic in their blood. Others were born to do the work. I belonged in the latter category, and for a while, I took my destiny as an emerging witch very seriously. I believed I could live up to the expectations that came with the Finnigan bloodline.

But in the end, I wasn't brave enough, didn't have the nerve.

I escaped Santa Solana to study graphic design in the Bay Area. I cut off my red hair and dyed what was left of it black. I wore combat boots and torn jeans and shapeless hoodies—not a proper look for a Finnigan woman who prides herself on her luscious copper locks and elegant dresses. But something always pulled me back. This town, and my aunt's work, haunted me in memories and dreams from the very moment I hopped on that San Francisco-bound bus. I never imagined my return to Santa Solana would take place under such sad circumstances.

With Aunt Clara gone, Maribelle is my last remaining link to my lineage. Ever since I arrived, days ahead of the funeral, my cousin hasn't left my side, bringing me up to speed on the town's comings and goings, catching me up on years' worth of gossip. This is how we, the Finnigans, grieve. We throw ourselves into the mundane tasks, we talk and cook and clean and go meticulously through our lists of chores, while our sadness murmurs in the background.

"The Cressons have recently moved to . . . *the house.*" Maribelle's voice drops. She looks away from the man and his children.

A shiver licks at my spine. I know the house she's referring to.

The house with the arched roof has long held a special place in the hearts of the Santa Solana children. Coming up its ramshackle porch on a dare, ringing the rusted bell, listening to the silence . . . The house used to be a rite of passage, drawing in the local kids like an anglerfish lures smaller things into the dark with its luminescent rod.

But if the house was the glowing lure, who or *what* was dangling it?

The year I turned twelve, I came close to finding out . . .

My memories of the encounter are muddled, uncertain. I don't know *what* I saw. But something did happen. I escaped danger, but I didn't get away unscathed. I lost my drive to learn Aunt Clara's witch work. The house with the arched roof drove a wedge between us, and my apprenticeship started to feel like a burden.

I went through a phase, obsessing over the house's history. I was determined to find the root of its malaise. I scoured Santa Solana's archives, spoke to the town's historical society, and befriended a retired librarian who fancied herself a digital sleuth. But the house with the arched roof did an excellent job of evading the news and staying off the radar. All that I could find about it was that it was built in the 1920s for a composer who was married to an opera singer. The rounded arched roof was designed for the acoustics. The pair had no children and lived happily into their 90s. When no kin could be identified after their passing, the state came into possession. The house stood empty after that. Nothing wrong with it on paper. But its vibe always felt off. Thinking of it as a home to anyone, especially to children, makes my guts turn with disquiet.

"They've lost their mother recently, before moving here," Maribelle whispers close to my ear as the stern-faced workers lock the crypt. "Jonathan is desperate to hire someone to look after the kids. Aunt Clara's been helping out over the past month." She gives me a meaningful look. "I think she was trying to . . . cleanse that house. The father is oblivious. But something's happening to the kids. Just look at them."

I zero in on the children. It's their shadows. Threadbare, muted. *Wrong.* That's what got my attention before. I just needed Maribelle's prompt to see it, this evidence of malevolence.

For as long as I remember, I could always tell when someone's been affected by evil. Whether it's a neighbor's sloppy curse work that latched on to its unsuspecting victim or a touch of frost on one's face left by something from beyond the veil, evil always leaves a mark. More often than not, it eats away at the shadow like acid burns through metal.

I look away from the Cressons, but the children's damaged shadows have imprinted on my eyelids. Sometimes I wish I didn't see such things, but we can't change who are.

"But she warned him about the house?" I keep my voice low. We're far enough from the mourners to not be overheard, but I don't want to risk it. Not everyone in Santa Solana is excited to have me back. Some look at me with disappointment, even hostility. As if I didn't just fail Aunt Clara when I left, I failed them all.

"She did. Jonathan dismissed her as the town's eccentric, but he was grateful she helped with the kids. No one else is willing to go anywhere near their place, let alone babysit. Aunt Clara wouldn't tell me what exactly she's been doing in the house, but . . . I suspect she was working to have that door closed."

The door.

I remember Aunt Clara telling me how our world is full of holes, *doors*, the thinning spots in the veil.

As a kid apprentice, I assisted Aunt Clara with customers. I held burning candles, while she chanted incantations into the charged air. I wiped the sweat from her brow with a silken cloth when she couldn't stop grinding dried out animal bones into fine powder. And I stirred the brew in the pot as she measured out the ingredients. But one aspect of her work she was less willing to expose me to was the "closing of doors". She was picky with those cases, only agreeing to the ones she felt were most dire, requiring urgent intervention.

Some doors, she explained, *can close on their own. Others will fester and rot and grow bigger and bigger until things that dwell on the other side slither in on their rank, reptilian bellies.*

That kind of talk scared me. I'd have nightmares about dead, ravenous things that bide their time, waiting for a door to open.

Aunt Clara had this antique globe dotted with a pattern of crystal-headed pins marking the spots all around the world where the veil was thin. One of the pins was in the vicinity of Santa Solana. Maribelle and I long suspected that it had to be in the house with the arched roof. But when that particular door opened or why remains a mystery. My aunt had years to deal with it, but left it alone, even after my close brush with the house. Perhaps the Cressons' arrival finally pushed her to act.

And now she is dead.

Maribelle's been vague on the details of Aunt Clara's passing other than that it was a heart attack. Sadly, heart issues aren't uncommon in the Finnigan line. The work of a witch takes a toll on one's health.

"She was waiting for you to come back home, you know," Maribelle says. "I think, in a way, she knew she wouldn't be able to finish her work in that house. She was hoping you would."

"Me?" I say, too loud for this mournful day. A few heads turn our way. "I'm only in town for the funeral, you know that."

Maribelle reaches inside her bag and retrieves a large envelope, the plastic kind lined with bubbles.

"She left you this. I think it's to help you . . . close the door."

"I want no part in this . . ." I plead as my cousin offers me the envelope.

But my dead aunt wanted me to have this. She wanted me involved. Disobeying her final wishes feels like playing with fire.

"I've been away for too long. I forgot everything she taught me," I say. "You know about this stuff more than I do."

"I may know the theory," Maribelle concedes. "But I'm useless when it comes to practice. I wasn't blessed like you. And you can never really forget this. It's in your blood, Emma."

I know she's right. But what a wicked irony. Having the Finnigan legacy bestowed on me, the girl with the wrong temperament for the job. Maribelle, level-headed and fearless, would be a better choice. But alas.

"She was supposed to be looking after those kids tomorrow," Maribelle adds, still waiting for me to take the envelope, now splattered with raindrops.

I bite my lower lip and draw blood.

I can almost sense it, the moment my fate is sealed, when I accept the envelope from my cousin's hand.

A broken comb, a bag of dried bird bones, and an elegant, curved knife.

A witch's implements, objects imbued with power. The contents of Aunt Clara's envelope are now in my backpack. But their presence offers little comfort. My apprenticeship is a thing of the past, a bricolage of memories. And memory alone doesn't make a witch. Practice does.

In my time as an apprentice, I'd never assisted Aunt Clara with the closing of a door. But I saw her prepare for it, charging everyday objects with magical intent. And I helped her recover after, when she came home a shell of her former self, falling exhausted into a fitful sleep that lasted a day and a night. She didn't talk about what she'd done, but she'd whisper in her slumber of places beyond the veil. Places of dark fairy tales, wilting and stuck in perpetual twilight. And she murmured of things that inhabited those places, hungry things craving vitality, the heat of a human body, the glow of memories.

But it's been years. A part of me doubts any of it was ever real. Was my aunt really a witch or just an unconventional woman who put on a good show?

Still, I shudder when I come up to the house with the arched roof.

It's as miserable as I remember. Bleak and peeling, battered by the eternal drizzle of Santa Solana. The porch creaks under my heavy-soled boots as I ring the bell. An atonal sound echoes inside, bringing back a memory from the darkest depths of my childhood. The door slides inward while my finger is still on the bell. As if the house was expecting me.

Leilani Cresson stands in the doorway. She's about nine or ten. Her mistrustful gray eyes give me a look-over.

Her shadow looked threadbare yesterday, but when I sneak a look at it now, I barely hold back a gasp.

There's hardly any shadow left.

Whatever happened between the funeral and this morning took a toll on this kid. Her shadow's deterioration is evidence that something *is* going on, despite how I feel about portals between worlds and Aunt Clara's legacy. I just hope there's something I can do to help Leilani and her brother. And I hope I'm not too late.

"You shouldn't be here," Leilani says.

She's tiny, small for her age, but she speaks like an older woman, her speech clipped and precise, and her eyes too old and knowing.

"Hello to you too," I say, ignoring her dismissive tone. "You must be Leilani. I'm Emma Finnigan. I live a few streets over"—I point casually behind my shoulder without looking —"in the house with the green tiles. Is your daddy home?"

Leilani stares at me.

There's a sound of steps. A man appears from the depths of the house and comes to stand next to the girl. It takes all my composure not to react to his malnourished appearance. Dark shadows circle his eyes, and his skin is so sallow, it has a greenish tint. I wonder how long ago he became a widower —must be more recently than I thought. He wears his grief like a mourning mask.

"Jonathan?" I ask instead of a greeting. "We spoke on the phone earlier. Clara was my aunt."

"It's so good to meet you." He takes a step back, inviting me in. After a moment's hesitation, I follow him into the dark lobby. I expect an immediate psychic attack by some supernatural force, but all is quiet. More sad than anything.

"Clara's passing is a terrible loss. I'm so sorry." Jonathan Cresson speaks like a man dying of thirst in the desert. The raw sound of his voice weighs down my heart.

"Thank you," I say. "She's been like a mom to me. I lost my parents when I was a kid, not much older than Leilani." I glance at the girl, silent and watchful by his side. She studies me with a spooky precision. "Aunt Clara took me in, she raised me. She's always been like that, selfless and ready to help."

"She's been a godsend," Jonathan says. "It's always tough

to start again at a new place, especially with kids. Clara's been looking after us."

"Why did you move here, if I may ask?" I look between him and his daughter.

"I lost . . . everything." He exhales, then runs a hand through his short hair. "My wife, my job, and then there was a foreclosure. But I was offered a new job in Sacramento. I work from home, but I do have to commute once a week, and it's just easier to get a hotel there for the night . . . It's so much cheaper to live in a small town. When I came across this listing, I couldn't believe my eyes at first. They were practically giving it away for free."

I have more questions, but he changes the topic.

"Leilani here is my oldest. Marty is somewhere . . . I'm so grateful you could help out. It's been impossible to hire a local to babysit. I thought teens here would jump on the opportunity, but no."

"We don't need a babysitter," Leilani states, drilling into me with those too-old eyes of hers. "We can look after ourselves."

"I know you can, kiddo," her father says, a forced smile on his lips. "But I'd feel so much better if there was a grown-up in the house with you. I can't really leave you and your brother all alone, can I?"

"We're not alone," the girl insists. A shiver crawls over my skin. "And strangers are not allowed inside," Leilani goes on, still looking at me.

"I'm not a stranger, though, am I?" I say, taking over from the girl's father. "I told you my name, you know where I live . . ."

"I've never seen you before. You don't live in that house," she snaps.

"Leilani!" Her father gives her a wide-eyed look.

But Leilani got me there. "It's okay," I say to the girl. "You're right, I haven't lived in that house for years, but I used to. My Aunt Clara just died, and I came back for the funeral. I believe she was supposed to mind you and your brother tonight while your father's at work."

I study the little girl, and she studies me back, still doubtful. Her father is silent and slack, not much help. His exhaustion creates an almost palpable aura of despair around him.

"You know what, Leilani? Have it your way," I say with an exaggerated sigh. "Your house gives me the creeps, anyway. And you seem old enough to look after your kid brother, make supper for the both of you, and keep the place running until your father comes home tomorrow. You've got it all under control, so I'll be on my way."

I turn on my heels and take the first step down.

"Wait!" Leilani's voice quivers, shedding its grown-up veneer to show a glimpse of the scared child inside. A child who has lost her mother. "You can stay," she says.

"Okay, then," I say. "I'll stay."

Another cold tremor of unease licks at my spine.

Jonathan Cresson hands me his credit card and a piece of paper with emergency numbers.

"They are both picky eaters, but they love pizza," he says.

We're alone in the lobby, with Leilani having retreated into the depths of the house.

This all feels so normal. A change of shift, a parent going away, leaving a minder in their stead. It's easy to pretend like the house doesn't creep me out or that I don't have a bag of bird bones in my backpack.

There's so much I want to tell Jonathan before he takes off, but the weight of words flattens my tongue. I understand what brought him here; desperation can trap people into some strange choices. And on the surface, this spacious, unique house *is* a catch. Despite it being empty for as long as I remember, it's in a pretty good shape. But can't Jonathan tell his children are not okay, that their demeanor is not only due to grief? He may not be able to see their threadbare shadows, but he must sense something's wrong, right?

Lost to my thoughts, I miss my moment to question him. He leaves the house, the door closing softly behind.

I pocket Jonathan's credit card and look around. This is my first time inside the infamous house. The reality of it is hitting me fully.

The house's exteriors may be peeling, but on the inside, the walls are eggshell-white, the floors are natural wood, and the furniture is Scandi, stylish, and dare I say, welcoming. But though this space is beautiful, it still feels . . . off.

Memories, old as dirt but very much potent, flood me now, as if the house is pulling them out of me, one glimmering string at a time.

I was twelve and hiding my sorrows behind a brave face, determined to show Aunt Clara and the whole world I wasn't a sad little orphan. There was a gang of local Santa Solana kids I was desperate to befriend. They were older, cool, and beautiful in that raw way of feral cats, faces painted with aimless determination. I wanted to be one of them. I wanted to *be* them.

I invited myself to their Halloween outing, and I dragged Maribelle along. The plan was to come to the house with the arched roof, ring its ancient bell, share a giggle, and run away.

That's not how the evening went.

The older kids, an inseparable trio of two girls and a token boy who was in love with both of them, went inside and didn't come out. When I opened the rotting door of the house and scanned the vast, empty hall that stretched beyond, a voice called to me from the dark.

Emma. Emma?

Clear and sweet. Just like Mom did when she came by my room to tuck me in at night.

"Mom?" I called back into the dark.

Even though I knew it was impossible—there was no way it was my dead mother in there, inside this empty house that gave me the heebie-jeebies.

But I wanted to be with Mom in the dark. I craved her touch, could already sense her familiar smell . . . I'd have given anything to hug her again.

The rest of that night is in patches.

Me, taking another step toward the dark threshold. Maribelle, pulling me back. Her fingers so hot against mine, like skin to an open flame.

My level-headed cousin saved me, stopped me from walking into a web lovingly woven by some human-eating spider. A spider that knew my name and spoke in my dead mother's voice.

Someone inside the house screamed, a bleeding, razor-sharp sound, and then Maribelle and I were running.

We ran all the way to Aunt Clara's house without stopping or looking back.

The three kids who went inside the house that night were found later, semi-conscious and rambling about mazes and ghosts. One of the girls—I overheard a hushed conversation at school—kept repeating the name of her older sister who'd drowned years ago on a holiday gone wrong.

Something changed after that. The kids of Santa Solana became less naïve, like a part of our collective innocence had been lost that Halloween. The house with the arched roof was no longer just a spooky presence at the end of a suburban street. It was an active site of unexplained phenomena. It harmed kids once. It could do it again.

"Marty loves pizza but hates red sauce," Leilani says. I flinch at finding her right by my side. How long was she standing there silently before speaking up?

"Well, that might be a problem," I deadpan, hiding my turmoil behind a confident smile. "Does he know what pizza actually is?"

"He likes Alfredo sauce. Or no sauce at all," she reports, ignoring the question.

"Sure, got it. No red sauce."

"Marty, come out here! Meet Emma, our *nanny*," Leilani calls into the depths of the house. I can't tell if she's being sarcastic with her usage of "nanny" or if it implies she's accepted my presence in the house.

A boy, smaller in stature than his sister but wearing an expression of a man already burdened with life's responsibilities, joins us in the lobby. He stands next to Leilani, his eyes a haunting copy of hers, his shadow like a rag with holes.

"Your sister tells me you're not a fan of red sauce?" I say with a smile Marty doesn't return. "What do you like on your pizza, then?"

"Cheese," he says, voice like an echo from a well.

I feel for him. Both of us lost our mothers at a young age, but his grief is fresh. Just like mine was that Halloween when a thing using my late mother's voice tried to lure me into this house.

"Cheese it is!" I say to the children, hoping they won't notice my anxiety hiding behind the cheerful tone.

The presence of Aunt Clara's implements in my backpack weighs heavily on my mind. I have no plan of action, only my memories from an apprenticeship long ago combined with hope that my Finnigan instincts will kick in any moment now. *Once a Finnigan, always a Finnigan. Born a witch, always a witch.*

After placing an order for two cheese pizzas with white sauce, I set the children in front of the living room TV. I have no idea what kids like to watch these days, but Leilani solves that riddle for me—*Peppa Pig* it is.

As we wait for dinner to arrive, I study the Cresson children for any signs of . . . what? Possession? Of being under the influence of something dangerous or evil? But they're just . . . children. Despite their concerned faces and frowns, they look healthy. Only their threadbare shadows tell a different story.

Marty keeps staring off into space, while Leilani focuses a little too hard on the TV.

On the coffee table nearby, there's a family photo. It takes me a moment to match the two solemn children in my care to the happy faces pictured. Marty's grin lights up his face, and though Leilani is more reserved, she also shines from within. I recognize her features in the woman in the center of the photo: same dark eyes, brown hair. The children's mother. I don't know her name, and I'm afraid to ask.

On the screen, Daddy Pig is making a birthday breakfast for Mommy Pig. Peppa and her little brother George watch and giggle and oink-oink-oink. Next, they prepare a celebratory cake, but—oh no!—there are only three candles! Mommy Pig is older than three . . . When Daddy Pig whispers Mommy Pig's real age into Peppa's ear, she appears shocked and whispers: *So old!*

"When is your birthday, Leilani?" I ask to see if the children are paying attention to the story.

Both of them remain quiet, lost in their own heads.

Pizza arrives, but the kids barely even move from their spots on the couch. The only time Leilani turns around is to study the corridor that stretches away from the living room and into in the dark. Marty is no better. Too still, too silent. Waiting.

The dinner is quiet; they munch on their pizza slowly, like mechanized dolls, so lifelike, they're uncanny. It feels like they're waiting for something. And like the house waits also.

Later, after Leilani and Marty brush their teeth and retreat to the bedroom they share, two single beds side by side, I watch them settle in.

"Do you want me to tuck you in?" I ask.

"No, thank you," Leilani replies for the both of them. "Our mommy will do it."

I stare at her, speechless.

"Your mommy . . ." I finally push out, but Leilani is already turning away to face the wall.

It feels cruel to remind the children of their loss. So I don't.

"All right then," I say. "Sleep well."

I leave them to it, trying not to think about the night ahead.

I set up in the guest room downstairs and lay out Aunt Clara's objects on the blanket. I study them in the unreliable light of the reading lamp that flickers as if in sync with some heartbeat.

An old, wooden comb, one tine missing. A plastic packet of dried bird bones (if the hand-written label's to be believed). And a small knife, its black blade like sharpened glass.

It definitely feels like a test.

Carefully, I run a finger along the blade's length.

Obsidian. Not glass.

And *athame*, not just a knife.

Aunt Clara used an athame like this one, perhaps this exact one, for ceremony as well as, on rare occasions, for blood magic. A prick of a finger was enough to enhance a potion or to empower a spell.

Her house smelled like burnt sage and smoked birch bark, and her cookbook contained recipes for food and magic both. She tried to teach me how to open my perception and fine-tune my witch's sense. But I was already checked out by then, counting down the days to my eighteenth birthday and the freedom that came with it.

Still, I listened carefully whenever Aunt Clara talked about things what dwell beyond doors. A world outside our understanding, where shadows have teeth. *As above, so below. Blood is not water. Like calls to like.* She liked speaking in metaphors, my aunt.

She once told me that kids were more susceptible to disturbances in the veil. *To a child, a door to another world feels like standing on a precipice and looking down.* Kind of like it felt to me when I nearly entered this house in my twelfth year. Is that what it feels like now to Leilani and Marty?

Mommy will tuck us in.

Leilani's words fly through my head like disoriented bats.

The little girl is unintentionally creepy. But is there more to it? When she mentions her dead mother, does she actually mean she can *see* her, interact with her? I did hear my own mother's voice coming from inside this house . . . but I was grieving then. And yet, Leilani is grieving now.

With Aunt Clara's blood in my veins, does it mean I can just close my eyes and locate some impossible door inside this house? And then what?

The only way to find out is to face whatever is waiting for me in the dark.

With Leilani and Marty safely in their beds, I leave the guest room and go exploring. Without thinking, I stuff the objects Aunt Clara left me into my pockets.

The house is too quiet for its age. I've lived in my share of old houses, bunking with friends, renting a room from strangers, and all those were noisy places. Squeaking floorboards, creaking window frames. A cacophony of rot and decay. But this house is silent. Listening, waiting.

Across from the living room lies the corridor that kept drawing Leilani's attention the entire evening. I listen to the silence that lives here and imagine I sense a weak pulse. A faraway heart punching out an uneven rhythm.

I smell . . . rain and forest, a terrible untamed wilderness. A greenish light streams from the corridor, pulling me in. My blood sings in response, senses awakening.

After leaving Santa Solana, I went to great lengths to stay away from places that felt even remotely like this. Now I'm walking toward one willingly. I've denied my true nature, but I can't anymore.

I hear . . . steps and catch a whisper of movement up

ahead. A floating ghost in teddy bear pajamas, a boy bathed in a greenish glow.

Marty. Out of bed and wandering in the dark.

I go after him, determined to drag him back to bed if I have to. But he's not alone—there are two sets of footsteps. I follow the Cresson children into the corridor, where the green glow is coming from. Leilani's serious whisper carries in the dark as she instructs her brother to watch his step.

I reach the corridor in time to catch a glimpse of the children disappearing through a door. A door that shouldn't be there. Its outline is glowing, emitting ethereal light.

The items Aunt Clara left me vibrate inside my pocket as I break into a run, following Leilani and Marty, while my survival instincts scream at me to turn around, to go back.

When I grab the edge of the glowing door, it's like touching a live wire. The contact singes the tips of my fingers. I swallow a scream.

The unbearable scent of wilderness hits me anew, assaulting my senses.

But I don't back down. My witch's blood sings inside me.

I open the impossible door wider, and I step through.

It burns. It burns like hell.

The door tears me apart and then puts me back together.

I feel neither warm nor cold. Moss squishes underneath my feet, and feathered branches brush against my face. But there is no birdsong, no animal noises in the brush. It's too quiet, just like the house. Aside from the barely-there shuffle of the children up ahead, I hear nothing else. This world feels flat, lifeless. And yet it exists.

I can pretend I'm dreaming, I can lie to myself. But as I tread through this twilight realm, following Leilani and Marty, I choose to embrace my new reality. Something's been asleep inside me all these years. I left my aunt, left witchcraft, and left Santa Solana because I was scared. Hearing my dead mother's voice coming from an empty house all those years ago terrified me into stillness, like an enchanted sleep some wicked sorceress had cursed me with. I was afraid that if I opened myself to my legacy, if I embraced what comes with being a witch, I'd make myself vulnerable, an easy target for the hungry things that dwell in the shadows.

But now, as the air vibrates around me and my aunt's magical implements buzz in my pocket, the warmth of confidence spreads through my chest. Perhaps it's my ancestors watching over me, their silent guidance bolstering my instincts.

I'm in a maze, I realize with a start, a hedge labyrinth. I clear one turn after another, only to find myself in yet another muted green corridor identical to the one before.

But the children seem to know where they're going, and so I follow them, drawing closer and closer to the labyrinth's erratically beating heart. Its sound drowns out everything else, and soon, that's all I hear, pulsing against my ears.

We reach the center of the maze, where an eerie pond lies still, its surface unbothered by a single ripple. At the water's edge lies a fallen statue, broken viciously at the knees. It looks like some toppled god, its head missing. This place has the aura of an altar, but an abandoned one, overgrown.

What's left of it is blackened stone, slowly eaten away by time and elements.

My vision wavers, and then I see her by the water's edge.

She's facing me but looking at the children: a pale woman with emaciated limbs and writhing black hair to her waist. Her feet are twisted, elongated, and her hair never stops its movement. She's wearing white, a shapeless funereal gown.

A gnawing discomfort spreads through my body at the wrongness of it, of *her*.

I can't stop looking at this being that inhabits the world beyond the door. Is she the thing that haunts this house, that calls to the young ones in the voices of those they've lost?

I no longer remember my mother's voice, but I bet this thing does. I bet it has means of knowing exactly what her victims want to hear.

The longer I watch her, the more I note the strain of her skin against her body, hinting at the thing that dwells underneath. I worry she might see me, but she only has eyes for the children. What should I do? Rush this creature? Throw Aunt Clara's packet of dried bones at her? Stab her with the athame?

My fingers reach into my pocket, where the implements await their moment. They've been buzzing the entire time I walked through this hedge, as if reminding me they're here and eager to be used. But when I brush my fingers against them now, they prickle against my skin with electrical spark. *Not yet.*

"Mommy!" Marty runs straight into the woman's waiting embrace, determined and unafraid. Leilani is not far behind.

Mommy?

This otherworldly being is gaunt, pallid, all wrong. But then my gaze slides to the water at her twisted feet, and I see what the children must be seeing. In the reflection, the being is alive, glowing with vitality. I recognize Leilani's features in her face, and Marty's eyes. The reflection matches the image of the woman from the family photo in the Cressons' living room. The children see their mother, not a monster who wears her skin like an ill-fitting costume and who looks at them with a predator's hunger in her bottomless eyes. Her mouth trembles in anticipation, opening to show rows of blackened teeth. But to the children, her rictus is a kind smile.

What is she, this thing that can reach into our world and lure the children in? I rack my brain, trying to remember Aunt Clara's lessons from years ago.

We are never truly alone, she told me one night, not long after my parents' funeral, when she found me crying into my pillow. *Our dead walk among us.*

What do they want? I asked through the tears.

Same things we want, she replied thoughtfully. *Love, companionship, justice. We're not that different, the living and the dead. But . . .*

But what? I asked. My tears had dried up; now I was curious.

There are other things too, she said. *Vile, evil things that wait patiently on the other side, eager for a door to open. They are hungry, and they are drawn to powerful emotions, the sad kind. Grief can open dangerous doors, Emma-girl. It's okay to shed a tear or two, but don't let your heart break completely. Because once it does, there's no putting it back together, and the door it might open will not readily close.*

She never gave names to those hungry things that dwell behind doors, but books and imagination eagerly filled the gaps. The beldam. The fetch. Lamia. Stuff of folklore and myths.

And now, one of those things is right before me.

Has she always been able to reach through this door, or did something change that night I was twelve, when I gave in to my sorrow, allowing this creature to sense my pain?

Was it my grief that elevated the house with the arched roof from a spooky Halloween spot to a real-life haunted mansion?

My heart is pounding, and I'm afraid the creature will hear it. But she's all too preoccupied with the children.

Leilani and Marty hug the emaciated being. Her long nails curl, digging into the children's backs, but they don't seem to feel it. They smile and laugh at the monster.

They dance with her, holding hands, circling the fallen statue. They splash pond water on one another and run around giggling. All the while, the twilight never becomes night. No stars appear, and all remains inert aside from the presence of children. The labyrinth's dark heart keeps counting down seconds and minutes like some hellish metronome.

At last, the children grow tired. They collapse next to the woman, resting their heads on her lap. She croons at them, their eyes closing. And as they sleep, this being that wears their mother's face uses her long, twisting nails to pull glowing strands from their heads. As each new strand breaks free, the creature sucks it into her mouth.

"Leave them alone!" I shriek, not very witch-like. The hedge maze shrinks around me as I run at the creature.

She lifts her head, her eyes meeting mine. Her blood-thirsty gaze, irises like ink blots claiming the white, threatens to consume me.

The creature stands up, unfolding to full height and towering over me as the children slowly come to their senses at her twisted feet. Her mouth opens as if to say something, but instead, it keeps expanding. It grows and grows until all I can see is a black abyss in the middle of what used to be a face.

Now, Emma!

My aunt's implements quiver inside my pocket. My fingers buzz in response. And as if Aunt Clara directs my hand, I fetch the packet of bird bones and tear it open just as the creature rushes at me in a predatory attack.

I throw the bones at her, and they transform in midair, coming together like mercury, becoming wings and claws and beaks. A small army of birds unleashes itself on the creature. Their screams tear to shreds the silence of this space. The first bird dives toward the beldam's oily strands of hair, its clawed feet digging into her scalp. The other plucks away at the skin of her face, ripping a large chunk off to reveal what hides underneath. Rotten flesh and blackened bone and spiderwebs and larvae.

I force myself to look away, use this distraction to get the children away from her.

"Leilani! Marty! Come with me!" I yell and grab their hands, but they just stare at me, their eyes still dazed. Sluggishly, they move, a sleepwalker quality to their features.

I drag the children away from the pond and into the maze. I hope I remember the way out.

"Mommy . . ." Marty cries for the monster, but I don't let go of his hand, no matter how much he resists. I need to get him and his sister away from the beldam, to break her hold on them. But Marty pulls and wiggles against my hold.

"That thing is not your mother," I tell him as I reach for his sister's hand. "It uses her face to trick you!"

"No, no!" he cries, and Leilani is no better. They're driven to this state by their grief, and they're about to push me away and run back to the thing that wants to devour them.

"Listen to me!" I gather them into a loose embrace, looking between them. "I lost my mom too, when I was just a kid. And long time ago, I thought I heard her voice coming from this house. I nearly gave in. I wanted to see her again so much. But it wasn't her then, and this is not your mom now! But your dad loves you. He'll be devastated if something happens to you. Please, please let me take you home."

I pull them deeper into the maze as I talk, and they let me. Whether it's my words or the widening distance between them and the creature, something snaps, their expressions shedding some of the fog that clouded their features. Now they look scared. Marty has tears in his eyes. Through the thick cloud of birds, Leilani stares at the beldam as if she's finally seeing its true nature.

Together, we run.

The hairs on the back of my neck rise. I turn and see the horrible thing gaining on us. How was she able to defeat the birds so quickly? For something so gaunt, it sure moves like a hurricane through the maze.

The comb! It's as if I hear Aunt Clara's voice in my head, her spirit moving my hand. The comb vibrates in my hand, practically flying out of my grasp. I throw it behind me.

Glancing over my shoulder, I see the comb's tines meeting the ground and taking seed, turning into trees so tall and dense, they stop the creature's pursuit.

I think of fairy tales then, of how things in them are never what they seem. Dead mothers look after their orphaned daughters, magical helpers keep watch, and simple objects take new form, serving the protagonist in their quest. Only this is no fairy tale, and we're not running through a magical forest. A being that feeds on children's grief is gaining on us, and I don't want to think about what happens when she gets close enough to pounce.

But we're nearly there, nearly back at the house. The glowing outline of the door hangs in the air, a disembodied mirage. Our salvation.

But as I shove the children one by one through the door, I realize that I have no way of closing it behind us.

What's to stop the beldam from following us into the house? Or from simply biding its time, licking its wounds, and returning another night to feed on the children again?

The creature must sense my fears because it screeches in victory as it snaps the trees in half like twigs. Against this awful wall of sound, I hear my mother's voice. It calls to me; it offers comfort. Mom is waiting for me at the heart of the maze. We can be together again.

Marty is crying. His sister holds him, but her face is turning wistful, giving in to the same enchantment that's taking over me.

"It calls to us," Leilani tells me when I meet her desperate eyes. "In Mommy's voice."

"I know," I say. "I hear it too . . . But we need to close this door!"

"It can't be closed," Leilani whimpers.

The vile, hungry being is nearly done breaking its way through the trees. Soon, she'll be here.

"Let's see about that!" I only have one more object left from Aunt Clara's arsenal.

I take the obsidian blade from my pocket and study it in the glow of the door.

I wait to hear Aunt Clara's voice in my head, for her spirit to move my hand. But all I get is the rapid pulse of my own heart, punctuating the telltale approach of evil.

I have to figure this out myself.

The same blood that flowed in Aunt Clara's veins flows through mine, the Finnigan blood. It's not too late to claim my heritage. Time is irrelevant where a witch's legacy is concerned. Blood is what matters, and my intent.

I use the obsidian athame to slice the skin of my right thumb. I feel it immediately, the singing rise of power. I have a lot to figure out about myself. But for now, I let my instincts guide me.

I press my bleeding finger to the glowing outline of the door. Electricity zaps the air, and the smell of wilderness dims, the glow darkening where I smeared my blood.

This is how I close this door. This is how I stop the thing that haunts the maze.

I seal the entrance with my blood.

As the last inch of the door's outline vanishes, the being on the other side slams into what used to be a portal. The impact throws me back. I land on my behind as the dark corridor of the house with the arched roof swims in my vision.

I hear her, sense her fury. This beldam, a demon, a *thing*.

We will meet again.

Her voice is a snake's hiss against my neck. I can hear her licking the drops of my blood that seeped through the door to her side. She smacks her lips. She's got my taste; she knows me now.

Bring it on, I hiss back.

The door is closed, but the thing on its other side is trapped, not killed. She'll try to find me. But when she does, I'll be ready.

The house with the arched roof might become harmless for a time, but one day, it'll be dangerous again. Someone else's grief might reopen this door. And so, I must remain nearby to keep an eye on it, until I'm strong enough to destroy the thing in the maze once and for all.

My late aunt's legacy is no longer some ambiguous thing. It's as real as Marty Cresson's fazed expression, as his sister's scared eyes.

"Is it gone?" Leilani asks.

"For now, yes." I take her hand as well as her brother's and lead them back to their bedroom. If they're lucky, the beldam in the maze will be nothing but a memory tomorrow, a scary dream ready to be forgotten.

Later, I collapse in the guest room. Tired, depleted. And when I sleep, I dream of the terrible thing on the shore of a dead pond.

She's waiting.

ABOUT KATYA DE BECERRA

Katya de Becerra writes atmospheric young adult horror thrillers featuring determined characters, complicated families and enigmatic places. Critics called her debut *What The Woods Keep* "a thoughtful and compelling horror fantasy" (The Bulletin) and "a narrative that will keep readers enthralled" (Booklist), while her second novel *Oasis* earned a starred review from Booklist. Her third novel, *When Ghosts Call Us Home*, earned a starred review from Kirkus, which called it "haunting, intense, and eerily spooky." She is also co-editor of the anthology *This Fresh Hell,* which reimagines and subverts horror tropes in new and unexpected ways. As a child, Katya wanted to be an Egyptologist, but instead she earned a PhD in Cultural Anthropology and now works at a university, where she teaches and researches as well as supervises graduate students in Anthropology, Creative Writing and Education. Katya is a short version of her real name, which is very long and gets mispronounced a lot.

CONNECT WITH KATYA

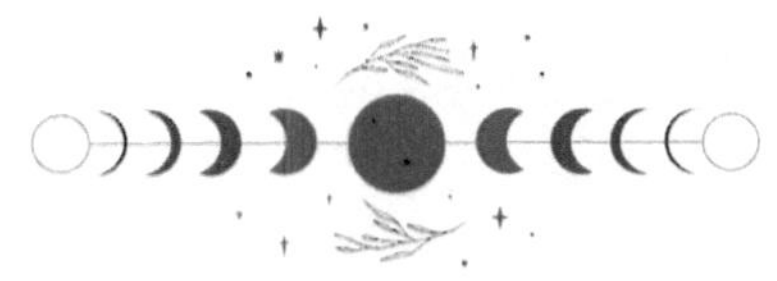

katyadebecerra.com

instagram.com/KatyaDeBecerra

facebook.com/KatyaDeBecerra

twitter.com/KatyaDeBecerra

Read Katya's blog by visiting katyadebecerra.com/category/blog

MORE FROM KATYA

Novels

When Ghosts Call Us Home

Oasis

What the Woods Keep

Anthologies

Sherlock is a Girl's Name (forthcoming)

This Fresh Hell

Thinly Veiled Saturday Mornings: Castle of Horror Anthology Vol. 10

Emporium of Superstition: An Old Wives' Tale Anthology

Clamour and Mischief

Thinly Veiled 80s: Castle of Horror Anthology Vol. 8

Femme Fatales: Castle of Horror Anthology Vol. 6

The Only One in the World

You Can Close Your Eyes

By Elle Beaumont

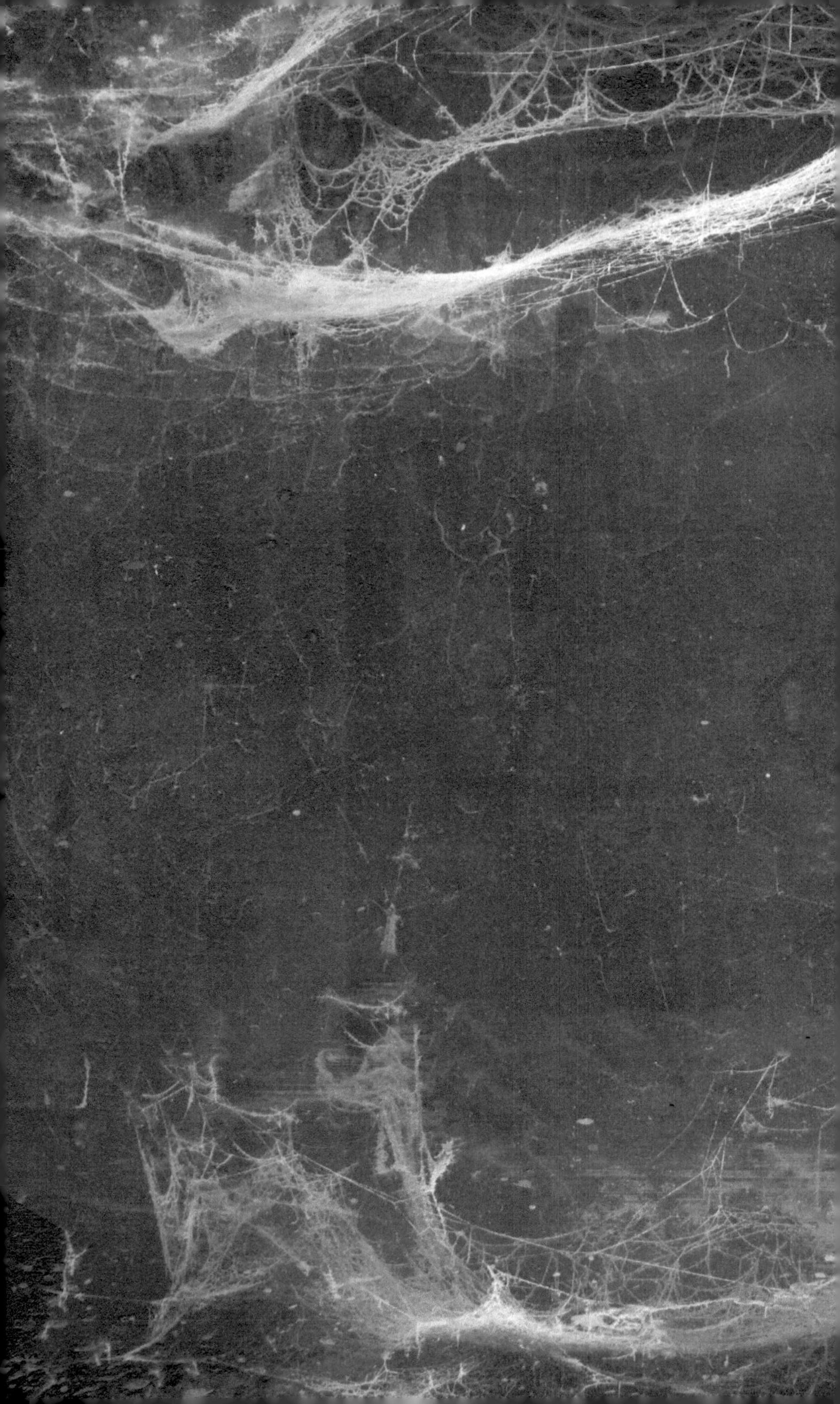

1

The notification came through on Eva's phone just as she pulled into Fort Phoenix's parking lot and turned in to a spot. The view, as always, was stunning. Although weak, the sun beat down on the New Bedford harbor, and the waves glittered like a sea of diamonds.

The reservation was relatively empty still, as the tourists had yet to pile into New Bedford and Fairhaven, nor had the locals emerged from their winter hibernation. Winter and even spring weren't the kindest to the inhabitants of Massachusetts.

Eva turned her car off and flicked through the job listings on Nannyfinder. Unfortunately, her last family—the Peabodys—had moved back to California, which meant she was in need of a new employer.

Eva actually enjoyed long-term nannying jobs. She had

practically raised the Peabody crew, having lived with them for four years.

Now, it was back to square one, and she'd be lying if she said she wasn't heartsick for her kids.

Eva sighed as one listing after another led to an out-of-state job. She didn't want to leave Massachusetts. Everything she knew and loved was here—her parents, linguica cheese rolls, and the Atlantic coast.

A listing caught her attention as she readied to swipe out of the app.

Seeking a live-in nanny for a special girl. New Bedford, MA. Yearly salary of 70k.

Eva tapped on the ad, and up popped an image of a girl around nine. The child hadn't smiled at the camera, just stared with blank blue eyes. She sat in a wheelchair, dressed in a blue floral dress, and her blond corkscrew curls inspired envy.

This would be good, right in my neighborhood. But that 70k has to be a typo . . .

Rather than let another moment pass, Eva hit the phone icon and let it ring through. Her call went to voicemail, but she left her contact information and decided it was up to fate now.

She placed her phone into its holder on the dashboard, but before she withdrew her hands, her phone lit up and rang.

Unknown Caller

Telemarketer or the one who placed the ad?

Eva pried her phone from the holder, dreading the robotic voice on the other end, and answered. "Hello?"

"Is this Eva Shaw?" an older woman's voice came through the line.

"Speaking?"

"This is Sarah Medeiros. I'm returning your call about the nannying position. If you're available this afternoon, we can set up a meeting for you and Rachel."

"I'm actually available right now. Per the map on the app, it doesn't look like I'm too far away." The wonderful thing about Nannyfinder was that it showed the radius of her potential clients, and this one was close by.

"Oh, that's perfect! Here is the address to the house." She rattled the street name and number off, and Eva tapped it into her car's GPS.

"You're right near Buttonwood Park," Eva murmured, recalling all the times she'd been to the zoo in her youth. And the time she fell into the scuzzy pond with her preschool teacher, and the time a swan nearly took her nose off . . .

"That's right. Two blocks from it, actually. I look forward to meeting you, Eva."

"Likewise. See you soon."

Eva ended the call and slid her phone into the holder once again. She turned her car back on and pulled out of the parking lot, reminding herself not to forget to ask about the salary when she arrived.

Your destination is on the right.

"And so it is," Eva mumbled as she pulled up to the curb. A beautiful olive-green Victorian home sat on a well-groomed, postage-stamp-sized lot. But what the property lacked in land had been made up for with brilliant landscaping. Magnolia and cherry trees bloomed, and the dark purple tulips were beginning to unfold as well.

Eva parked in the driveway and opened the car door. She rounded the front of the car, and before she got to the footpath to the house, a woman, perhaps in her fifties, approached.

"Eva?" the tall woman inquired, her dark red brows furrowed in question.

"That's me. You must be Sarah?" Eva took in the woman's auburn hair, which was pulled back into a neat braid. It gave her an earthy-crunchy appearance, and the floral blouse she wore only made that vibe stand out more.

"Yes." She smiled, tilting her head to the side. "So glad you could come out today. You were the first to reply to the ad." Sarah turned away and motioned toward the door. "Come on, let's head in, and you can meet Rachel. She just ate lunch, and we were getting ready to go outside."

It was the perfect day for it. The sun shone above, and it was warmer than normal—in the 80s—which was highly unusual, but Eva wouldn't complain. She enjoyed the warmth, especially if it meant she could lay out at the beach.

Sarah led the way down the brick path and toward the storm door on the side of the house. When she opened it, the smell of mint tickled Eva's senses. Strong but not unpleasant.

She stepped inside after Sarah and glanced around. It was like Eva was transported back in time to the Victorian era. The walls were covered in white floral wallpaper, and on the ceiling, wherever there was a light, were ornate medallions. There was also a distinct old wood fragrance. Eva couldn't place it, but there was an unsettling feeling creeping inside of her, and for no reason.

Several pictures decorated the wall, who Eva could only

assume were old family members—all women. Faded with age but still distinguishable. A woman with clever eyes and hair coiled on top of her head in a bun stared at her. Beside it, another younger woman with sharper eyes made Eva think of a hawk waiting to swoop in on her prey.

Between that look and an inexplicable feeling of dread unfurling in her, Eva was certain the house was haunted. She didn't believe in ghosts, but alarm bells blared in her head, and everything screamed "run" solely based on the aura of the house.

It was nonsense, though; she chided herself.

It's just an old house. You've seen far too many movies.

Sarah crossed the hallway and entered the small living room. A small fireplace with a white mantle stood out to Eva, bringing to mind a cozy Christmas morning with stockings hung by the fire. But it warred with that nagging sensation within her.

She pulled her attention from the hearth and glanced over to the window, where a blond girl in a wheelchair sat. Guilt spread through Eva for not having noticed her before.

"Oh, is this Rachel?" Eva smiled and closed the distance between them.

"Yes, it is," Sarah said from the doorway. "Rachel, this is Eva. She'll be taking care of you while I'm out of the house."

Rachel's round, blue eyes stared up at her, and just like the picture Eva had seen, there was no hint of a smile on her face or in her eyes.

"Hello." The girl's gaze flicked to the window again.

Inwardly, Eva cringed. Rachel was going to be a complicated ward, she could tell already. Sometimes, when it came to a child with a disability, Eva felt they were harder to reach, to grow closer to. Eva assumed it was self-preservation. New wasn't welcome. New was too different and out of their routine. New wasn't safe or predictable, and she understood that. It was par for the course of being a caretaker.

It'd just take time.

"I don't blame you for looking outside. It's awfully beautiful with everything blooming."

Sarah sighed as she stepped closer to Eva. "Thank you," she said quietly.

Perplexed by this, Eva cocked her head and regarded her. "For what?"

"For not asking *why*."

Why what? Eva wanted to ask but bit the tip of her tongue. She could only assume that it was, *Why Rachel regarded her so shortly? Why she was in a wheelchair?* It was important information to know, especially if it meant she could help the girl more, but the talk would come, and it would be a moment to share with Rachel or Sarah in a more private setting.

"Is there anything important I should know?" Eva stepped away from Rachel, allowing her to have the space she clearly wanted.

"Good thing you asked." Sarah lifted her hand and pointed toward the room across the hall. "I need to show you a few things."

"Sure, of course." Eva cast a lingering glance toward Rachel, but then followed as the slender woman led the way across the hall and into the kitchen.

Pale yellow counters lined the right side of the room, putting Eva in mind of the '70s and not the Victorian era. Dark wooden cabinets hung above the garish Formica counters, contrasting in style.

Not here to judge the interior design, Eva.

"This door, with the crystal knob, it's the basement. No need to go down there; I'd prefer if you didn't." Sarah smiled as she spoke. The words were said softly, but there was no mistaking the demand in her voice. "Nothing is down there, but I should point out that the handle and lock are tricky. If you're not careful, it'll lock you down there."

Eva's brows rumpled, and she shook her head. "That doesn't sound like a fun way to spend an afternoon. Got it. No going down in the basement."

"Perfect," Sarah said as she turned toward the sink.

Above it, a window overlooked the front yard. On the sill sat a small glass jar of pills.

Sarah reached for the bottle and tapped her nails against the side. "Rachel is taking this supplement. She *must* take these three times a day. It doesn't have to be with a meal." She put back the container and placed her hand on her hip. "I think that's it. Do you have any questions?"

"I went over the form online, and I think the only one I had was about the hours?"

"Twelve hours a day. Seven to seven. Monday through Saturday."

That was a long, long day. But that salary whispered to her . . . Her mind screamed possibilities: a vacation, a better apartment, a new wardrobe.

"I just want to clarify some information that I saw online." Eva bit her bottom lip. This was the part she always hated. Asking people about the payments or negotiating a raise.

"Of course. What is it?"

"Was the seventy thousand dollars a year a typo, or . . ."

Sarah laughed. "Not an error. Rachel is a unique ward, and so I believe your time and efforts will be worth that."

Unique? "Aren't they all? Each one differs from the last. But now that it's settled, when do I begin?"

"Tomorrow."

"Perfect. I'll see you tomorrow at seven sharp. I'll just say bye to Rachel."

Sarah nodded. "Thank you for being patient with her."

Eva turned on her heel and left the kitchen. She didn't enter the living room, just popped her head in.

Rachel hadn't moved from her spot next to the window. "You're still here?" the girl asked. "I'm supposed to be outside already." There was an even sharper edge to her tone this time around.

"I'm sure your mother will take you out as soon as I leave. Thanks for being patient while I interrupted your schedule."

Rachel turned to look at her, pinning her with cold eyes.

There was an odd glint in the girl's eyes, one that didn't match the nine-year-old. Eva had handled belligerent children in her time as a nanny and had earned several glares, but none had the depth or coldness behind them that Rachel's did.

She turned around to catch Sarah wincing. "It'll take some time, I'm sorry."

Time was all Eva had.

2

B ack at her small apartment in Fairhaven, Eva propped her phone up on a tripod and tapped on her contact list. She poked her sister's name on the screen, *Lily*, and FaceTime chirped at her. In a moment, her round face filled the screen.

She plopped onto her plush couch and grabbed her tacos from their wrap. "Heya. Looks like we're stuffing our faces at the same time."

"Find a new job?" Lily asked as she popped a fry into her mouth.

Eva had told her sister about hunting for another long-term nannying job. "I did, actually! And I start tomorrow."

Ranch dressing dripped from Lily's fry and onto her shirt. Eva made a face and shook her head.

"Ooh, how much will you be making?"

"Is that all you care about?" She shrugged a shoulder, sighing. "Salary is seventy thousand a year."

"Rolling in the dough now, are you?" Her sister grinned. "You could sound happier about it."

It wasn't that Eva was unhappy. Only, when a child was less than enthusiastic about a new caretaker, it always made things hard in the beginning. "It isn't that. It's the girl. She's going to be hard to win over."

"I have faith in you. You're amazing with kids, and anyone would be lucky to have you watch over them."

Eva smiled. Her sister didn't know how much those words meant and how badly she needed to hear them.

"Why do you have to be in California right now?" she grumbled, missing having her built-in friend local and within a five-minute car drive.

"Something to do with learning?" Lily winked and waved a fry around.

For the rest of the phone call, Eva let her sister catch her up on life, gossip, and ambitions.

But she couldn't help but think about her growing sense of oddness of her new place of employment. Even though she had only been inside once, she had never had anyone forbid her from stepping into a certain room. And if the basement door truly locked, wouldn't there just be a key secured down there to ensure a way out?

Eva pulled into the parking space outside the Medeiros' house. Two ravens sat in a weeping cherry tree, croaking back to one another. However, the moment she opened the car door, they flew overhead, close enough she could see the gleam in their beady, black eyes.

Her mother had always told her that ravens weren't to be feared but that they relayed messages, warnings even, of loss and death. Eva wasn't certain what she believed in, but she hoped it didn't mean a loss for her.

That was the tricky thing about omens. Death could mean the end of something, or it could mean a true death.

Eva shuddered. *Let's hope not.*

She chewed on her bottom lip as nerves fluttered in her stomach. Eva shoved the anxiety aside and left the comfort of her car. As she rounded the hood, Sarah was already walking toward her.

The older woman smiled. "Good morning. I'm in a rush to get to work, but Rachel is in the living room. I left a list of her usual schedule and the pills she must take. Make certain she doesn't skip her pills."

Eva nodded. "Got it! I'll make certain she gets her pills." Maybe it was her imagination, but Sarah's tone seemed to harden at the end of her words. *No, don't be silly. She's just in a rush, and you're only reading into it . . .*

What was it about this job that had her on edge? Maybe it was the absolute need to have it because she'd be asking to move back in with her parents by the end of the month if she didn't get another job secured.

Eva stepped into the house, shrugging her purse off and hanging it in the entry hall. Her footsteps thumped against the hardwood floor, and it creaked in complaint as she moved toward the living room.

Rachel sat in front of the bay window again, watching as hummingbirds wove in front of the glass before settling on fresh blooms.

"Hey, kiddo."

"Don't call me that," Rachel snapped and turned to glare at her.

Eva flinched but stepped forward. "Okay. I won't call you

kiddo, just Rachel." She pressed on, trying to smooth whatever feathers she had ruffled. "It's going to be beautiful out today. I thought maybe we could head outside after lunch?"

Anger swirled within the depths of Rachel's blue gaze. "Eva, I don't want you here. *She* wants you here. If I were you, I'd run away from this house."

A chill ran up Eva's spine, and she nearly laughed out loud—not because she found this amusing but because she was so damn uncomfortable. This was a joke, right? Someone was pranking her, and that was why the rate was incredibly high.

"Rachel, your mom just wants what is best for you."

"She's not my mother!" Rachel shoved her hands to the wheels of her chair and spun around. "You know nothing about us."

Come to think of it, Eva hadn't once heard Sarah refer to Rachel as her daughter. Not even the in-depth file she'd sent over via the Nannyfinder app mentioned it.

"That is true, Rachel. However, I hope to learn more about you. I'll be taking care of you while Sarah is at work." She looked away from the girl and toward the floral couch, trying to think of some way to diffuse the growing tension.

"Whatever." Rachel folded her arms and stared across the room.

Eva sidestepped toward the couch and sat down. She pulled her phone out of her back pocket and tapped on the nursery block icon for the nanny app. It swirled and swirled, but nothing loaded. She tried her browser, and even that wouldn't load.

This house had to be a dead spot. They were in a city, for crying out loud!

"You should have brought a book," Rachel offered and

reached for her cup on the end table next to her. She smiled smugly and sipped at the contents.

Eva gnashed her teeth and swallowed the need to chastise the girl. There had to be some way to soothe her, some way to ease whatever anger bubbled within her. She didn't have to psychoanalyze her to know she was angry.

Angry that her caretaker worked and left her with a stranger, perhaps?

Whatever the reason, Eva would have to have a conversation with Sarah when she returned home.

By some miracle, she was able to pull up a book on her phone. Even when she tried to focus on something other than the sound of Rachel picking at her nails or slurping at her drink, she couldn't.

Eva nearly leaped out of her skin when a clock chimed noon. *Pills. Pills. Don't forget her pills.*

She raced to the kitchen and grabbed the bottle of tablets. She saw Rachel wheel into the kitchen doorway from the corner of her eye.

"I wouldn't drop them if I were you," Rachel singsonged, then laughed.

Eva swallowed roughly. Despite the girl finally laughing and even smiling, none of it came as a relief. There was a hard, cruel glint in Rachel's eyes, and when she'd laughed, gooseflesh covered Eva's arms.

Why are you so freaking creepy?

After fetching a glass of water, she approached Rachel and tipped her hand to let the pill fall into her cupped hand.

Rachel's eyes never left hers. Even as she placed the pill in her mouth and swallowed. "I don't think you'll last here very long."

Maybe she was right. If the girl was going to be this difficult, then even for seventy thousand dollars a year—it wasn't worth her sanity.

"That could be true. But why do you think Sarah was so quick to pick me if I wasn't a good fit?" Eva nearly patted herself on the back for keeping her tone neutral.

"Desperation." Rachel flicked her hand and drank more water. "It drives people to do crazy things."

Don't I know it?

She sighed. If there was a way to conjure more patience, she needed to find it now. Eva pinched the bridge of her nose. "Would you like to go outside now?"

"Nope."

Eva sucked her bottom lip into her mouth and fought against biting down. She mentally raked over the file on her phone, recalling nothing about removing her from the premises.

"What about if we went to Fort Phoenix?"

"I don't want to." Rachel spun in her wheelchair and went back into the living room.

Seven o'clock couldn't come soon enough.

Rachel shook Eva's knee.

"Wake up, fool." It was the girl's voice, but *not*. She sounded older and crackled. "It's time for you to leave."

Eva had fallen asleep? Strange. The last she knew, she'd

been reading. Eva blinked, but when she looked at Rachel, her face was sagging as if it were melting off.

Her cheek drooped, peeling away from her cheekbone, and the girl—woman—laughed at her.

Somewhere, a door shut.

A door shut.

Eva jolted awake. She ran her hands down her arms, then hurriedly looked toward the window where Rachel still sat. The girl's face was normal—held in a scowl, but normal.

It was a dream. A stupid, awful dream.

"You snore awfully loud."

"I didn't mean to—"

Footsteps carried down the hall, and a moment later, Sarah came into view. She smiled at Rachel, then at her. "How was the first day?"

"What do you think?" Rachel griped.

Terrible. Terrible. Terrible.

The money was one thing, but sanity? She'd pass on this job. A day was more than enough with this girl. "I'll be honest, I don't know if it's best I—"

Sarah glanced at the girl. "Rachel is trying to be difficult to scare you off. It's what she does. I'm sorry if she was cruel to you today." She reached out and grabbed Eva's hand, squeezing it. "Please don't leave. Not yet. Give it . . . a few more days."

Eva didn't respond. She smiled awkwardly at Sarah and withdrew her hand. If she agreed to a few more days in front of Rachel, the girl would surely act even more devilish.

"May we speak outside?"

"Certainly." Sarah motioned toward the hall, and Eva followed behind her.

She plucked her purse from the hanger near the door and

stepped outside. "Sarah, I don't want to cause any tension between you and—"

"Rachel will do her best to push every single one of your buttons. But she will warm up to you. I just know it." Sarah reached into her coat pocket and pulled out her wallet. She flicked through it and grabbed some bills. "Here. For your extra troubles."

Initially, Eva thought she saw hundred-dollar bills flashing in the wad, but she could've been wrong. Why on earth would Sarah pay her extra? Eva tried waving her off, but Sarah only shoved the money into her hand. "Thank you." She sighed, and her shoulders relaxed. "If I'm to stay, do you have any suggestions at least?"

Sarah tapped a finger to her lips and nodded. "There is a family album in the living room, inside the end table. She enjoys looking at the pictures and reading the newspaper clips inside. It holds a lot of our family's history in it. She should perk right up!"

Eva rubbed at her arm. She wanted to continue with the job, if only for the money, but honestly, the sourpuss of a child for twelve hours straight was mind-numbing and draining.

"I'll see you tomorrow morning." Sarah smiled and walked off.

When she had disappeared behind the closed door, Eva unfolded the bills and realized it was two hundred dollars.

Between the tip and her pay, that was six hundred dollars for one day of dealing with Rachel.

Eva flicked her fingers against the bills and walked away, shaking her head. How could she say no?

3

Eva jolted awake, her mouth open to scream, but no sound came out. She darted from her bed and rubbed at her eyes, trying desperately to shake the nightmare off.

What nightmare? She blinked and scanned her room, then, in a flash, it came back to her. Sarah was smiling as she brushed Rachel's hair, but the girl's face was wrinkled and as dry as a prune. Her teeth were blackened, and her blue eyes were milky.

"You should never have stayed, Eva. But now . . ."

Eva raked her fingers down her face and tried to shake off the remnants of the dream. The dregs of it clung to her, clouding her mind, and threatened to pull her back under. Even her subconscious wanted her to run away from the job. But making it something mythical was outrageous. Rachel was just an unpleasant little girl. "It's nothing, just a nightmare." She reached for her phone by the bedside and tapped the screen. A visual break from rehashing what happened would help, and hopefully she wouldn't fall asleep in the same nightmare.

12:32

Six hours until her alarm went off, but there was no way she could close her eyes right now.

With no hope of drifting off to sleep, she typed: *Sarah Medeiros New Bedford*

Blue listings popped up—hundreds of them—but none that Eva wanted. She chewed on her bottom lip, typed in *West End*, and waited.

Sarah's picture appeared next to an article.

Local Dartmouth real estate agent, Sarah Medeiros, had been reported missing for four days. Authorities were notified by a concerned neighbor. Not long after the detectives began their search, someone tipped off they'd seen Sarah at Fort Phoenix in Fairhaven, Massachusetts.

According to Ms. Medeiros, when asked, all was well, and she had only been away dealing with extended family.

On further investigation, when we approached the concerned neighbor, Martin Delano, he stated that a little girl had appeared as if out of thin air. Reportedly, the child is, in fact, Ms. Medeiros' younger cousin. Soon after, they moved.

When we dug further, we discovered Ms. Medeiros moved to the old infamous Dead Eddy House in New Bedford. But when we reached out for comments, Ms. Medeiros and the girl were unavailable.

Oh. Pieces of the puzzle shifted into place, and she realized this could very well be why Rachel seemed so bitter. Perhaps she was. This seemed to be important information for Eva to know about her ward, and she wasn't certain why it had been kept a secret.

There has to be more to the story. Had her parents died or simply lost custody?

Eva scrolled and frowned as a screen popped up, prompting her to subscribe for a fee. She stared at the screen, wondering why on earth the authorities would get involved over a woman not leaping to answer phone calls.

"No. You're supposed to be soothing your fears, not fostering them." Fears of what, exactly? Eva didn't know. There was just an uneasiness building in her, and Rachel's grim predictions didn't make it any easier.

Tomorrow she'd try harder, and if the girl still wasn't receptive, then Sarah would have to find someone else. What was six hundred dollars a day when it came to peace of mind? Money was great, but if Eva spent the nights fidgeting, unable to sleep, was it worth it?

Eva's doorbell buzzed, stirring her from sleep. She snatched her phone up and eyed the time; it wasn't even six o'clock yet. She flipped her blankets off and sleepily marched out of her room, but before she got to the door, it flung open.

In stormed her mother, dressed in a blue paisley shawl, flowy black pants, and Birkenstocks. Her salt-and-pepper hair was in a single braid that draped over her shoulder. "My love!"

"Mom?" she squeaked.

"I haven't heard from you in a few days, so I wanted to stop by."

"At a quarter of six in the morning?" She blinked at her.

Sometimes, even her mother's oddness surprised her. Just when she thought she'd seen it all . . .

"Oh, is it that early? I was wondering why some shops weren't open yet. I was just at a yoga session. You should join me someday."

Eva nodded slowly. Yoga wasn't her thing. Running? Now that she could manage. But if twelve-hour shifts were in her foreseeable future, all she would want to do when she got home was sleep.

"Did you need something . . ." Eva closed the door as her mother strolled into the living room.

"No. I just wanted to see my firstborn. And your sister said something about a new job? I know how upset you were about the Peabodys leaving." Her mother sat on the couch and patted the seat next to her.

"Of course Lily did." She sighed. Leave it to her sister to steal her thunder. Eva plopped down next to her mother and brushed her hair back. "It's at the old Eddy House."

"The Dead Eddy's House?" Her mother's eyes widened.

"What?" Eva couldn't help but laugh. "It's on Maple Street."

"That's the Dead Eddy's House." She placed her hand on top of Eva's knee. "It got its name because the entire family was murdered and they don't know who did it. They say their ghosts haunt the house to this day."

Unease crept into Eva. Dread feathered along her skin as she mulled over the history of the house.

"It's for seventy thousand a year, though."

Her mother hummed and withdrew her hand. "That's an awful lot of trips to St. Maarten. Which, by the way, I booked a trip for June." And just like that, her mother was off on another tangent.

She leaned into her mother, curling her arm around hers. Scatterbrained or not, she loved the woman, and she amused Eva to no end.

Eva opened the Medeiros' door and nearly walked into Sarah. She stepped back, sucking in a surprised breath, and placed her hand on her chest. "Sorry about that."

There was no hint of a smile in Sarah's eyes, but her lips twitched into the semblance of one. "Eva, dear, I made a fresh pitcher of lilac lemonade and chocolate cake. Be sure to eat that. I don't want it going to waste."

"Sarah, I had a question—"

"I'm terribly late for work. Don't forget to try the album?" Sarah stepped outside, moving around Eva. "Just one more day. If you're really having a difficult time, then I'll re-list my ad."

She nodded. Eva could handle another twelve hours in the house, and if she was lucky, maybe she could get Rachel to go outside with her. "Of course."

Sarah's mouth formed a thin line, and she walked down the remaining stairs. "I'll see you this evening." She turned away and walked to her car.

When Sarah pulled out of the driveway, Eva took a moment to steady herself. This entire situation was weird, and she had dealt with her fair share of odd people.

Eva stepped into the house and ventured into the kitchen. She eyed the counter, wondering if a note had been left for her, but nothing. Only the chocolate cake.

Her stomach rumbled, and she helped herself to the cabinets, fetching a plate. She found a fork and knife in a drawer, then set to slicing herself a piece.

"Rachel, do you want a piece of cake?" she asked but wasn't certain why. The girl no doubt would answer with a hiss or other insult.

"I'm not hungry," the girl's flat voice called out.

Shrugging, Eva piled the sweet treat into her mouth. The rich, dark chocolate exploded on her tongue. It was *so* good. No way it was a boxed confection. She devoured the rest of it and set to washing the dish and cutlery right away.

When she was done, Eva walked into the living room to find Rachel reading a book. Upon further inspection, it was a novel about the Puritans. *Odd choice for a little girl.* But she commended her for reading outside of the typical books.

Eva glanced at the end table, then at the bronze knob on its door, and remembered Sarah mentioning the family album. She moved forward, kneeling before the mid-century piece, and thought about how disconnected the entire house's decor seemed. There was no true theme, just a mish-mash of various centuries ranging from Victorian to mid-century.

She opened the table and heard Rachel muttering to herself.

"Don't touch things!" the girl snapped.

Eva plucked out the album and offered a small smile. "I heard you like to learn about your family history."

Rachel jutted her bottom lip out. "I already know all about it."

"Maybe, but I don't. I'd like to learn."

A mixture of emotions passed over Rachel's face, and Eva couldn't pinpoint them all, but there was no mistaking a sudden dark glimmer in her eyes.

"Very well."

Eva sat on the couch and placed the leather album on her lap. She opened to the first page and noted the same women who were in picture frames on the walls in the hall. "'Sarah and Rachel Towne oppose Boston Globe's research into the Salem Witch Trials, calling Edward Sullivan's research a sham and mockery of history.'"

"The sisters—my family—descend from the Salem witches. Sarah and Rachel were hated for opposing such a big company in 1874." Rachel's lips quirked into a delighted smile. The first authentic smile Eva had ever seen.

"That's a cool bit of history to have in the family. My family is mostly new immigrants, but we're from Scotland. We had our own witch trials then too."

Rachel gave a dismissive grunt and shook her head. "Every culture has hunted a witch at some point."

That was accurate enough. Still, it wasn't right.

Eva turned the page, and this time, it highlighted two different women in the early 1900s. "'Sisters Prudence and Chastity begin a column in New Bedford, and they focus on the history revolving around the Salem Witch Trials.'"

"Mmm." Rachel tapped her fingers on her book. "We've always had ties to the trials. They burned one of our family members at the stake. So, call us a little obsessed."

Eva frowned. "That's terrible." Although so long ago, it was still a wretched thing to do. And so many were innocent. So many had nothing to do with witchcraft, whatever that entailed.

The mood in the room changed drastically, and Eva closed the album. "Why don't we head outside? I know it's early yet—"

"I think that's a good idea," Rachel said, snapping the

book shut with such force, Eva almost leaped out of her skin.

Well, this is an improvement.

Eva crossed the distance between them and reached for the book in Rachel's grasp only to pause midway. "Do you want me to put that away for you, or do you want to read outside?"

"I'll leave it inside. Just put it on the hutch." Rachel motioned to the built-in hutch behind her. "I want to enjoy the weather before it turns."

Such an odd thing for a little girl to say. She sounded more like Eva's grandmother than any child she'd watched before.

"Of course." She rounded the wheelchair and leaned forward to push the break off. Rachel was *almost* in a pleasant mood, but Eva wasn't about to push it. She pushed through the living room, to the kitchen, and headed for the door.

She maneuvered it open and pulled the chair through the doorway and onto the ramp leading into the backyard.

Eva carefully moved from the incline to the paved path and continued onto the grass, heading toward a wooden bench with black iron legs. Above it, a red maple's new leaves rustled, not fully formed yet.

It was more peaceful out here than in the house. Eva didn't understand why, but inside, it was almost like dozens of people were screaming.

Get out of here.

You don't belong.

Run!

"Eva?" Rachel's voice grabbed Eva from the screeching in her head, startling her. "I asked if you wanted to know how I got this way?" She motioned to her legs and the chair.

Maybe Sarah was right and all it would take was a few days for Rachel to settle in. "If you're ready, Rachel, I'm willing to listen." She placed a hand to her chest and offered a reassuring smile.

"It's not that interesting of a story." Rachael sighed and looked away, her fingers fiddling with the skirt of her navy dress. "I ran up the basement stairs when I was told not to. It was as if someone grabbed my ankle, and I twisted, falling down the stairs. When I hit the floor, I knew it was bad." She frowned and grew quiet after the admission.

Eva wasn't sure what she should do at that moment. Rachel hadn't shown herself to want physical affection in the short time they'd known one another, and she didn't enjoy being coddled. That much she knew. Even so, her heart ached for the girl. What a terrible accident!

"Thank you for sharing that," Eva said after a moment. It was all she could safely say and truly mean it.

Rachel nodded. "There is some birdseed in the shed. Would you mind grabbing some and refilling the feeders?"

"Of course." Eva set off across the lawn, to the shed painted the same shade of green as the house. When she opened the double doors, she scanned the immediate area and found the bird seed.

Eva scooped up the bag and carried it to the feeders, refilling them with the cup inside.

"While you're up," Rachel started, then pointed toward the bird bath across the lawn. "Can you refill the water there? They make such a mess."

Apparently, Rachel's willingness to chat also included a desire to order Eva around. *Whatever.* If it kept her relatively happy and opened her up, Eva would do it.

When she was done cleaning the birdbath and refilling

the water, Eva wandered back to the bench and sat down with a sigh.

Although Rachel didn't open up again and talk, they sat in relative quiet until Eva's watch chimed that it was a half hour before noon. "We should probably head in. It's almost lunchtime."

The girl nodded her head. "I guess so."

Eva stood and unlocked the brakes on the wheelchair. "What are you thinking about lunch?" She pushed the chair across the lawn and wheeled it up the ramp, only stopping to maneuver the door open. The hinges whined in displeasure as she forced it as wide as it could go, then she pulled the chair back indoors.

When Eva spun Rachel around, she frowned as the basement door popped open. It should have been locked, per Sarah's instructions. "Why is that open?" she asked out loud but didn't expect Rachel to answer.

"It shouldn't be." Rachel sounded confused and even annoyed. "It should be locked."

"Stay here." Had someone snuck in the front door? She approached the door. Aged wooden stairs led down to a dimly lit basement. A dirty stone wall foundation faced her, and a single light bulb with a pull string gleamed at her.

"Why is the light on?" Without thinking, she started down the stairs, but she couldn't see beyond the railing. It was too dark.

"Eva, maybe you shouldn't go down there!" Rachel's voice raised an octave.

She turned around just in time to see her wheel dangerously close to the edge. "I'll be fine, please back up. I'm just going to—"

Something clattered to the ground, and it sounded as if it

were rolling closer to the stairs. Eva gritted her teeth and continued down into the basement. The weak light hardly illuminated any sort of path, but from what she could see, the floor was red clay, and she assumed the floor spread the length of the house.

Eva stopped walking when she bumped into something hard. She patted at it, feeling the cold metal under her hand. "Oh, stupid . . ." she muttered to herself, then reached into her back pocket and grabbed her phone.

She turned the light on and gawked at the cage. There was a pile of clothes in it. A pair of jeans and sneakers. Next to it, a smaller cage with a stuffed animal inside. *Strange . . .*

Eva moved her hand, following the light's path. Nothing but cobwebs greeted her.

"Eva, I'm scared. Come back up here," Rachel called to her, sounding as if she were on the verge of tears.

It must have been a rat. Something was bound to squeeze through the cracked foundation. Yet, despite telling herself that, her neck prickled with the feeling that someone or something was watching her—and waiting. The more she thought about it, the faster her heart pounded.

Without looking over her shoulder, she rushed toward the stairs again and tried to calm herself. But she couldn't swallow, and it was hard to focus on climbing the stairs.

"You shouldn't have gone down there, Eva," Rachel crooned and leaned forward. "You were told not to."

Heat crept up Eva's neck, and then, like a switch, it fled her body, leaving her cold and clammy. "Rachel." She forced her name out, then on the last stair, she saw the floor rise to meet her, and all went black.

4

Eva roused, feeling a wet, cold cloth on her forehead. She sat up and glanced around the room, remembering she had fainted in the kitchen.

"Oh, we're so glad you're okay." Sarah stood up from the wingback chair in the corner of the room and bent down to press her knuckles against Eva's cheek. "You gave Rachel a scare. She called me right away."

The memories were still hazy about what had happened before, like a giant hole in her routine had been carved out. "I'm sorry."

Sarah nodded and glanced over at Rachel, who frowned at her cousin. "You kept waking, mumbling something about the Eddys . . . But when I tried to bring you to the ER, you said you were fine."

"Did I?" *I don't remember that . . .*

Her head didn't throb, but there was a fogginess she couldn't deny. She remembered nothing prior to the floor rising to meet her.

She swung her feet off the couch and carefully stood. Eva

wasn't dizzy, and nothing ached. Other than forgetting things, she was fine.

"I'm okay. Thank you for watching over me. I should probably get home."

Sarah's eyes pinched at the corners. "It's morning, dear. You slept yesterday away."

Eva's heart thundered in her ears. "Oh." A whole day? She frowned and rubbed the spot between her eyes. "I suppose you need to head off to work."

"Only if you think you can handle Rachel again."

She thought so. Although the memories weren't there, she had the feeling they'd actually gotten along well yesterday.

A flash of lightning illuminated the dark living room, and then the low, house-shaking thunder rumbled through.

Rain pinged off the windows, sounding more like hail than water droplets.

A lousy day meant they'd be stuck inside.

"We will be just fine."

Sarah smiled. "Perfect." She reached beside the couch and picked up a glass. "Here is some lemonade. It'll raise your blood sugar before you can eat. If you need anything, just call me."

Eva took the glass and took a swig of the lemonade. It was floral but not overly so. She swallowed and lifted it. "Thank you."

After Sarah left, Rachel surprised her by actually speaking.

"How are you feeling? Truly?"

"Out of it, but I'm okay. I just feel weird." Eva couldn't place her finger on it. The closest she could compare it to was falling asleep in the afternoon and waking thinking it was the next day. But even that wasn't accurate. She felt detached from her memories, which was silly.

"How so?"

"I recall little from yesterday." Eva took another swig of the lemonade, hoping it would wake her up.

"Oh, that's a shame. We actually got along yesterday." Rachel grew quiet, then quickly added, "I think you should quit, Eva. I'm not the easiest, and it's really long hours. Your friends and family must miss you?"

Eva laughed a little. Sweet child. Not really, but she'd take it. "My parents are pretty occupied with their own lives, always planning their next trip. And my sister is in college all the way out in California." She shrugged and put the lemonade down. "My last job was pretty demanding. I was a live-in nanny and forever running the kids around. I don't have any friends, and certainly no boyfriend to speak of."

"Just think about it." Rachel didn't say a word after that.

Eva sorely missed her Peabody kids. They were brilliant, wonderful, and so weird, but she adored them.

This bloody house, though, was bizarre and hummed with a warning that even her ward was reiterating.

Six o'clock rolled around, and Eva scooted into the bathroom. Pink tile lined the walls, accented by a soft teal. It was a choice for sure. But the awful linoleum flooring was enough to make Eva want to gouge her eyes out. *Ew.*

This bathroom screamed "lost in the '50s".

"I don't want to do this anymore, Sarah!" Rachel's voice

rose loud enough that Eva could hear her. Was Sarah home already?

"I know you're tired of this," Sarah said lowly, "but Eva is perfect. You said it yourself. She has no one. We can live like we used to. You're my *sister*, Rachel. I can't stand to see you live like this. Broken and miserable!" Sarah choked on a hysterical sob.

"We've been at this too long . . . We weren't meant to live to two hundred. Our grandmother would be ashamed of us."

"She would have wanted us to live! Burning at the stake, what life is that? Imagine what we could accomplish! Imagine what we could build for ourselves."

"What have we built for ourselves in two hundred years? Nothing. Because we hide away like rats! I'm done, Sarah. How much longer before another hunt begins? The real Sarah's family is already sniffing around."

Sarah growled in frustration. "And what are we supposed to do with Eva?" Her voice drew closer.

Eva's heart raced. This was a joke. It had to be. But something in her very marrow said it wasn't.

When she finished going to the bathroom, she washed up, then carefully opened the door, hoping she could scoot out the kitchen door without Sarah noticing.

Except, there stood Sarah, face pinched and a wicked gleam in her eye.

"I should be heading home," Eva stammered.

"That won't be necessary." Sarah barred her path, but Eva bolted forward, pushing past her—but she wasn't quick enough to get away.

Sarah grabbed the back of her head and pulled her toward the door, slamming her head into the framework.

Eva's vision darkened, but adrenaline coursed through

her, driving her on. She swung around, her fist connecting with Sarah's jaw.

"You little . . . I'll enjoy watching you suffer. It's people like you who chased us through the centuries, you know? Why we have to keep switching lives. But we always come back here, to our home."

"Enough, Sarah!" Rachel cried out.

Sarah wiped some blood from the corner of her mouth, ignoring Rachel, and Eva backed away, closer to the kitchen door.

"You were flighty from the beginning, which is why I thought to prepare your body and mind ahead of time. That cake and lemonade had enough herbs in it to perform the spell on three people, let alone one."

Spell? "You're . . . witches." Eva raced to the door, but a blast of air knocked into her back with enough force that she hit the floor.

Real witches. Eva needed to escape, now!

"You may try to resist, but your transformation is inevitable," Sarah drawled, then muttered strange words under her breath.

Eva's eyelids grew heavy, and she tried crawling toward the door, but her muscles locked up. The last thing she remembered before she fell into darkness was the beat of the ravens' wings and their black beady eyes, taunting her with the promise of *death*.

5

"What do you want me to do, Rachel? Kill her? We have no choice but to let her live out her days as the little girl. Your body isn't aged like usual and therefore this one will survive the change." Sarah's stern voice roused Eva, and she swallowed a sob as she pieced together the article she'd read a few days ago.

Sarah had assumed control of the *real* Sarah's body and discarded the prior body. It explained the disappearance and then the emergence with a new ward.

Rachel growled in frustration. "I wish you would listen to me for once!"

Sarah waved her off. "You'll feel better when it's done."

Eva tried to open her eyes, but they were so bloody heavy, she couldn't manage it. She attempted to move her hand, but all she was capable of was wiggling her fingers. They brushed against cool metal, and when she jerkily shifted her hand again, she felt more metal.

Her heart pounded in her ears. She willed her eyes open and stared ahead. She was in a freaking cage.

She wanted to scream, but her mouth wouldn't cooperate.

"Ssstop ttthis," Eva slurred, trying to move her arm to undo the cage, but it was no use. She could scarcely lift her wrist from the bottom of the tray.

"Did Rachel tell you how she got hurt?" Sarah hummed, tapping her lips with a finger. "The last girl tried to run."

The last girl? Eva tried blinking away the fogginess, but everything was blurry, and the dim lighting didn't seem to help.

"Stop this, Sarah. If you respected my wishes . . ."

"Enough arguing, Rachel," Sarah snapped at her. "It's time."

"Fine, but this is the last lifetime. I'm done."

Sarah hissed but didn't argue. Whether or not she agreed with whatever nonsense the woman was saying, Eva didn't know or couldn't discern.

Where is my phone? The SOS button would still work.

Eva tried fumbling for it but couldn't feel the bulge of the phone in her back pocket.

Sarah shuffled across the floor and murmured something to Rachel, then picked her up from the chair she sat in as if she were only a doll.

"It'll be over soon," she whispered, then bent down to lower the girl into another open cage. "And then you can live."

Eva's eyes rolled back, but she jerked herself awake and willed her feet to move, hoping to kick the door of her cage open. But all that she could manage was a weak twitch.

"And now for the fun part," Sarah said with a laugh, then closed her eyes as she lifted her hands, palms facing upward. "Quod quondam fuit meum, nunc ad te pertinet, et in commutationem me tibi offero." She started quietly at first, and then, as a distinct hum filled the air, her voice grew louder.

Eva's skin itched, and it almost felt as though something was probing her mind, tickling the inside of her skull. She gritted her teeth, wrenching her eyes shut. "Ssstop." With every ounce of strength she had, Eva clawed at her head, hoping to break up the sensation.

Exhaustion swept through her, and blinking took more effort than it should have. "What . . . what is hap . . . happening?" Her head fell back, and she knew no more.

The sound of wooden floorboards creaking stirred Eva. She blinked away the last dregs of sleep and lifted her hand to wipe her eyes. *What a bizarre dream. What is with these lately?*

As she stared at the ceiling, a familiar medallion stuck out, and she screamed as realization dawned on her. It wasn't a dream! She rolled over, tumbling off the couch, and stared at the worn wooden floor.

Shoes shuffled into her view, and as she glanced up, she saw Sarah smiling down at her as if nothing had happened. "Good morning, dear. Have a little tumble?" She laughed. "I'm so glad it worked."

"What worked?" Eva's brow rumpled, and she wondered why her voice sounded odd. Why did her legs feel strange? She peered over her shoulder at her backside. Her legs were bare, and she was wearing a floral dress. From the corner of her eye, she saw blond curls.

What?

"Come on in," Sarah said over her shoulder, then glanced back as she grinned down at Eva. "She's awake again."

Who was here with her? She twisted around, trying to get her legs to cooperate, but it was tiring and useless.

As the newcomer stepped into the living room, dread lanced through Eva. The individual was tall, with dark hair and hazel eyes. She wore jeans and a sweater.

It was *her*. Except not.

"Rachel," Sarah said to *her*, to *Eva*. "Meet your new sitter, Rachel Shaw."

A scream bubbled out as she thrashed on the floor, pounding it, hoping to wake herself, but this wasn't a dream.

"Don't worry. Your family won't notice much of a difference, they never do. That is the glorious part of the spell, it steals your memories." Sarah squatted before her and gripped her chin. "It's also a good thing you work such long hours. That can affect any would-be personality flaws." She laughed, then laughed even more when Eva swatted at her hand.

"You wretched . . ."

"Sticks and stones, little one. This is your home now." Sarah withdrew and left the room, leaving her with Rachel.

Tears welled up in Eva's eyes. She wanted to launch herself at her. Tear into her with all her might.

"For what it is worth, thank you. I will take care of your life and of you. I vow it." She bent down to help her up, lifting Eva into the wheelchair. She didn't smile, nor did she say another word.

What could she say, when this was now her life?

It was her new reality.

ABOUT ELLE BEAUMONT

Elle Beaumont loves creating vivid fantasy and science fiction worlds. She lives in Southeastern Massachusetts with her husband and two children. When not writing or chasing around her children, she enjoys making candles. More than once, she has proclaimed that coffee is life-blood, and it is how she refrains from becoming a zombie.

CONNECT WITH ELLE

www.ellebeaumontbooks.com

facebook.com/ellebeaumontbooks

instagram.com/ellebeaumontbooks

bookbub.com/authors/elle-beaumont

Stay up to date and receive some free books by signing up for her newsletter! ellebeaumontbooks.com/newsletter

Join Elle's Facebook group and hang out with her

facebook.com/groups/ElleBeaumontStreetTeam

MORE FROM ELLE BEAUMONT

Standalones

Die From a Broken Heart

The Dragon's Bride

The Castle of Thorns

Demons of Frosteria

Frost Mate

Frost Claim

Slaying the Frost King

Immortal Realms Trilogy

Seeds of Sorrow

Tides of Torment

Wages of War (Feb '24)

The Hunter Series

Hunter's Truce

Royal's Vow

Assassin's Gambit

Queen's Edge

A Mother's Love

By D.M. Siciliano

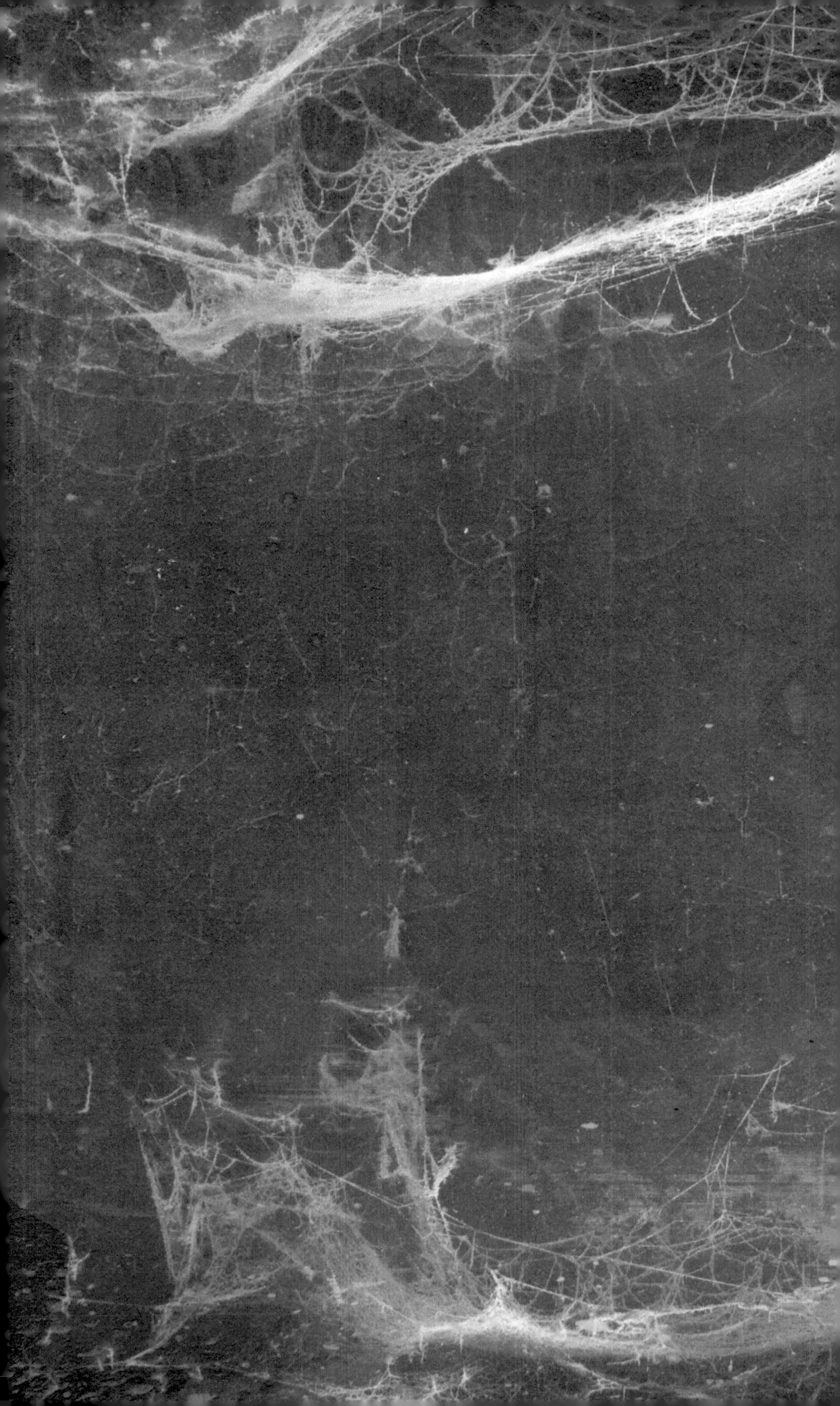

1

Succinct. Good pay. Alexandra liked that. What Alexandra chose to ignore was what was written *between* the lines. She'd never met Ms. Winters, but the word around town was that she was a bit of a hermit. Some described her as odd, others called her a witch, yet no one, strangely enough, knew she had a child. None of the rumors mattered to Alexandra—only the money did. As the new girl in a small town, she'd take what she could get.

Alexandra rode her bicycle to the Winters house, down the end of Walnut Street, where the road had wasted away to harsh gravel. Before turning down the street, she paused, uncertain. *Why is this road unpaved? Am I even in the right place?* She pulled her cell out of her pocket and glanced at Google Maps. *It's down there. Why does it look darker down that street?* She glanced hesitantly down the bumpy road before deciding to continue. Alexandra's vision bounced around with the jostling of her tires on the uneven road. She brought the bike to a stop and gazed upon the house, an over-whelming feeling tickling her skin. It was not an awestruck moment because of the beauty of the house or grounds surrounding it, but the disrepair and contrast of the house to the only other house on the street. Across from it sat a modest ranch-style house. There was a long, paved driveway and a sizeable yard. The lawn was tidily manicured, the grass appearing freshly mowed. Bushes surrounding the front and sides had a proper, even trim. Even the sun was shining over that house, whereas it wasn't above the old Victorian.

Alexandra set the bike aside and paused before stepping onto the walkway, taking in the state of the exterior. Bits of yellow paint hung off the house, chipped off over time, now giving the house more of an aged, gray tone. What once must have been a glorious Victorian was now a pale memory of its former glory, just like the lawn around it. The windows sagged as if they were weary, tired of holding their place in this dilapidated house. Worn and rotted shingles sparsely covered the roof. A thought trickled through Alexandra's mind, like the scurry of spiders across her skin, and she shiv-ered, thinking, *Are the rumors really worth the money?* She pulled out her cellphone and snapped a few pictures of the house. She debated sending them to her roommate but remembered the confidentiality she'd promised Ms. Winters.

Community college wasn't the most expensive thing in the world, but coming from a relatively poor family hadn't afforded Alexandra any luxuries. She had to pay for school all by herself, along with the apartment she shared with her roommate. Her savings were tapped out, and there wasn't enough money for a car. There was no one in town she could ask for a ride either, since the only person she knew at all was her roommate, and they'd just met a week previous.

The Winters's lawn was dry and dead, brown and bristly. A gangly and sickly tree with no leaves grew by the path leading to the front door, as if it were late fall rather than spring. Everything was either dead or dying on this property.

It gave Alexandra another chill, and she rubbed at her arms and shook off the shiver. As she glanced down the path, she noted there were quite a few earthworms dead and dried out from the day's sun. Absent were the birds. No chitter or chirp could be heard among the property. Not a single bird picked through the lawn or nested in the trees. Yet across the street, several sat in the lush green oak near the sidewalk. *What have I gotten myself into?*

A sigh of wind kicked up and whooshed her bangs over her eyes despite her glasses. She swept her hair back and off her face and startled.

In the doorway stood a woman dressed in black.

They stared at each other for a moment, neither blinking nor flinching. Finally, the older woman's harsh features softened, and she spoke. "Hello. I'm Ms. Winters. Eleanor Winters." Her voice was low and resonant. "You are the nanny."

Alexandra wondered if that had been a question. "I am. Alex. Alexandra," she stuttered as she replied to the intimidating presence before her. "Nice house." Alexandra could feel herself blushing at her foolish words. It was *not* a nice house. Probably hadn't been in a very long time.

The woman was much older than Alexandra had originally expected. When they had spoken on the phone, she'd guessed the woman to be no older than forty, maybe forty-five. Now, doubt rolled through her mind as she stared at the lines on the woman's face: her lips tight and puckered with wrinkles, crow's feet in the harsh corners of her eyes, and deep creases above her brow. Her skin sagged in a way that only old age would suggest. Ms. Winters squinted her eyes even tighter as she ran them up and down the length of Alexandra, soaking her in. The weight of her stare caused Alexandra to flinch and look away.

"Come in," Ms. Winters said as she beckoned her closer with a bony finger before turning and entering the house.

"Yes, ma'am." Alexandra noted the woman's gait. She leaned slightly to the left, possibly an arthritic hobble, one hip raised higher than the other. Her back also held a heavy set of age to it, rounded at the shoulders and neck.

Ms. Winters paused but did not turn as she said, "It's impolite to gawk, young lady. Follow me." And with her next words, she did turn around enough to make eye contact and spoke softly. "I was in a house fire when I was younger and fell down the stairs making my exit, fractured my hip. Doesn't hurt, but it looks like it does." She put her hand on the affected hip, turned back around, and led Alexandra onward into her home.

The house opened into a grand rounded room. To the left, a long sweeping stairway bent around toward the bottom and greeted the room. To the right was a vast hallway.

Ms. Winters shouted down the long and tenebrous hallway, "Ophelia! Would you like to meet your nanny?"

No response.

"Ophelia?" she called much softer. She turned to Alexandra and whispered, "Maybe she's sleeping. She's also quite shy, you'll come to see. A little frail as well. She doesn't have friends or play outside. Ever." This last word she said sharply. "Ever," she repeated in a whisper. "She's a good girl. You won't have to do much. Basically, just be here with her. She's too young to be left alone. But you won't have to clean up after her or make her any meals. Very easy job here. You can do your own thing most of the time." Ms. Winters nodded and added, "As I mentioned, discretion is a must. She's a delicate one."

Alexandra followed her. "Is she sick? I mean, like, is there something that keeps her from going out?" The floorboards creaked as she stepped.

Ms. Winters ignored her and stopped in the doorway of the sitting room. "My dear?"

Alexandra persisted. "Does she have any allergies? Can she play, or is any exertion out of the question? What is her bedtime?"

Ms. Winters finally responded, "She loves to play! Hide-and-seek is her favorite! She's very sneaky."

I wonder why she keeps avoiding my questions. Alexandra contemplated as she peered out the bay window that looked out onto a sizable backyard. The grass was withered, dry, parched. Dead. One tree remained in the middle of the yard, still clinging to life. On one side, the tree was drying and dying, but the other still held some green and browning leaves—odd. She didn't realize she'd spoken her thoughts out loud until she heard her own voice, "What on earth could cause a tree to do such a thing?"

Ms. Winters ignored her question. "Ah, she's right here. In her favorite chair, looking out over the yard. She'll do this for hours and hours and always be content." The woman moved around the chair and motioned for Alexandra to follow.

"Such a good girl. So quiet. Never know she's here," Ms. Winters gushed.

But once Alexandra saw who—or rather what—sat in the chair, she gasped. There was not a little girl but a doll propped up in the chair. One of those celluloid dolls that hadn't been made in decades. The ones with the eyes that opened and closed when you moved them. The doll couldn't have been more than two feet tall, and she wore a beautiful Victorian-style dress. The sleeves were puffy, a faded pink that tapered at the wrist and exposed her tiny, unmovable hands. The neckline was high, coming up to her chin, fitted tightly with a puff of lace crowning her face. The dress was cinched tight at the waist with a shiny white ribbon, then billowed out as it came down her legs. The dress was trimmed in faded white lace, the bulk of it spilling down her chest and finishing the hem of the dress. Her stockings were the same pink of the dress. Upon her feet were white shoes that looked like a strange cross between clogs and Mary Janes.

Alexandra stepped back and bumped into a bookcase, dislodging one of the books from the shelf. It hit her on the head.

"Sorry." Alexandra bent to pick it up but couldn't take her eyes off the doll. It had wavy blond shoulder-length hair and gray eyes the color of a New England winter sky, one of which was a bit more open than the other. Its button nose and parted lips exemplified the delicately etched features. The lips parted as if she were about to speak. The doll's head sat a bit askew, and those empty, unblinking gray eyes stared at nothing.

"Are you for real?" A sick fascination gripped Alexandra, and she almost reached out to touch the doll's face, to be sure it was indeed plastic composite and not real flesh. Ms. Winters's heavy eyes fell upon her and snapped her out of her gawking.

Ms. Winters scoffed at her. "What are you doing?" Her face furrowed in concern, and again, her advanced age showed. The lines crept around her eyes and moved up her forehead. Her lips tightened and disappeared into her face. In that moment, Alexandra was certain the woman was at least seventy-five years old.

Maybe the rumors were true. *Witch.* Alexandra's roommate had warned her, but she'd written it off as silly tales a small town tells out of boredom. Now, she wasn't so sure.

Alexandra didn't know what to say. She recovered. "She's just . . . what a . . . lovely child."

A vision of the doll creeping around the house playing hide-and-seek sneaked into Alexandra's mind, and she couldn't shake it. *Get out of your head. Don't make this weirder than it is. It's just a doll. An inanimate object. You're being paid to sit for a doll!* Alexandra smiled, and she knew it was too forced, too big. "I'm sure we'll get along fine."

A smile spread across Ms. Winters's face, and it broke the spell. She appeared a forty-year-old woman once more. "Yes! Yes, I'm sure you will." She bent and kissed her *daughter* on the top of her head. Her daughter did not flinch, did not move. Why would she? "I must be going. I have some medications to pick up and lots of odds and ends. You two will be fine?"

"I'm certain of it." It was the oddest job she'd ever taken but promised to be the easiest—nannying for an inanimate object.

"Wonderful. Let me show you where I keep the emergency details."

Alexandra struggled to keep up with the older woman, whose gait seemed to vanish, her pace up that hallway much quicker than she'd moved so far.

"Here." Ms. Winters pointed to the refrigerator. Most people's refrigerators were covered with magnets and kids' drawings and pictures, but Ms. Winters's held nothing except for the list of phone numbers.

"And again, don't ever let her go outside. And don't let anyone in." Her face was very stern.

"Seems it will be a calm and easy evening. If you like, I could water the lawn for you as well."

The older woman batted the idea away with the back of her hand. "No need. But I almost forgot, help yourself to some tea. It's imported and quite good. You're a tea drinker, no?"

"I enjoy a cup of tea from time to time, yes."

"None for the little one though." She winked, and Alexandra was confused as to which part of that might have been the joke: caffeine for a child or a beverage for a doll. Before she could comment, Ms. Winters grabbed her coat and ducked out the door.

Alexandra put an ancient-looking copper tea kettle on the stove and waited for the usual scream of the pot. It had the slightest dent in one side, and the spout curled in and then up. It reminded Alexandra of a snake about to strike.

When the whistle sounded, she tossed loose tea into the cup and poured the steaming water over it. The aroma was one she couldn't place: herbal, spicy, almost a hint of woodiness. She put a dollop of honey in it and sat down at the dining table, then cracked open her psychology textbook and notebook. Except she could not focus. Everything about her current situation felt so wrong. She got up and glanced into the fridge. There was no evidence of a kid living here. No milk. No Capri-Suns. No cheese. No bread. She went to the pantry and opened it up. No canned or boxed foods. No chips or cookies or candies. *Does this woman really believe the child is real or not?*

She sat down at the table and wrapped her hands around the hot cup and let the heat soak into her. She dipped her face over the steam and breathed in the calm, soothing scent. The first sip tasted as it smelled, and it eased her as it went down her throat. She tipped her head back and leaned against the chair. Her eyes felt swimmy, and her mind clouded. She hadn't yet begun her study session, so she couldn't figure out why she was so tired. She glanced at her watch—6:43 p.m. She'd only arrived at 5 p.m. *Where has the time gone?* Confusion draped over her like a warm blanket, threatening to rock her off to sleep. A noise pulled her back.

"Hello?" The voice was soft, frail, and childlike. "Hello?" It sounded as if the word came out of a misshapen mouth. Lips that fought but failed to move correctly, unable to shape words through hard lips, tongue, and mouth.

Ophelia. Alexandra's pulse quickened. She giggled aloud and pushed the silly thought away as she slapped her hand over her mouth. How could a doll be calling to her like that?

"Hello? Mama?" The voice faltered and cracked, and the shape of the word "mama" didn't seem to come out right. It sounded more like *mmmemmmme,* as if the words dragged through immovable lips.

Alexandra jumped to her feet and stepped into the hallway. Nothing. No one. She swallowed down her creeping fears and moved to the sitting room where she last saw the doll and peeked her head inside. "Ophelia?" she called out softly. She sighed when there was no response, certain she could go no farther. "Ophelia?"

Movement in the chair by the window caught her eye. The chair slid back a couple of inches, screeching across the hardwood floor. A flash of golden hair stuck out from behind the chair as the figure moved. Alexandra's pulse jumped into her throat and threatened to choke her. A barely audible whisper made it past her lips. "Ophelia?" She hoped there'd be no answer.

"Mama . . . that you?" The squeaky voice ran fine needles across Alexandra's flesh. "Mama, can't see you."

Footsteps clicked and clattered away. The celluloid doll stepping upon wood preceded the sight of her. Ophelia came around the chair and faced Alexandra. Her head still held the crooked, unnatural tilt. Her eyes still darted up and to the side at nothing. She held her arms straight out, unbent, at her sides, and her legs did not bend either. Ophelia shuffled but a few inches at a time. Her right foot led while the left dragged a bit behind. With each step, her head bobbled, her hair swished in front of her face. Never once did her eyes move. "Hello?" Alexandra watched the doll try to speak, mouth opening and closing unnaturally.

Alexandra screamed. Her mind reeled. Tired. Frightened. Her vision clouded.

Frozen, Alexandra struggled to comprehend the unbelievable sight in front of her. She reached out for the wall. Her hand missed. She slipped, falling to the floor. One of the doll-child's eyes locked on Alexandra, and she shimmied closer.

Ophelia again cried out, "Mama."

The doll's mishappen mouth moved. Its jaw dropped and

lifted, but its lips remained stagnated. It seemed wrong that a plastic mouth should or could move that way, and yet it had.

Alexandra's vision blurred, and when it cleared, the doll stood over her. As she glanced up, she grew more confused. *What on earth?* A human child looked down at her. *This can't be.* No plastic, no wandering fake eyes, no arms that wouldn't bend. Emotive, grayish eyes stared at Alexandra, blinking furiously.

Ophelia's brow furrowed. Her mouth pursed and unpursed, as if she wanted to say something.

Ophelia reached out. In her soft, human hand was a lock of hair the same color as Alexandra's. Alexandra extended her hand, yet the girl pulled away and hid the hair in her pocket. Alexandra gawked at Ophelia. So human. This was no lifeless doll. Alexandra felt dizzy, nauseated. The room went black.

Someone shook her awake. Alexandra groggily opened her eyes and saw Ms. Winters standing over her. But over her *where?* She seemed to be in the living room, sprawled out on a couch, tucked under a blanket.

"Falling asleep on the job, eh?" Ms. Winters said through a crooked smile, her low voice chilling Alexandra. Ms. Winters reached for the blanket and pulled it higher up over Alexandra.

She sat up quickly, embarrassed at being scolded. The blanket fell to the floor. "I—I didn't mean—"

"Hush, child. It's late. I don't mind at all. Glad you were

comfortable enough here to nap. Take a minute to wake yourself up and get yourself home safe."

"Yes, ma'am."

"I take it Ophelia was no trouble?"

"She was a doll." The words came out before she could stop them. She cringed. "I did have an odd dream. Oh, never mind. I better be heading home. See you tomorrow?"

"Yes, dear." She handed Alexandra an envelope with money inside.

Alexandra trudged to her bike, kicked the stand up, and attempted to ride. At first, she struggled and almost tipped over. Perhaps she was more exhausted than she first thought. She couldn't keep the front wheel straight. Slower, she rode away, feeling a bit groggy and confused by what had transpired at the house. Ophelia coming to life had to have been a dream.

In bed, she pulled the covers up high and tried to fight off the chill that had seeped into her bones. Shivering, she wrapped her blankets tighter and closed her eyes. Visions of the doll stood before her. One moment, it was a doll—unbending, unflinching. Then it was a doll trying to maneuver arms and legs and mouth to work. And before she faded into sleep, it was a girl. A real live girl.

Diffuse light trickled in through the crack in the blinds, and Alexandra peeled her eyes open to the disturbing sound of her alarm on her phone going off. Her joints ached, and her feet didn't want to carry her. In the shower, she sleepily stood like a zombie as the water rained over her. She wondered why she was so tired until she recalled the fevered dreams of the doll standing over her. The little girl holding a lock of . . .

She combed out her long brown hair and suspiciously eyed the amount of hair left on the comb. Twice as much as normal. Ophelia had been holding a lock of her hair! She climbed out of the shower and weakly dried herself off. Her limbs were so heavy; the shower had done nothing to revive her, and the loss of her hair only made things worse.

After her regular breakfast of oatmeal, her stomach rumbled and did a flip, gurgling at her, threatening to return her breakfast. She gulped.

"You look like crap," said her roommate, Cassidy. "Dark circles. You sleep funny? Go out to a party without me?" Cassidy waggled her brows and gave Alexandra a wicked grin. "Drink too much?"

"No. No party. Slept fine. Lots of weird dreams. About that house. Nannying for—" She remembered the discretion part of the agreement.

"What? Oh, the nanny job for the old witch? You took it?" Her roommate shook her head and made the sign of the cross. "Maybe it's my fault, maybe I should have told you more." She hesitated, then continued, "There's a story that the same woman has lived in that house for two hundred years. Two hundred years!" She shook her finger as she repeated the last words. "Some say it's not possible, but who knows? She looks *exactly* like her mother, and her mother's mother . . ."

"You're not helping. She's not a witch. Odd. But nice enough." Alexandra was no longer sure of that. *Hadn't I seen her looking both old and then young on a few occasions?*

"Ok." Cassidy shrugged.

"And how would you know what her mother and her mother's mother looked like?" Alexandra's tone was sharper than she'd meant it to be. "This is how vicious rumors go."

Cassidy rolled her eyes. "You know, there are people in this town who know more about her than you do. You're new here. They've seen the odd things she does. Her coming and going at weird hours." Cassidy paused, as if considering saying more, and then added, "I'm just saying. Ask around if you don't believe me. But I'd stay away if I were you."

Alexandra decided to skip classes. With her slow start, not feeling well, and growing concerns and questions about the Winters family, there were bigger mysteries at hand. Cassidy's warning held steady in her mind and wouldn't let go.

Fresh air on her face did her some good, and she began to feel better as she pedaled to Mr. Maples's house. Her last odd job had been helping the old man clear out his attic. She parked her bike and walked up to the stoop, then rang the doorbell. Shuffling from within preceded Mr. Maples slowly opening the door. He wore slippers and his usual sweatpants and sweater. Alexandra had never seen him wear anything else.

"Mr. Maples, hi."

"Alex, what a nice surprise. What can I do for you?"

"I hope I'm not bothering you. I just wondered if I could ask you something. Some questions."

"Sounds ominous." He raised his hands and wiggled his fingers in the air.

Alexandra laughed. "Nah. It's just for school," she lied.

That seemed to be enough for him. "Come on in." He opened the door and made a grand sweeping gesture with his hand, then shuffled in his slippers behind her as she stepped into the living room. "Have a seat."

They both sat, and Alexandra dove right in. "You know Ms. Winters. How long have you known her?"

"I've known her, or more like *of* her, for forty-nine years. Mrs. Maples and I moved here when we were thirty. It was our first house. And our last, I guess." He sighed and a frown fell over his face. "I miss her."

"I know you do. I'm so sorry."

He only nodded.

"How old was Ms. Winters when you moved in?"

He thought on it for a moment, his hands rubbing his stubble on his chin as if it would jog a memory. "I suppose about the same age as us." He thought harder, his eyes squinted. "Or maybe she was already in her forties. You know, now that you mention it, that woman doesn't quite age with time."

Alexandra thought that was both a strange and accurate comment. "Do you know how long she's lived in that house?"

"Well, I think she inherited it from her mother when she passed. Spitting image, I hear."

"So, her mom lived there her whole life?"

"I think so. I don't know for certain. What's this about?"

Alexandra hated lying. "Like I said, school project. About the history of the town. First residents and stuff."

"Interesting. Sorry I don't know much more about the family. She keeps to herself." He shrugged, and Alexandra knew that was all the information she'd get.

"Thanks for your time." She rose and made for the door.

"Alex? It was the Smiths."

She turned back. "What about the Smiths?"

"First residents."

"Right. Thanks. Good to see you."

"Take care, Alex."

She hopped onto her bike and pedaled much faster to Mrs. Smith's house. A month previous, Alexandra had helped her do some gardening when she pinched a nerve in her back.

Charlotte Smith answered the door with her three-year-old, Timothy, tucked behind her. He peeked his head out shyly. "Hi, Alexandra," said Charlotte. Timothy just glared.

"How's your back doing?"

"Much better, thanks. But if I have to bend over and pick up one more toy off the ground . . ." She turned and looked down at Timothy. "Who knows if it'll last?"

"Let me know if you ever need anyone to watch him now and then."

"Thanks. What can I do for you?"

"I know you're busy, but can I ask a few questions about the town? I'm doing a project on the history of this town and could use some help. Mr. Maples said your family was the very first here."

"Sure, come on in." She led Alexandra inside, and Timothy raced into the living room. Toys were strewn everywhere. It was like a minefield. He dove in.

"Both women sat. "When did your family move to town?"

"My great-great-grandfather came in 1898. Lived here his whole life. His brother and sister both followed at some point, but I'm not certain of the years."

"No worries, I can try to look those records up at the

library." She bit her bottom lip. "I don't know why, but I thought the Winters were the first family."

Charlotte tipped her head to the side as if debating the answer she wanted to give. "Hmm, I don't know exactly when, but yes, they were one of the first families. But their history is sort of cloudy. No one seemed to know them well. All recluses. Just like the current Winters.

"There's a rumor, though, that they moved to town after a tragedy. I think maybe it was Eleanor's grandmother, or great-grandmother more likely. Like I said, I didn't know them closely."

"Eleanor is the current Winters, right? What happened?"

"Yes. There was a fire. Their whole house burned down. Apparently lost two little girls in the fire. Both under ten years old."

"Oh my God. How awful! So that would have been the current Ms. Winters's mom's siblings?"

"I guess. Sorry I don't know much more than that. Eleanor keeps to herself. Always has. Doesn't do much in town in the day. Seems like she only comes out at night."

"Is that why everyone thinks she's a witch?" The words came out before Alexandra could stop them.

"Burned houses. Lost little girls. Strange woman. Witch. Yeah, that's kind of the thing." Charlotte stood. "Where is Timothy? I'm sorry I can't help more. I've got to see what he's up to. Good luck with your *project*." But the way she said it suggested she knew Alexandra was lying.

Alexandra typed away on her phone, sending a text to Cassidy:

Dude, I think I'm nannying 4 a witch

Told u

U knew about the fire?

Yup

And the little girls

Yup

I'm nannying 4 a doll. IT'S A DOLL. Thought the old lady was crazy but now I think u were rt.

A doll? WTF. I need deets

I'll fill u in later. Gotta run

Careful

Ms. Winters met her at the door, whistling a cheery tune.

When Alexandra glanced up, she caught Ms. Winters staring at her expectantly. "Alexandra. Nice to see you. Come in, come in. Ophelia is in the sitting room again, by her window. Should be another calm night."

Alexandra wanted to ask why any woman in her right mind might keep a doll. She wanted to ask how old Ms. Winters was, or if she even had a mother, or if she'd been living there the whole time. Instead, she nodded and agreed. "She is such a well-behaved, quiet girl."

Ms. Winters smiled and waved her into the kitchen. "There's some homemade chicken soup in the fridge. Ophelia said she had a touch of a stomachache this morning, but she seems right as rain now. I think it's the jitters of having a new sitter. Help yourself if you like."

"Oh, that's so nice of you. I started the day a bit slow as well. Maybe Ophelia and I are feeling the same thing." After she said it, she realized how absurd it was. Ophelia was nothing more than a doll. This old woman might see her as a real child, but Alexandra knew better. "My mother never made me chicken soup when I wasn't feeling well. I just got the canned stuff."

"Poor thing. Homemade is the best," said Ms. Winters.

"What about your mom? Did she make you soup too?"

"Taught me everything I know!" She reached out and swept Alexandra's bangs out of her eyes. "Could use a trim, there, couldn't you? I could help you with that if you like?" And just like that, Eleanor had changed the subject, and Alexandra had lost some nerve.

"Oh, I don't want to be any trouble." As if to contradict her words, her bangs slipped down over her eyes again as she bashfully lowered her head.

"Don't be silly. You're not going to be able to see soon enough."

The warmth that came off Ms. Winters at that moment took Alexandra aback. She nodded and said, "Thanks."

"When I get back, we'll get it done, lickety-split." On her way out the door, Ms. Winters grabbed her black hat and set it on her head. She took a couple of steps toward the door and paused, turning back around. "Almost forgot! It's supposed to rain." She reached down and grabbed her umbrella, which was also black, and disappeared out the door. Alexandra put a hand over her mouth and bit back laughter. Ms. Winters surely was dressing the part. But would a witch want to call attention to herself like that? Or maybe a witch wouldn't care.

Alexandra headed to the sitting room to find Ophelia. As she approached the door, a soft humming filled the hallway.

She cracked open the door. The humming stopped. She paused. But nothing else happened.

The doll sat in her chair facing the window, one little hand resting over the arm of the chair, betraying her presence. Alexandra wondered how many hours Ophelia sat in this same spot. She wondered if Ms. Winters placed her in a chair at the dining table and pretended to feed her each meal, and if she carried her up the stairs to a bed every night and tucked her in like a real child. Did she sing nursery rhymes to the doll at night? Ask her about her day?

Alexandra moved behind the chair and spun it around quickly to face her. The doll shifted to the side with the abruptness of the movement. "Hi, Ophelia. I wanted to check in on you. Looks like you're content here." The doll's left hand clenched the arm of the chair. And then it didn't. Alexandra doubted what she'd seen. As she stared closer, one of the doll's eyes fluttered carelessly.

Alexandra jumped back.

"So, I guess I'll just let you be. I'm gonna get some soup and some studying done. So . . . if you need anything . . ." She stepped back. "Okay, then."

She turned to leave the room and again knocked into the same bookshelf as last time. A picture fell off the shelf. The sharp sound of cracking glass cut through the silence. She cringed and bent to pick it up.

In the frame was a picture of Ms. Winters sitting in the living room on the sofa with the doll Ophelia in her lap. Ms. Winters wore all black, and Ophelia had on the same dress she wore now. The picture looked as if it could have been taken recently. As she lifted it from the ground, Alexandra noticed another picture underneath. Carefully, she slid it out of the frame.

Alexandra studied the picture, noting the similarities. Ms. Winters in a black dress. Sitting on the same couch. Fingers of a real girl were laced around Ms. Winters's hand. A smile creased the child's lips, and her eyes glanced at her mother, and her mother looked lovingly back at her child. Alexandra gasped. Peered closer. She took out her cellphone and snapped a picture of it and blew it up, examining the differences. Similar dress and trim, but there was no doubt this was a real child. And Ms. Winters looked different as well. She was younger. Much younger. Ms. Winters, at one time, must have had a real live child. She remembered her earlier conversation with Charlotte. Wasn't it Ms. Winters's grandmother who'd lost two children in a fire? Was this actually Eleanor's grandmother, or was it Eleanor Winters, the unageing witch?

She put the picture back behind the other and reminded herself to apologize for breaking it. But her interest had been piqued. She plucked through the books on the shelf until she saw a rather large one sticking out—a photo album. She flipped the book open and found more pictures of both Ophelia the doll and Ms. Winters, and Ms. Winters and the real child. What shocked her more were pictures of another little girl, this one younger and smaller than Ophelia. The pictures of this girl were all of a real child, no dolls. This little girl existed. It must have been Ophelia's sister. There had been two real girls, once upon a time. *Ms. Winters must be using this doll as some sort of therapy to deal with the loss of her little girl, that's all. It's just a doll for a sad woman.*

Alexandra went to the kitchen and pulled the container of chicken soup from the fridge. She ladled a couple of scoops into a bowl and put it in the microwave. All she could do was think about those pictures. Who were they, really? And which Ms. Winters had the two real girls, and which Ms. Winters was she nannying for?

The microwave dinged and brought her out of her reverie. She placed the steaming bowl on the table and sat down. It smelled delicious; carrots and onion and chicken wafted in the air, and a ravenous urge overcame her. Her stomach growled. She tested the first spoonful to make sure it wasn't too hot, then shoveled it into her mouth faster than she should have. She slurped at it and gulped it down. She tipped the nearly empty bowl back and drank down the rest of the broth. Her stomach growled and called out for more, and she obliged.

Mid-second bowl, the front door opened, and Ms. Winters called out, "Hellooo. I'm home. How's my girl?" Her footsteps clicked across the floorboards as she moved toward the sitting room.

The picture!

Alexandra scrambled to her feet, wiped a bit of soup from the corner of her mouth with her sleeve, and hurried down the hallway after her. "Ms. Winters?" By the time Alexandra got there, Ms. Winters was holding the picture in her hand.

"I'm so sorry. I was coming to tell you. I bumped into the shelf, and it fell. Can I replace it for you? Buy you a new frame? This one is really old."

"No," Ms. Winters snapped. "It's irreplaceable." She ran her hand lovingly over the picture and over the broken glass. Her fingers came away with a little trickle of blood. "I lost so many things in the fire . . ." Her voice trailed off, and Alexandra struggled to hear the last word.

"Let me at least get you a bandage."

"No. No, it's fine." Her voice and face softened as she looked at Alexandra. "It's stopped bleeding already." She showed Alexandra her finger. "Besides, we need to trim that hair of yours." She smiled, and there was such warmth coming from it. She seemed so motherly at that moment that Alexandra softened to her. "Come, come." Ms. Winters led her back to the kitchen. "Best lighting in here." She pulled one of the chairs away from the table and into the middle of the floor. "Sit. Let me grab my scissors." A few moments later, she returned with them and opened and closed them. *Snip-snip.* That one action sent a strange heaviness creeping through her gut that had nothing to do with food. *Calm yourself, she's trying to be kind. She's just a mom at heart. And the poor woman lost her child . . . Your own mother never showed you such kindness.*

She sat still and let Ms. Winters do her work. Rather deftly, she snipped here and there, evening things out and clearing the bangs from Alexandra's eyes. When she was done, she tapped Alexandra on the shoulder and beamed. "Much better! Go down the hall and take a look. You look lovely." Again, the warmth radiated off Ms. Winters. *I feel sorry for her, really. Poor, old, confused woman. If she needs a doll to get through her own pain, who am I to judge?*

Her bangs were trimmed, nice and short, perhaps a little too high on her forehead. But she could see. And she needed to be able to see clearly if she was going to solve this mystery.

Ophelia stood behind her, brushing Alexandra's hair with a Victorian, sterling silver, antique brush. She sang a song, cheery and playful. "Alexandra's falling down . . ."

At first, the brush went through without a problem, but as Ophelia continued, somehow, Alexandra's hair became more tangled. Ophelia tugged and pulled, harder and harder, through Alexandra's ratty hair. She continued her singing, her words getting harsher. "Falling down." And rougher. "Fall-ing . . ." She raked the brush through Alexandra's tangles. "Down!" Darkness crept into her tone. Chunks of Alexandra's hair came out at a time, yet Ophelia kept yanking.

Alexandra woke with a start. In her bed. Just a bad dream. Sweat covered her neck and chest. Her stomach flipped and turned. She flipped on her bedside lamp.

She ran her fingers through her hair and came away with a knot of tangled hair in her fingers "NO! This can't be real! It was just a dream!" She bolted out of her bed and raced through her open door. The world swam as she opened the door to Cassidy's room and flipped on the light. The room swayed as if she were on a boat, and Alexandra fell forward onto her friend's bed. "Wake up!"

"What the hell?" Cassidy sat up.

Alexandra held out her hand, showing her roommate the hair. "I had a dream about Ophelia brushing my hair, and I also let Ms. Winters give me a haircut, and look, my hair is falling out! They did this somehow!" She sucked in a long breath after her run-on rant.

"Maybe you shouldn't go back." Cassidy reached out to help her friend right herself.

Alexandra pulled herself to a seated position. "I need to. I need answers, once and for all. This town has been sitting on the idea of a witch for too long. If she's up to something awful—and I think she is—I need to catch her. Stop her."

"I don't understand."

"Screw the discretion on this job. I need to tell you what's been happening there. This is no normal household. I thought I was babysitting for a sad woman who maybe was grieving the loss of a child and using a doll to mourn and somehow process it. But it's not that. The doll. It's real, really a child. At least sometimes." Alexandra fumbled with her words but managed to fill her roommate in on the strange happenings of the house. When she was finished, she reached out to Cassidy, imploring, the tangle of her hair falling to the bed. "Will you help me?"

"Okay, I'm with you."

The next evening, Alexandra arrived at the house with a small gift. Ms. Winters opened the door, and Alexandra handed the package to her. "I'm so sorry about the frame. I bought a new one."

Ms. Winters nodded and opened the door wider. "Maybe we should take a picture of you and Ophelia together. She hasn't stopped talking about how much she enjoys having you here." The woman lingered at the door, adding, "And how much she loves your hair."

The words sent a chill that tiptoed across Alexandra's skin. She recovered by asking, "When did you take that picture? It's such a nice one. Is it your favorite? Do you have a lot of other pictures, any more like that? Is that Ophelia's favorite dress?"

Ms. Winters looked Alexandra up and down as if she were sizing up a slab of steak at the butcher. "I don't recall," she replied, squinting. "Lots of questions tonight."

"I was just trying to be conversational."

"Sorry, I've got too much to do tonight for chitchat!" She grabbed her coat and stepped out the door and called back, "See you in a bit!"

Alexandra pulled the window curtain by the door back just enough to watch Eleanor drive away. She paused, then waited a little longer to be sure the woman was truly gone. *Where does she really go, and what is she doing? This excuse of midnight gardening doesn't hold up.* To the stairs she went, taking two at a time, moving quickly. She faltered, almost missing a step, and grabbed the banister and noticed a full moon carved into the wood. She looked to the next and the next, and it was carved with a waning gibbous moon. Each after that went through the phases in order, right through the waxing gibbous moon and back to full again.

Standing at the top of the stairs, she tried to talk herself into the idea of snooping. When she and Cassidy had talked about finding some sort of evidence of wrongdoing or witchcraft, it had been the best idea in the world. Now that it was time to enact the plan, however, she second-guessed herself. What if she got caught? What might the retribution be? *Maybe she'll fire me. Maybe she'll do worse.* What was she hoping to find that would sate her curiosity? *Maybe I should forget about all of this.* She ran her hand through her thinning hair and came away with more loose strands. *No more.*

She steeled her courage and glanced at each of the doors in front of her. There were two to her left and two to her right, and at the end of the hall stood a giant bookcase with a window next to it.

She tiptoed forward. As she wrapped her hand around the first knob, her heart quickened and her palms began to sweat. The feeling was both awful and inspiring.

She twisted and pushed the door open.

The sleigh bed was positioned against the wall, and beyond that was a window. The sun had set, and only a spray of moonlight through clouds fell over the room. The bed had been made to perfection: a dark, soft, purple comforter pulled neat and even, not a wrinkle upon it. Several pillows lay at the head, and one large floral-patterned throw blanket lay folded across the foot. Nothing "witchy" there. *What do I think I'm going to find, anyway? What could cement in my mind that she's a witch?*

Alexandra stepped into the room and noticed even the carpet was a deep shade of onyx. The scent in the air was woody, almost like the tea she'd drunk, like being outside in nature. On the vanity dresser, a five-sided glass jewelry box rested. She opened the pentagonal box. It held only a few small pieces of dark jewelry; most of it looked antique. She moved on to the closet. Inside, several dresses, shirts, blouses, and pants hung, all very neat and orderly, all ranging from black to dark purple and blue.

The pace of her heart quickened the deeper into the house she went and the more she spied. She was terrified of being caught but drawn to continue in hopes she'd find answers. She closed the door to the woman's room and headed to the hall. The floor beneath her creaked; she froze and cringed, waiting. Waiting for what, she wasn't sure. Who could hear her? *The doll.*

She labored about the house as if the doll were truly a girl and she'd be caught or tattled on for snooping. She suppressed the notion and pressed on. *There has to be a reasonable explanation for all of this that I'm missing. Otherwise . . .*

The hallway appeared darker than before.

Alexandra rushed to the window at the end of the hall and peered out at the blackening night. The moon had tucked itself away for the night, giving way to thick clouds. Bloated, the sky was a blackish purple that threatened a storm. Light rain tapped at the roof and against the window. The drops increased, speeding to a frantic pace. Her heart quickened its pace as well. She swallowed hard. "I can do this. I've come this far," she whispered to herself.

She turned away from the window and rain and moved to another room. She opened the door. Her hand trembled as she turned the knob. She held her breath, then exhaled, relieved she'd found nothing more than a bathroom. It smelled of lavender, and this room, too, was done in purple.

She closed the door and headed across the hall to another room, which opened as if it were waiting for her. A soft pink paint covered the walls, and the thick shag carpet matched it perfectly. The pink canopy bed had silky ribboned sheets hanging from the frame. A rocking chair sat under the single window. It was all so perfect, quite a dream bedroom, or rather, she thought, something one might see in a *dollhouse*.

A placard on the wall above the headboard read *OPHE-LIA*. Everything in the room looked pristine. Of course it would be though; nothing living lived here. Ophelia was just a doll. Alexandra pictured Ms. Winters tucking Ophelia into bed, kissing her hard, cold forehead, and even reading her a bedtime story while her dead doll eyes stared up at the ceiling.

Chills skittered up her spine. She shuddered and raced out of the bedroom, slammed the door behind her, and leaned against the hard wood. Lightning sparked outside the window. Thunder boomed as the storm moved closer. Rain pelted the windows.

Alexandra felt as if she were close to discovering something, but what, she didn't know. Unable to quit, her pace quickened along with the intensity of the storm to the next room.

Red curtains and pillows and a fluffy red comforter covered the bed. Plush red carpet to boot. On the wall above the bed hung a placard with the name *VERONICA* printed on it.

There was no other daughter—girl—doll or whatever in the house, so who did this room belong to? Who was Veronica?

"The other daughter!" Alexandra slapped both hands over her mouth as she cried out, remembering the other girl in the photos and the *two* daughters who perished in the fire all those years ago. But how did the timeline add up? It couldn't have been Eleanor's daughters that had perished, but that was what the pictures had suggested.

Alexandra closed the door, her courage dwindling. Yet there was another room she needed to look into.

"Mama?" A chill crept up her spine when she heard that sickly soft voice calling from downstairs. The doll was a real girl, and she was crying out.

Alexandra was clearheaded in this moment, unimpaired. *This cannot be a dream; I can't be imagining it.* Alexandra swallowed her fear.

"Mama? Ma-maa."

"I can't be hearing this. I can't be hearing *her*." Alexandra covered her ears. "She's just a doll." But as she thought it, she knew she was lying to herself. It wasn't just a doll. It was *alive*. It was time to face the facts. And get whatever proof she needed in the process.

Alexandra gripped the knob of the last room, twisted, and entered.

An old Singer sewing machine sat under the window. Rain drummed against the pane. The storm had increased in intensity.

Long threads of cloth were strewn about, and the mannequin to the left of the sewing machine wore a work in progress—a red dress, almost complete. A long appliqué of lace lay by it, some already stitched around the neckline. The cuff and hem of the skirt were pinned, prepped for lace to be added there as well. Perplexed, Alexandra stepped closer. Something felt wrong with the dress. It was . . . too small for Ophelia. It was as if the old woman were making a dress for another child. Another doll? *Veronica!*

Thunder rocked the house, and the floor shook beneath her feet. Lightning ripped outside the window, sending flashes of light through the otherwise dim room. Alexandra peered into the hallway in time to catch movement by the bookcase at the end of the hall. She gasped. The doll—the girl—whatever *it* was stood there.

Ophelia stared at Alexandra with those dead eyes, one eyelid fluttering. She reached out those awkward bent arms.

"Mama. Mama, the storm scared me." The voice came like nails scratching down a chalkboard. Uneven. Too high-pitched. "Mama, hold me."

Alexandra's voice squeaked, "Not Mama. It's me. Alexandra."

Ophelia tipped her head to one side like a bird, listening.

"What are you doing? How did you get up here?"

Ophelia shifted her head to the other side.

Alexandra waited—for what, she wasn't sure. Fear had a way of interfering with rational thought.

A skin-prickling giggle erupted from the doll just as lightning flashed several more times in quick succession. "HIDE-AND-SEEK!" Ophelia screamed.

Lightning flashed—one, two, three times—and when it stopped, Ophelia was gone.

Thunder growled and rolled through the floorboards again, and Alexandra thought of a pack of angry dogs, giving warning before an attack.

She turned away from the bookcase. Ran toward the stairs and skidded to a rough stop at the top of them, bracing both hands on the banister.

Ophelia stood at the bottom of the stairs, her head tipped upward, eyes looking at nothing, calling out, "Mama."

Alexandra whimpered. Even though she was here to prove that something foul was afoot, she wasn't prepared for this reality. She had to get out of the house.

Lightning flashed again.

"I'm not your mama!" Alexandra screamed. She ran her hand through her hair, and more of it came away in her grasp. "It's you! Why are you taking my hair?"

"HIDE-AND-SEEK," Ophelia said once more, her voice now deepening unnaturally.

Slam! Alexandra took her eyes off Ophelia and stared down the stairwell toward the entrance.

"Alexandra?" Ms. Winters called out.

When Alexandra looked back down the stairs, the child was gone. She said a silent prayer and made her way down the steps slowly. Her knees shook and wobbled. A sneaky fear crawled up her spine that Ophelia might be lying in wait, ready to jump out at Alexandra and make her fall to her death.

"I came back early because of the storm. My, it was such a fright out there. Trees down, thunder banging so loud, I could feel it in my bones. And yet, just like that, here it is tapering right off." She paused and looked long at Alexandra as she made it down the last step. "What on earth? Are you alright? Is Ophelia alright?" Not waiting for a response, she raced down the hall to the sitting room, and Alexandra kept pace behind her.

That little demon isn't in there. She's been chasing me through the house, tormenting me, was what Alexandra wanted to say. Instead, she kept her mouth shut.

"Ophelia?" Ms. Winters's voice cracked with concern.

Incredibly, Ophelia sat in the chair, looking out into the yard and the storm. Eleanor turned back to Alexandra. "I thought maybe something had happened."

"I—I think I just feel off still," Alexandra said. "And I got a little spooked with the storm and the creaky floors and—" *How she's possessed and you're a witch and this is all wrong.*

"Oh, I understand. Say no more. Will you be okay getting home?"

"Totally fine." Alexandra didn't hesitate, and regardless of how bad the storm had been outside, she didn't want to spend another second in the house tonight. She was already scooping up her belongings when Ms. Winters spoke again.

"I've got to get Ophelia to bed, but you take some of that chicken soup home and get some rest. You look like death."

"Yes, thank you. Good night." Alexandra bit back a response a third time: *I may look like death, but you and your creepy daughters have escaped death for how long?* She left the soup and trekked home.

Alexandra sat at the kitchen table with her head buried in her laptop.

"Dude, your hair. It's falling out. You've got this one spot that's pretty bald." Cassidy reached over the table to point it out, and Alexandra flinched as if she were about to be hit.

"I know. I can't stop though. Not yet."

"What's got you so intent?"

"I'm trying to find anything else I can on the original Winters. I went to see Charlotte Smith, and she filled me in on a lot of it, but the timeline doesn't work. She said Eleanor's grandmother lost two little girls in a fire, but I think it was Eleanor."

"What do you mean?" Cassidy sat across from Alexandra.

"Well, I'm babysitting for one of them. I mean, I thought it was a doll. I took the job not knowing, then I just assumed it was sort of harmless, like Ms. Winters thought the doll was a real girl, but it turns out she is. Ophelia is a real girl. Sort of." She shook her head and knew her roommate wasn't following. She wasn't even sure if she herself was following.

"Oh my God. It's true, then. I thought so . . . The Martin's kids, Stevie and Brice? They live around the corner from Ms. Winters, and sometimes their ball ends up in Ms. Winters's yard. They've told stories that sometimes there's a little girl in the window watching them, and sometimes the little girl just disappears. Like, in a heartbeat. Sometimes, they'll see her in an upstairs window, but, like, moving too fast to be natural. Everyone pretty much stays away from that place. Even the grass and trees are all dead there." Her words were a jumble, and Alexandra struggled to keep up. "Last year, the Martins lost their dog, and Stevie swore that Ms. Winters did something to it, but no one could prove it. That was a little while before the girl started popping up in the windows. And around that same time, there was this girl in high school, a couple years younger than me, that started nannying for Ms. Winters. Recluse, so no one really knew her or hung out with her or knew her story. But she got really sick, like, overnight. Started with stomach problems, really tired all the time, wicked dark circles under her eyes . . . and her hair started falling out!"

"Holy shit! Like me?"

"Like you."

"What happened to her?"

Cassidy whispered, "She died. No one could prove anything."

"We've got to stop this witch," Alexandra said. "Let's reach out to everyone who knows anything about her. I've got a plan."

The next night, Alexandra accepted a request to nanny on her night off. But this time, she brought backup. "I'll text you when she leaves," she said to Cassidy. "Wait here."

Cassidy parked her car down the street, and Alexandra rode the rest of the way on her bike through the drizzling rain. The clouds were black and bloated.

Alexandra loomed outside the front door, her raincoat deflecting the drops that fell on her as she put on her happiest face and opened the door. The house was dark and exceptionally chilly when she peeled off her raincoat inside the front door. She asked Ms. Winters, "Ophelia in her favorite chair?"

"No, heavens no. I shouldn't have left her to sit in that chair when I left last night. That girl caught a fright! All that lightning in front of that window. No, no, she's in her room."

That girl isn't scared; she's evil, Alexandra thought. The image of Ophelia propped awkwardly in her bed on fluffy pillows made her shudder.

Ms. Winters noticed. "You alright?"

"Just cold tonight. I'm glad Ophelia is comfy upstairs. I have a ton of homework to do."

"Ah, yes, she'll be an angel. I'm certain of it."

"It's cold in here," Alexandra said. "Do you mind if I warm this place up? Start a fire?" She waited for a reaction to that one word, and it didn't take long.

Ms. Winters whipped around, her eyes wide. "No. No fires! Not ever. Ophelia doesn't like them. They're—they're dangerous for children. Ophelia got burned years ago . . ." Her voice trailed off, and it seemed her mind had too.

"Oh, I hope it wasn't too bad. I haven't noticed any scarring," Alexandra pried further.

Eleanor's eyes grew wet. "Thank you again for working tonight. I have one last-minute errand to attend to before the new moon."

Alexandra bit her lip and chose her words carefully, fishing. "The moon? Yes, I saw those lovely carvings on the stairs. All phases of the moon, right? What is the significance?"

Ms. Winters was quick with her response: "My garden. Moon phase gardening. I follow the cycles of the moon when planting." She waved the conversation away as if she thought it silly or tiresome. "Anyway, I'll be back in a few hours."

Alexandra waited, watching Eleanor grab her coat and umbrella and exit. At the window, she watched Ms. Winters get into her car and drive off. She grabbed her phone and texted, *Driving by u now. Come. Door open.*

Cassidy sent the thumbs-up emoji.

A loud thump sounded from the floor above as if

someone had dropped something. Alexandra jumped. *Ophelia.*

Thump. Uneven footsteps clattered above.

She glanced up the steps. "Hide-and-seek?" she whispered.

Not waiting for her friend, she raced upstairs and found the door to Ophelia's bedroom open. The glow of a lamp shimmered over the dust motes in the freshly disturbed air. Someone had just come through here.

Alexandra paused in the doorway but didn't see Ophelia.

She glanced at the window, half expecting to see the doll rocking back and forth in the rocking chair, dead eyes staring up at nothing. She closed her own eyes and sighed, steeled her courage, and walked closer to the bed. She kneeled, lifted up the bed skirt, and peered underneath. For a moment, she had a flash of fearful imagery, of being pulled under the bed by her ankles by stiff, lifeless fingers. But there was no one under the bed.

The hair on the back of her neck rose. She dropped the bed skirt and sat up.

Someone was behind her. She took a deep breath and turned slowly, expecting to see the creepy child-doll. "Cass."

"Let's sort this shit out." Cassidy nodded and helped her friend to her feet.

A sound, *clickety-clack, clickety-clack,* like the one Ophelia's feet made on the hardwood floor came from the hallway. The girls raced out of the pink bedroom.

No one was there. But the sound continued.

They moved with deliberate speed down the hall toward the source of the sound but stopped in front of the bookcase. "What the—?" Alexandra whispered.

A soft glow of light emanated from beneath the bookcase.

Alexandra dropped to the floor and laid her head on the cool hardwood floor. She peered at the crack between the bottom of the bookcase and the floor. A shadow tripped across the light that shone out. Not sure if it was her imagination, Alexandra waited, and a few seconds later, another shadow spilled through the light, along with the distinct sounds of Ophelia's feet clicking on the floor.

"What do you see?" Cassidy whispered.

Alexandra jumped at the sound of her friend's voice, her nerves frazzled. "Ophelia is back there, somehow," she replied.

It wasn't a bookcase at all but a trick door. Determined to see what was going on, she swallowed her fear and fumbled to her feet. She nodded at Cassidy, then traced her hands along the smooth bookcase, searching for something uneven, some latch, some hidden way to open it. Cassidy followed her lead.

"Mama," Ophelia mumbled from the other side. A squeaking, high-pitched giggle froze Alexandra's heart. She nervously ran her hand through her hair and came away with a handful.

Her hand was shaking, but Cassidy reached out to still it. "You good?"

"I'm not crazy, you heard that, right?"

Cassidy nodded.

"We can't let this witch win." Alexandra ran her now steady hands across and over the bookshelf until something clicked.

She caught her breath.

Silence.

She stepped back and noticed the bookcase didn't sit flush against the wall but rather jutted out a few inches on the left. She grabbed hold and pulled outward, and the book-case opened like a door. A rancid, pungent odor raced out of the room and assaulted her. Her eyes stung with it. She glanced at Cassidy, who had flung her hand over her nose and mouth.

The twosome stepped inside, and Alexandra gasped, raised her hand to her mouth to stifle the rest of her surprise. Both girls stood covering their mouths.

Inside stood Ophelia, her back to them. She tapped one of her feet and hummed a song. It reminded her again of "London Bridge is Falling Down", a song she used to hear and sing as a child. *Just like in my dream*, Alexandra remembered.

The doll-child stood with her back to Alexandra, facing a workbench. Her little hand gripped something and swung it to and fro to the beat of the song she sang.

Alexandra moved to see what Ophelia held. It was another hand. An arm, attached to another doll's body. A smaller doll lay upon the table. Naked and missing one arm. The workbench lay within a chalked circle. Upon the workspace, at the new doll's head and feet, were large wax candles. Hanging along the wall were random body parts of dolls: legs, arms, hands, torsos, heads. Lining the outside of the circle were newly dead things: mice, rabbits, raccoons, squirrels, flowers. There were also some critters sliced open and pinned to the wall, like a strange dissection lab, parts of the insides removed. The odor of piss and decay coated her nostrils and tongue and made her gag. It was as if the sight of it intensified the smell. On a small table by the wall were a red bonnet and red shoes. *Veronica.*

It lay lifeless on a small wooden table. As Alexandra stepped closer, she noted its near baldness. Yet, clinging to its head as if freshly glued was *some* hair. The shade and length of this new doll's hair was so similar to Alexandra's that she reached up and ran her hand through her own, mostly to reassure herself it was still there.

She came away with a few more loose strands. She looked at the lost hair, then back to the new doll. All this time, as Alexandra's hair had been coming out, the witch had been collecting it and giving it to this doll. Alexandra never considered this might be the reason the witch was all too happy to give her a haircut. She recalled Ms. Winters saying Ophelia loved Alexandra's hair. Cassidy reached out and closed her hand around Alexandra's and her hair.

It was all too much.

"You little demon!" Alexandra shouted at the doll.

Ophelia stopped singing. Her foot stilled as she turned, only her head, all the way around, spinning like an owl's. One dead eye locked on Alexandra; the other floated in her head. Her mouth-hinge dropped open. She spun her body around to face Alexandra. The doll's mouth moved awkwardly as she spoke, almost like she was chewing. "Play-time?" One of her eyes shifted, looking at Cassidy, while the other stayed trained on Alexandra. "Alexandra falling down . . . falling down . . ."

"Nope. Not me. No chance."

"Hide-and-seek?" The girl squeaked as she spoke. Her mouth curled into a smile that was too big for her face. Her doll mouth contorted before Alexandra, the celluloid material seemingly melting away into skin. Yet her eyes were still made of that composite, and neither one of them looked directly at Alexandra. One drifted off at nothing, and the eyelid moved wildly. The other remained still. Her smile widened more. In her mouth were teeth. Real teeth. The top two front teeth were a little too big.

Stop smiling. Stop smiling. You creepy little thing. Alexandra stood taller.

Cassidy squeezed Alexandra's hand too tightly as she muttered, "Holy shit. Holy shit. Holy—"

"I know. I know," she said to Cassidy, then turned a stern tone to Ophelia, pointing a finger at the girl. "No playtime." She was doing all she could not to run away screaming.

Ophelia's face contorted into a pout. Both of her stormy eyes were now trained on Alexandra. *When had her eyes changed to human?* Her cheeks were rosy and fleshy. But her arms and legs were still that unbending celluloid. She moved, her steps clicking as she walked toward the girls. "But I want to play!" she screamed.

"Who's that behind you? Is that Veronica?" Alexandra held a severe tone, but inside, she was shaking.

Ophelia nodded vehemently. She brought her hands together and clapped them. But it was an awkward thing. *Click-clap, click-clap.* "Do . . . you . . . like . . . her . . . hair?" She dragged the words out, making a strange song, the last word holding and hitting a sour, high pitch. She continued her clapping, and the *clickety-clack* and *click-clap* of her doll hands suddenly changed to the sound flesh hands make. At last, she stopped and interlaced her hands in one another and rested them in front of her. Her little human thumbs began to twitch, and she fiddled them over and over.

Alexandra recoiled at the sight of a doll turning to flesh, then thought better of it. She took out her cell phone, fumbled with it a bit, then hit the Video button. They needed proof. Her feet clattered again on the floor as she stepped closer to the table. As Alexandra filmed on, the doll's legs began to flex instead of lumber on with no functional bend to her knee joint as she had just moments before. Her knees bent and maneuvered like a real human's, raising one leg, bending, setting it down, and then on to the next. At first, Ophelia did this in a painfully slow manner, and it seemed to Alexandra as if she were watching a film play out in slow motion.

The doll spun back to the table and grabbed something with blinding speed. When Ophelia turned back around, she held a dagger. And she was no longer a doll. Her eyes were wide and wild. She lurched at the girls, stabbing at the air. "Veronica says thank you! She needs more. Come close." The girl giggled and lunged forward, her dexterity now frighteningly adept.

"You're getting this, right?" Cassidy said as she swiped at the child, knocking the knife out of her hand, cutting her own hand in the process. Blood trickled from the wound.

"Yes." Alexandra tried to hold steady, but her hands were shaking as she videoed the girl.

Ophelia eyed them both, pouted again, then bent and picked up the knife. She licked the few specks of blood off it with a tongue that was too long for a human.

"Enough!" Alexandra yanked Cassidy out of the room and slammed the door shut behind them. They leaned against the door. "Got it."

"Send it."

"Done." Alexandra hit the Send button on the video, and off it flew to every phone number in town she and Cassidy knew. They were all waiting.

Ophelia started with a cry for Mama, but it turned into a howl of fear. High wailing, like a sickly human. The keening went on.

Knock, knock. Ophelia was trying to get out. "Mama, stuck. Mama, help," she cried over and over. The door vibrated against the girls' backs. The force of it was unnatural and shook them more than it should have. *What if she bursts through?*

"Let's go!" Alexandra grabbed Cassidy's hand, and together, they flew down the stairs and out the door. The *ding, ding, ding* of incoming texts rang out as they escaped. The rain had stopped. Petrichor filled their nostrils. Car horns ripped through the silent night. The girls waited outside the Winters house.

A car screeched to a halt, the driver-side door opened, and Cassidy's mom got out. She signaled cars to pull over and flagged everyone out. Another car with Cassidy's boyfriend and friends parked. Charlotte and her husband. Mr. Maples. The Martins. So many other cars pulled up, people spilling out. Mr. Maples reached into his trunk and pulled out torches, passing them along to everyone as they filed by.

Cassidy spat, "I fucking told you she was a witch. She's gonna burn."

Cassidy's mom pulled out her phone. "Look what that witch did to Angie's dog a little while ago." She held up her phone and played a video that had passed around for the past hour or so. Ms. Winters threw the pup a hotdog. After devouring it, the canine passed out. The Witch Winters quickly pounced upon it, brandished a knife, and sliced the animal open, ripped out its heart, then ran off into the night.

Horrified, Alexandra covered her mouth. "Poor dog." Her words were mumbled from under her hand. "No wonder they hated fire. I don't think this is the first time this has happened. But history tends to repeat itself."

The crowd of townsfolk had gathered around, waiting, holding their weapons.

"Burn her. Burn them all." Alexandra threw the first torch.

Ms. Winters's car pulled up, and she barely brought it to a stop before jumping out and racing toward the house, yelling, "My girls! Don't hurt my girls!" She disappeared into the house, and Alexandra could hear her shouting out, "Ophelia! Veronica!"

"Come out, witch!" shouted someone from the side of the house.

"Come out, come out, wherever you are." Cassidy sing-songed the words, dragging out the last, mimicking and taunting Ophelia.

The old woman reappeared in the doorway. She plead-ed, "Don't. Whatever you're about to do, I beg you. My daughters are inside. One of them is sick." She raised her hands as if she were surrendering to the police and gave them an uneven and unnerving smile, her teeth showing a little too much. "Not again, I can't lose them again. That's why I needed the dog. It was nothing personal." She looked at Alexandra as she spoke. "I'm sorry. I had no choice. It's all for my girls."

Tears rolled down the witch's face, but Alexandra remained unmoved. "My hair, you were taking it. And you were draining me somehow. Poisoning me with your soup and tea. Killing me slowly. Killing me to bring Veronica back."

Cassidy yelled, "You awful witch. How many have you killed over the years? You're going to pay!"

"You don't understand. It was all for my girls, my daugh-ters. I had to. The only way." Her tone suggested this was a more than acceptable reason for it all. She glanced at each and every person there and asked, "What wouldn't you do for your own child? You'd do anything, I know. And so would I." She sighed, her shoulders slumped, her age now betraying her. She appeared much older than the seventy-five years that Alexandra had at some point guessed. A hundred? More? "It's a mother's love," she pleaded. "The love for her children. Please, you must understand." She turned her eyes once more toward Alexandra, pleading, but Alexandra felt a cool resolution.

"Burn them," Alexandra whispered. She found her voice. "Burn them!"

The townsfolk chanted, "Burn them! Burn them! Burn them!" All that was missing were pitchforks. Instead, they carried torches. Cans of gasoline sat on the ground, sporadically placed between the members of the lynch mob.

A torch flamed to life, and another, then another. The night was full of fire and anger, and it stoked the anger within Alexandra. She watched as torches went sailing through the air, crashing through the windows of the living room, the sitting room, the kitchen, the witch's bedroom upstairs, then the hidden room. The room where Ms. Winters had been piecing together her younger child, draining Alexandra's life, using her hair.

Each and every window was broken. A trail of fire burned through the night and into the old Victorian, and a trail of fire burned through Alexandra as well as the full realization of events finally hit her. She ran her fingers through her hair, and another clump of it came away. She fell to her knees, but Cassidy was there to help her back up.

The witch howled and screamed, "Nooooo!" She raced inside and slammed the door behind her. The house caught fire, slower than it might have had the rain not played a part. But the slow burn of hell burns as hot as anything else. Flames licked from the inside out, dancing and slithering around and up the windowpanes. The witch continued her screaming from within.

Within a few minutes, the front door opened, and the fiery doorway spilled out its contents. Ophelia. She dragged something behind her. Most of it had already melted, but what remained was a hand, a charred arm, and a part of a torso. Ophelia was yet again a doll. And she was not on fire, but she was dripping, and the celluloid body of her sister had now merged to her hand as she dragged it on behind her.

Her jaw unhinged and dropped and raised as her words came out even more garbled than before. "Mmmmemmme. Mmmme . . . Burns. Can't see . . ."

Some of Ophelia's hair still clung in a singed and smoldering ruin to one section at the very top of her head. All else had fused to the sides of her face. One of her eyes had dissolved into her head, but the other still stared blankly.

Alexandra looked on, unaffected, as the doll took another shuffling step and crumpled in on herself, melting. Her neck disappeared, and her head began to liquefy into the hole between her shoulders. It reminded Alexandra of a turtle receding into its shell.

A sound escaped her as her head disappeared, but no words were discernable.

"What's that?" Alexandra mocked. "You want to play hide-and-seek? I think you're winning."

Ophelia's single remaining eye popped out of the hole that remained. The eye rolled slowly down the walkway as if it were taking a casual stroll. It almost got stuck in several cracks, then stopped feet away from Alexandra. Alexandra almost giggled when the doll's eye fell upon her for the very first time. Every other time she had looked at the girl—the doll—she'd had no idea where it had been looking. It always stared off into space, never quite landing on anything.

Until now.

With a wave of anger that had built over the past few days like the raging fire in the house, Alexandra lifted a foot and brought it down hard upon the staring eye, shattering it.

All the while, the screams of the witch echoed from within.

Some townsfolk threw more torches. No one left; all stood guard as the fire burned on and storm clouds dissipated. Soon, the hints of morning worked into the horizon.

As morning crept on and the sun burned through what was left of the clouds and rose higher in the sky, it was clear to everyone what they'd done in a rage last night.

The house was totaled; flames had devoured everything inside and collapsed the rest.

But no matter how long she screamed that night, and how long the townspeople searched the remains in the light of day, no evidence of the witch was ever uncovered.

ABOUT D.M. SICILIANO

DM Siciliano, a native of Western Massachusetts who now lives in Napa Valley, is a writer of horror, sci-fi, and speculative fiction.

Her first release, Inside, was a Best Seller, and several of her works since then have followed suit.

A former singer turned writer, Siciliano thrives on storytelling, especially anything extraordinary and paranormal. If we can explain it, she won't be writing about it.

Her wild imagination and self-proclaimed "biggest scaredy-cat ever" title inspires her daily to continue creating her dark tales.

CONNECT WITH D.M.

www.dmsiciliano.com

Instagram.com/DMSiciliano

www.facebook.com/DMSiciliano

MORE FROM D.M.

Inside

Under Another Sun

In Between

Emporium of Superstition

ACKNOWLEDGMENTS

Thank you for taking the time to read our anthology. We all had a blast bringing our tales of nannies and their horrifying wards to life. We do have to extend a big thank you to D.M. Siciliano for bringing this idea to us. Without her, this anthology wouldn't exist!

A giant thank you to our editors, Carla and Jess for taking the time to shape each story, then polish it to perfection. You're appreciated more than you know.

A shoutout to our wonderful Meg Dailey for writing our epic foreword and setting the tone for this collection.

And, to everyone who has had to watch their fair share of "creepy" children...thank you for enduring them and relaying some horror stories that have inspired us to no ends.

MORE BOOKS YOU'LL LOVE

If you enjoyed this anthology, please consider leaving a review on your favored platform!

Then check out more anthologies from Midnight Tide Publishing!

Heed the warnings, or you could be next.

A society of Old Wives' comes together in this collection of suspenseful stories. In between these pages, twelve authors draw on ancient tales your grandmothers warned you about. From demons living amongst humans, to ghosts lurking in the shadows, and even gods looming above, these recountings will surely inspire a fright.

Open the book, turn the page, for it may be the last thing you do.

Emporium of Superstition is an anthology full of superstition, suspense, and horror. If you love Survive the Night by Riley Seger, Stephen King, Joe Hill and American Horror Story, then you'll not want to miss this thrilling collection.

Available Now